EASTSIDE WITCH HUNT

(MIDLIFE SUPERNATURALS #2)

T.J. DESCHAMPS

Edited by
PAUL CARPENTIER

Edited by
ANGELA OHLFEST

For my children, you three inspire me every day to be a better mother and writer, and you keep me tethered to the Eastside community so I won't become a feral bog witch (There's always my golden years for that!). I hope someday the world sees all the beauty and chaos inside you as powerful. Show them through your own works and deeds.
Also, Roman, thanks for the Jada inspo!

Eastside Witch Hunt by T.J. Deschamps

Published by Tammy Deschamps

tammydeschamps.com

Copyright © 2022 T.J. Deschamps

Cover by German Creative

Formatting by T.J. Deschamps

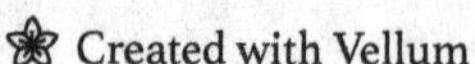 Created with Vellum

1

A man in an ill-fitted suit, standing on a literal soapbox, shouts from the street corner, "End times are nigh. Accept the Lord in your heart and you will be saved in the last battle."

At one time, no one would have listened to him, believing him mad. This man isn't alone. Another man in a suit, and two women in winter jackets and modest floral dresses with rain boots sticking out from the ankle length hems, hold up signs with Bible verses about Armageddon. What were once madmen's words ring true, a balm even, if they echo familiar teachings in times of upheaval. Facing the truth, facing the unknown, and accepting we don't know everything, seems like the mad choice.

News that all supernaturals exist and live among humans hasn't gone as well as I'd hoped it would. Obviously. Some have accepted it. Some have become fans, writing the members of the Supernatural Council of the Pacific Northwest letters, and printing our faces on t-shirts. We didn't want fame. We'd meant to take power away from the Angelic Anocracy, the shadow government of the entire world.

One of Soapbox Evangelist's companions, a woman in a long,

shapeless dress, holds a Bible up in one hand, a brochure in the other. "Thou shalt not suffer a witch to live," she hisses at our approach. Another cries, "Repent and be saved."

Her proclamation reminds me of the comedian Eddie Izzard's skit called "Cake or Death," where the character gives everyone the choice, "Church or England, cake or death," and makes as much sense. I look straight ahead, pretending to ignore her. I'm not foolish enough to actually ignore someone shouting at me, but I won't feed into her b.s.

The evangelists are not alone, but neither am I.

Phyr and Jada are with me. Phyr wears a glamour, an illusion to make him appear human. The fae sneers in their direction. He won't do anything. The local archangel Gabriel, my sort-of boyfriend, has my friend on a tight leash. If Phyr breaks any of Gabriel's conditions the fae had agreed to, he's bound not by the archangel, but by the Goddess Danu, to keep his word.

That's the downside of being a high fae. Danu makes us, even halfling fae witches like me, keep our word. We suffer pain if we lie—Danu's sense of justice. She meant to temper our power with these limits. It only made fae craftier.

The man and his companions' eye Phyr with, well, fear. Even in his human guise, Phyr is uncommonly handsome: black hair, sharp, imposing features, amber eyes that take everything in and discard it at once, and the lean-muscled build of a fae warrior. Instead of black leather armor, he still wears an Enchanting Treats t-shirt from our shop under a leather jacket, paired with jeans and black combat boots. Even with the frilly logo for our bakery, he looks like a badass. His sneer reveals straight white teeth, his fangs obscured by a glamour.

Jada snakes an arm through mine. Her voice is the barest of whispers. "They're everywhere."

We've had protestors and religious zealots in front of the bakery for the past few months. Most people ignored them, but some stopped and listened. Some people stop now.

I squeeze my daughter's hand and say in Kairska, the language of witches, "Do not be afraid, my sweet. They're only human."

The man shouts as we pass, "The angels and saints will weep! The beast and the harlot will terrorize the righteous! But, lo! Do not lose faith! Our savior comes!"

I'm not too keen on the way he emphasizes the word "harlot" with his eyes on me—especially since I'd once been Lucifer's consort. Could he see it? I push the thought from my head. Of course, a mundane person couldn't see past what's before him.

Phyr's hand goes to his hip, gripping the air. Invisible, Angel's Bane, his sword, rests there.

I give him a slight shake of my head. No. I will not lose my dear friend again over these idiots.

"Wouldn't you like to be saved?" the woman pleads with me. "It's not too late. Come to the Paradise Center! If you accept Jesus's sacrifice, his blood will cleanse you of all sin so that you may live in paradise."

"I prefer bath bombs to blood, thanks," I mutter under my breath.

Mundane humans have it all wrong. Well, mostly wrong. Lucifer had told me the true story, or at least his version of it. Their god abandoned the angels and humans to do who knows what. He promised to return before he left. That was eons ago.

When Lucifer was still part of Heaven's leadership, he'd wanted to let humans be and keep angels' things among angels. He thought his creator would come back if things got bad on Earth. What would later become the Angelic Anocracy believed it was their job to guide humans to believe in their god, and with enough of that belief, he would return.

Factions formed.

They fought.

Thousands of angels died, more than in any other war.

Lucifer, tired of seeing his brethren die over humans, allowed them to strip him of his Grace. He and his followers escaped to a realm called Hell.

The Angelic Anocracy ran a smear campaign to make sure he wouldn't attempt to garner human worship for himself. Turns out, the widespread rumor of Lucifer as this anti-god, anti-human villain called Satan gave him more power than he'd ever had as an angel.

Sometimes I wonder if Lucifer knew all along that becoming the villain would work out better for him. Sometimes I wonder if he'll ever get over the heartbreak of his father abandoning him and his angelic brethren, making him an outcast, a bad guy. He may have accepted the role to survive, but Lucifer wasn't happy about it.

Family squabbles. Am I right?

~

We enter Lucinda's Café despite the sign reading "closed," Magic of the protective wards I've set in place. A few months ago, the owner didn't need the wards.

Times have changed since.

Lucinda, the proprietor, and my best friend, greets us. She stands about five-foot two to my five-foot six. Her curly deep brown hair sits in a topknot. She's dressed in leggings and a hoodie. Lucinda is a triathlete and has the build of one. She's also a siren.

"Roxy is in the back. Why don't you join her?" Lucinda gestures to a set of double doors.

Roxy is Jada's bestie. She's eighteen, and used to be the biggest pain in my butt. I'd thought that the girl was a delinquent, with her cagey attitude and rough manners. Turns out, the alpha abjured her mom from the pack and the pack hazed the poor girl.

Gabriel, her father, is not only an archangel. He's in the unique position of being an alpha to the Greater Seattle shapeshifter pack.

Weird combo? You bet. However, I don't have room to talk. I'm not a full fae or witch, and my daughter is a witch, demigod, and fae. American melting pot, supe edition, I suppose.

Jada waves to the Supernatural Council of the Pacific Northwest, who all sit in overstuffed, colorful chairs and sofas that give the cafe a nineteen-nineties sitcom feel.

Princess, the honey badger shifter, sits on a couch. She's in her badass biker chick jeans and a leather jacket. Her dark hair is slicked back. A helmet rests between her black boots. Gabriel's beta, she's here to represent shifters.

Next to her on the sofa, Aurora, a tall willowy blonde, sips tea. She represents the cryptids' interests.

Opposite Princess and Aurora sits Cian, the auburn-headed construction worker-slash-Leprechaun. He represents the low fae unaffiliated with the high fae courts.

Next to Cian, a demigoddess of a Hawaiian pantheon and medical doctor, Leilani turns to smile at me. She possesses a lovely smile and the most gorgeous hip-length ringlets I've ever seen. She's also the bubbly, sweet type when she's not in giant lizard form.

Last, but certainly not least, is Gabriel, the Archangel of the Pacific Northwest lounging. Noticing my arrival, he pushes to his feet. My eyes go up and up to meet his gaze. He's six-foot four wall of lean muscle. How would I describe him? Angelic perfection with the raw animal magnetism of a shifter.

Rawr.

He also has wavy brown hair that he's let grow into loose curls. His eyes are green, and his lips are shapely and full. They feel really nice too. Right now, those pretty lips are set in a grim line.

Uh, oh. Disapproving face.

I'm the last to arrive at the council meeting. Shit. Gabriel hates tardiness.

Before I can apologize for our lateness, Phyr asks in a mild tone, "Did you see your fan club outside, Archangel?"

Gabriel's grimace deepens. "Yes. I was starting to worry they'd detained you." He answers Phyr, but his eyes are on me.

"If they threaten Miriam's person," Phyr warns, "I have sworn vows—"

I cut him off, "I can handle myself."

The pissing contests between these two have become the constant bane of my existence. I wish they would kiss and make nice.

Now, there's a thought.

"Did they threaten you?" Gabriel's voice lowers into a deep grumble, definitely not in a human range. His wolf has become more protective of me over the last few months, and we haven't even yet done the deed. I don't want to know what he'll be like once we do. I'm not into alpha-holes. Been there. Done that. Got the scars to prove it.

"Thou shalt not allow a witch to live" rings in my head. "They offered to make me clean with a blood of Christ bubble bath."

He snorts and some of the tension eases in his shoulders. Gabriel gestures for me to have a seat to his right. I settle there. Lucinda fixes herself in an overstuffed chair opposite the archangel.

Phyr remains next to the door. He appears at council meetings to stand watch, not as a representative with a say. A couple of months ago, we didn't need a guard, but not all mundanes are pleased about supes living among them. Obviously.

"I'm sorry about those creeps. They said some of the same crap to me and Aurora." Princess nudges her head to her girlfriend seated next to her.

"It's scary," Aurora confides. An almost seven-feet-tall blonde with long, willowy limbs. Her outfit befits the owner of a scented oil and candle shop: colorful broom skirt and loose peasant blouse. She's a gentle giant with hippie tendencies. Aurora wears a glamour to hide a Wookie-looking Bigfoot in those hippie clothes.

I spare her a rueful smile.

Laughter bubbles up from the back. At least Jada and Roxy are having fun.

"Shall we begin?" Gabriel asks, standing.

We all nod. The sooner we stop talking about the assholes outside and get something done, the better.

"I am here today as the Archangel of the Pacific Northwest. I cede my power of alpha to represent the Greater Seattle shapeshifter pack to Princess."

The magical transfer of power scrapes like wool on my skin.

Princess stands. "I represent all the shapeshifter packs of the Pacific Northwest."

Each of the council members stands and names who they represent. There's an air of solemnity because we all take our positions seriously.

Gabriel clears his throat. "I would like to update you on Heaven's stance."

A hush falls across the council. We regard the archangel with expectant gazes and clasped hands.

"The Angelic Anocracy is still not speaking to me directly, at least not officially. I've heard through back channels there is deliberation on whether they will remove me as archangel and replace me with a full seraph. If you choose to ally with the new archangel, then I would leave immediately. I promise I will take no action against you."

My heart aches for him. Gabriel loves his father. I can't help but feel personal responsibility for the rift between them. He broke the angelic code for me. I had Lucifer powerless. I could have ended the conflict between Heaven and Hell by murdering the King of Hell with my faelight. Instead, we made a bargain.

Also, Gabriel has had to make the same speech with all the shifter packs in the PNW. He's been an exemplary leader. No alpha broke allegiance to him. Still, some members of other packs have broken with their alphas and moved out of Gabriel's territory. None have challenged him. At least we have that. All of the shifters know he's not stripped of his angelic powers, his Grace, and his claim to alpha status is still legendary.

It's no surprise that no one leaves. We decided to defy the Angelic Anocracy and come out of the supernatural closet together.

"I cede the floor to Cian, representative of the low fae."

"I saw on the news," Cian says, his Irish accent slight but there, "that Congress is trying to decide whether or not supes are citizens. There's also talk of immigration doing deeper investigations of all resident aliens and marking the files of those suspected to be supernatural."

Phyr and I exchange a glance. He's here on paperwork Gabriel had pulled strings to get. I'm not as American as I'd thought either. I recently learned that I was born in my father's faerie. My mother is an American citizen, but I no longer go by the name that she gave me. Tatiana died, confirmed by my death certificate online. That's what I get for faking my death so thoroughly that my mother filed one.

"There are supes in the House, Senate, and the Supreme Court, as well as in the ACLU and other legal organizations that would battle any bill claiming us as anything but tax-paying Americans," Gabriel replies, unconcerned. "They know I can expose them all. We're fine."

Mutually assured destruction. Great.

"Enough supes to not be worried?" Lucinda asks, echoing the concern etched on everyone's face.

Gabriel clears his throat, looking as if he doesn't want to share what he knows. "The president is a shifter. We've spoken."

Princess chuckles at my startled expression. "Shifters run this country, Miriam."

I blink. So that's how the Angelic Anocracy ruled without being present except for regional archangels. This was new information. Also, being half shifter and an alpha would put Gabriel in a pretty position.

"Most shapeshifters don't want to be commanded by an off-world agency anymore," Gabriel adds. "Which works in our favor. This council might set precedence for an official type of office."

Had he planned on coming out longer than he'd let on? I exchange another glance with Phyr.

"A shift in the power dynamic is coming," Leilani sighs. "We all wanted it. We all knew coming out would be a catalyst to that shift, but it seems to be happening faster than we anticipated."

We discuss possibilities awhile, until the discussion takes its natural course and dies down.

I bring up a topic in my official capacity. "As representative of the high fae, I must ask, when are you going to grant fae permission to enter your territory?"

"I'll speak to Oberon on the matter. Arrange a meeting."

Bristling that he doesn't make it a request, I stare. Just call me Miriam, supernatural secretary.

"I have sad news. A cryptid has gone missing," Aurora says, breaking the silence.

Gabriel rubs his brow. "Who?"

"Robby." When we all stare blankly at her, the bigfoot shakes her head and throws up her hands. "Robert? You've all met him." With an exasperated sigh, she grumbles, "The moth man."

Gabriel pulls a face.

"Oh, him." I'd forgotten his existence until now.

Princess rolls her eyes. "Ugh, him? He was so whiny. We were protecting him from a crossroads demon, and he demanded raw, vegan organic dishes served on ethically sourced plates and cutlery."

I bite my lip to keep from laughing. Robby is a cryptid, and a suburban Pacific Northwesterner through and through.

Aurora holds up her hands defensively. "Yeah, yeah, I know he's a bit of a pill, but he's missing, and his people are asking questions." Her gaze shifts briefly to Phyr, distrust in her eyes.

"Are you accusing me of kidnapping him?" the fae prince asks in a mild tone.

Aurora brushes her tie-dyed skirt. "We found him in your faerie."

"Between my duties at the bakery, learning about this world, and spending time with my family, I assure you I don't have the time to kidnap an irritating mothman."

Gabriel sighs. "We all know Rhiannon trapped him before he could trap her." To the Princess, he says, "Beta, put someone on it."

She nods.

Cian pipes up again. "A halfling living in a trailer near Sultan runs a small cleaning business. She stopped showing up to work and won't answer her door, but her car is in the driveway."

That grabs Phyr's attention, and mine.

"Do you know her?"

Cian waffles a freckled hand in the air. "I know of her. She's a brownie. Her cousin says she started going to church, talking a lot about end times, and walking the righteous path. Then she was gone."

Princess leans forward. "Pack alphas as far west as Forks and east as Wenatchee, and one down near Eugene have reported members who started acting strange, withdrawing, and not participating in gatherings. The alphas did check-ins, but none of them were home. I would suspect they left their pack, like some do, but all their belongings are still there. Family photos, mementos. That's not seceding from a pack. What bothers me is the alphas aren't concerned. They think they'll just show up."

Gabriel adds, "Normally I wouldn't think anything of it either. Some shifters like to take a hiatus from the pack occasionally, go out to the woods, and just be their animal. Given there's also a cryptid and a brownie missing, maybe we should alert the alphas to put some hunters on it to investigate."

His gaze travels to the members of the council. "Anyone else have someone missing to investigate?"

I say, "I'm going to check in with the local witches, make sure they're doing well."

"I'll check on the nymphs and oracles," Lucinda says. "I'm due for a visit with them."

The meeting comes to a close. Gabriel resumes his position as alpha.

He touches my shoulder as we both rise. "Can we talk in private?"

THE ONLY PRIVATE place in Lucinda's Café is the back office where the girls are doing homework and gabbing.

Gabriel smiles at the scene and then looks over his shoulder at me.

I don't know what he wants me to see. Yes. Our girls get along. They've always gotten along. Then I see it from his perspective. They would make good stepsisters. Did Raf see it that way when he asked Gabriel to look after us before he ascended?

I shudder inwardly and don't like my future pre-planned, even if my former husband meant well. I've gotten over Raf leading a double life, one foot in the supe world and one in the mundane, but I would be damned if I partnered with someone because we made a good insta-family.

Gabriel clears his throat. The girls look up in unison.

He smiles. "Can we have a moment of privacy?"

"But I'm hungry," Roxy whines.

"I'll take you for sushi on the way home."

The girls collect their things.

Jada eyes us for a second, then closes the office door behind her.

Gabriel and I started dating a few months ago, but neither of us had ever actually dated before. We decided to take things slow. We had to. More and more, witches have been showing up in the territory, after having left their covens. I also have a bakery and two new members of my household. Well, Phyr has been my friend my whole life, but we've spent many years apart. Rhiannon, a witch I took in, is a lot.

It's also Jada's senior year and we're looking at colleges. She'd wanted to go to Howard University, but after supes came out, she decided to stay closer to home.

I lay none of this on him because he knows. He's busy too. He's been the public face of all supes. Handsome, gregarious, good at oration, Gabriel handled most of the press. Apparently, he's been talking to *the* president as well.

"Is there something wrong?" I ask, worried he'll want to delay his arrangement with my father. Again.

"Yes." Suddenly he's in my space, hands cupping my cheeks. "I miss you."

"Oh, yeah?" I hedge, grinning.

He angles his head so his face hovers just above mine. "Should I show you how much?"

He's so close that heat radiates from his body and his breath fans my face. He smells so good, evergreen forests and fresh mountain air in combination with an indescribable scent I attribute to angels.

My hand trembles a little as I reach for his beautiful face. The stubble of a beard rough under my fingers makes him feel real, instead of a perfect angel. I like real. Normal. I want what Raf and I had, something mundane but precious in its normalcy. With Gabriel, there are so many complicating factors: our positions in the supe community, our kids, our friends, and the conflicting interests we have from time to time.

I focus on his shapely mouth, wanting to bite his plump lower lip, or trace my tongue over the shapely peaks of his upper one.

"Show me," I command in a breathy voice.

He breaches the small distance, the contact between us electrifying. Power pulses from him. I'm more sensitive to it, in the same way I can feel the energy of a crystal, or the threads of magic that weave the universe.

He takes his time, a leisurely kiss appropriate for two people reacquainting.

Conversely, need coils within me, winding so tight I think I will burst. I deepen the kiss.

He makes a sound that's almost a growl. His hands find their way to my waist and then his calloused palms are smoothing all over my body, heat flaring in their wake.

My inner light pulses. So much of his wild lupine magic mixed with angelic might. I want to consume it. Consume *him*.

Something's not right. Still I kiss him harder, nipping at that juicy bottom lip. I rake my hands down his muscular back. The material shreds under my nails. Wet warmth soaks my fingers.

Gabriel breaks off the kiss wide-eyed. Blood trickles from his mouth.

My mouth tastes like pennies. I bring my hands to my face, noticing there's blood on my razor-sharp claws. Claws? I have claws. Sick realization that I'd *bit* Gabriel and tore up his back sinks in. The room spins. I shut my eyes to stop the vertigo.

A steel grip clutches my shoulder. "Miriam?"

I can't answer. If I open my mouth, I'll vomit.

"Miriam?"

I shake my head. The motion nauseates me.

"I'm going to get Phyr. He'll know what to do."

I open my eyes. The blood keeps running from Gabriel's injuries. My heart sinks.

"I should heal you." I reach to touch him, pausing at the sight of the bloody claws extended toward him. The blood smells good to me. Too good.

"I had ways of healing from injuries before I met you." Gabriel takes a step back, holding up his hands cautiously. "Just stay here."

I will not say it doesn't sting that Gabriel doesn't want me to heal him. Given that I like the smell of his blood, I don't blame him at the same time.

When he leaves, I close my eyes and take a deep breath, relieved. With his scent not as strong in my nostrils, I don't feel as out of control.

I take a seat at Lucinda's desk, careful not to touch anything with my bloody hands. All I want to do is go home, wash this off me, and forget. That's a lie. That's not all I want. Part of me hungers for Gabriel to come back, and begs me to follow him. It takes all my will to keep my butt planted in the seat.

Phyr enters the office, his face grim. He's lacking the leather jacket he'd sported earlier. Likely, he gave it to Gabriel to cover the shredded shirt.

Embarrassed by my behavior, heat floods my cheeks.

No illusion masks his bronze skin covered in tattoos—protective spell work. He offers a cup with the cafe's logo. "Drink this. It'll dampen the effects."

I take the cup and sniff. Not coffee. The liquid smells slightly sweet. A feral part of me, the same part that grew claws and sprouted fangs, wants to down it. Another part, a logical, witchy part, suspects the contents are something I don't care to drink. I narrow my eyes at the dark contents with crimson edges, then lift my gaze to Phyr, noticing a bandage around his wrist.

He frowns. "Yes. It's my blood."

I rear my head. "Why are you giving me your blood?"

He rubs his brow. "I really wish someone else would have explained this to you."

"Explained what?"

Phyr's face and body language emote he'd rather be anywhere than here. "There are bodily changes when a fae child transitions into adulthood. Drinking my blood, a fae who has gone through the passage, will make you less...scratchy and bitey when you're feeling amorous."

"Sounds like a cure for puberty." I sigh. As I eye the liquid dubiously, I recall a mate-bonding being a big deal between adult fae when I was a child. "I saw a bonding ceremony once. They drank each other's blood." And had sex right on the altar. The other fae watched regardless of age, but my mother dragged me away. "Will drinking this bind us?"

Phyr rolls his eyes. "I've shared the blood of many fae, and I am not bound to any of them."

"If drinking someone else's blood relieves the physical need to bond but doesn't actually bind you, what does?"

His gaze fixes on the cup as if he *could* will me to drink and get it over with—making me wonder why he's so eager to avoid the conversation.

I gesture at him and the cup with my bloody hand. "I want to know before I drink."

"There is a specific ceremony for mate-bonding. Remember when I found you on an altar dedicated to the ritual?"

I remember waking on a stone slab in a sheer gown covered in flowers. The memory triggers another of a bondmate ceremony. One of the fae was wearing a similar dress.

Oh, wow. The fae of that faerie assumed I'd come there to bond with their prince. Phyr, knowing how I'd lived my life through the pixies who followed me, must have had his doubts. No wonder he wasn't happy to see me.

"How could I forget?" I grin. "You kicked me awake."

He grins back. A bit of mischief sparkles in his amber eyes and some of the tension in his body eases. "I nudged you gently with my boot, well aware you didn't understand what you were being set up to do."

"Some reunion that."

"Indeed."

I take one last look at the contents of the cup before I drink. The taste isn't unpleasant. My fangs and claws retract, and my hands, albeit bloody, are my hands.

"Your change has finally come. Talk to your father," Phyr advises, unease in his features. "It is his duty to explain."

2

───────

❦

Seated at my dressing table, I hold a gilded mirror with beautiful floral embellishments on the back and handle. The comedic irony that I'm using a magic mirror like something out of a fairytale to contact my fae father isn't lost on me. I'm simply not in the mood to laugh at the absurdity of being a fairy princess.

I push my faelight into the mirror as I say words in High Fae that loosely translate, "Show me the blood of my blood. Oberon, your progeny awaits."

I must believe it will work. The mirror vibrates in my hand, letting me know the magic is working. The surface of the looking glass ripples for a moment before Oberon's image appears. My father's features are a study of sharp angles wrapped in smooth, pearlescent skin. Pink hair lays in loose waves past his shoulders. White antlers sprout from his head, regal as any crown. Oberon looks to be about twenty-five, but he is likely older than Earth itself. He arches his fine pink eyebrows, concern filling his features.

"You look troubled, daughter."

"I tried to eat my boyfriend, father."

The worry morphs into a wicked smile, replete with fangs where canines should be. "That nephil smells delicious. However, I have a treaty with him. Have Phyr teach you how to control your urge to devour the archangel, or anyone who would be inconvenient to eat. He'll know how."

An icy frisson skitters up my spine. Oberon is no worse than the father in my memories, but my time away from faerie has changed my perspective, my sense of right and wrong. I'm no goody two-shoes, but I also don't eat people. My mother had warned me that fae drank witch's blood for their power. I'd assumed she was lying, since she'd lived in faerie as my father's concubine. How much of her time was spent in terror?

"I don't want to eat him like food." I then describe what happened.

"Oh, that's much worse. Much."

"How could wanting to suck the life out of him be worse?"

"You are going through a change, Miriam. A transition from babe to adult that should have happened long ago. Gabriel is powerful, and you innately want that power for your offspring. Until you bond with a fae, this problem will continue whenever you're aroused."

I wrinkle my nose. Oh, sweet Danu. I'd lived for at least forty-three years without hearing Oberon say "aroused." An eternity without that word coming out of my dad's mouth again wouldn't be long enough.

An idea occurs.

"What about drinking Phyr's blood?" Not that I cared to drink my bestie's blood as a supplement, but desperate times and all.

"A temporary solution. Follow that path and you'll crave Phyr, body and soul."

"Why?"

"You've not recovered all your memories, then." Oberon sighs, appearing—uncomfortable? Fae speak freely of murder and sex, not to mention eating lovers. Why does he not want to talk about this? "When a high fae reaches maturity, their libido becomes insatiable. They become irritable as well. To quell the instinct to fight or mate, they bond with another fae."

I rub my hand over my face. "So, I can't bond with Gabriel?"

"No. The bonding instinct developed before angels or man existed."

"So, I have to bond with a fae in order to stop feeling this urge?" I refused to add, 'when I'm aroused.' I just couldn't. Living in the suburbs of Seattle made me prudish about talking sex with Daddy Oberon, High King of the Fae.

"Unless you can find a willing supply of the blood of many unmated fae on Earth, I'm afraid so, yes."

Rubbing the back of my neck, I ask, "Do you understand why the bonding ceremony would be disagreeable for all parties involved? I'm dating Gabriel." Gabriel's ex-wife, Kirsten, cheated on him repeatedly. She even cheated with an incubus, who likely used her as a spy for Lucifer. The pack believed Kirsten got away easy, with only being abjured. Gabriel had already come out of the supernatural closet for me in their eyes. "Shapeshifters will look at this as some sort of cuckolding."

Oberon sighs. "Their culture is primeval at best," says the fae who suggested my boyfriend smells delicious in the culinary sense. "I think the best course of action would be to discuss matters with—how did you put it? Oh, yes. 'All parties involved.'"

"Thank you for the advice," I reply, meaning it. Open discourse is the best action. The discovery of my former husband's deceit left me with a lot of unresolved resentment.

"I'm happy to oblige." He smiles, bearing fangs. I'm about to end the call when Oberon asks, "Dearest Tati, is there anything else you'd like to discuss? I have the time."

Is my dad trying to keep me on the line like an empty nester who misses their college kid? The notion tugs at my heartstrings. In my recovered memories, he had been an affectionate and doting father.

"I do, actually."

Oberon's face lights up. Unfortunately, I had fewer personal matters to discuss. Time to put on my diplomat hat. "Gabriel would like a meeting regarding the visas."

His face hardens. "Again? We've discussed terms."

He and Gabriel had sat down in my dining room with me as an intermediary twice. Gabriel kept pushing the date back when he'd allow more fae into his territory. They also had an agreement that there would not be an open-door policy. A limited number of fae would have access to this realm, and all those who entered would report to Gabriel weekly, as Phyr does. I understood Gabriel's reasoning. Fae aren't human immigrants. They'd earned their reputation as murderous tricksters. I also understood Oberon's waning patience. Gabriel wanted fae forces to back him if the Angelic Anocracy decides to revoke his position by violent means.

My head hurts. I rub my brow, hating politics. "Circumstances have changed."

"Is this a negotiation for fewer visas?"

I shrug. "I'm unsure, father."

"You are my diplomat and heir. He should present terms to you and then you relay those to me. Until there is an official romantic alliance between you two and I am family, his desire for direct communication with the High King is unseemly."

"Should I relay this to him?"

"I'll leave it up to your discretion, my dear. You must learn this art if you're to take my throne. Be well, my child."

"Be well, father."

I don't want his throne. The High Court will always have a special place in my heart, but I prefer this world. I assure my father I will do as he asks, then get off the magic mirror call. I forget I'm a freakin' fairy princess until dear old dad becomes Oberon, High King of the Fae.

Sweet Danu, my life is weird.

PHYR ANSWERS his bedroom door at the first knock. His glamour is gone. Bronze skin shimmering. Protective tattoos in High Fae script cover most of his bare torso and arms. He's in loose black pants and no shoes. A cell phone in his hand slips into his pocket. He rests a tattooed forearm on the doorframe. The bandage is gone, the wound already healed.

"Yes?"

"Why haven't you bonded?"

A grimace touches his lips. The rare display of emotion shows I've taken him off guard. "It's rude to ask that question among fae."

I arch an eyebrow at him. "When have we cared for propriety between us?"

"This is different." His discomfort is palpable.

Why does everyone hate talking about bonding?

He worries his lip, scratching the door frame with a nail lacquered black—Jada's work, no doubt. Phyr allows Jada to apply makeup to his face and paint his nails, braid his hair. I had to remind her Phyr was her fairy godfather, not a pet.

Releasing a long-suffering sigh, he relents. "I haven't ever felt the urge to bind myself to one fae, so I didn't."

"Is that still the case?"

He considers me for a moment before replying, "Perhaps."

Disappointment settles cold and hard in my gut because he is the only fae I'd trust or feel comfortable bonding with, but I also feel a modicum of relief. I wouldn't have wanted him to wait all this time for me. I'd lived my life, married, and had a kid. It seems incredibly unfair that he would endure the bonding instinct every time he became aroused because my mother had hexed my memory and taken me away.

"How are you—" I clear my throat "—handling not being bonded and not drinking fae blood?"

"I am not engaging in sexual intimacy." He spreads his hands. "Your archangel's rules, remember?"

"Oh," I say. "Sorry. I will talk to him, if you like. It's unfair."

He rests a reassuring hand on my shoulder and squeezes. "Don't be sorry. I made a choice to be here with you and Jada, and I'm happy with my life as a simple baker."

"Yes. But, for how long?" I ask, voicing a fear out loud. I, too, have enjoyed our rekindled friendship and running a bakery with him. Losing Phyr because of Gabriel's rules would break my heart.

His hand falls away. "This isn't about me or my desire to bond. You want to have sex with Gabriel, and bonding with me would allow you to do that without desiring to bond with him." His tone is soft, and his features lack the usual teasing smirk when it came to discussing sex.

Guilt knots my stomach. "I'm sorry. It's selfish of me. I won't ask you to do this."

I should leave it at that and return to my room. Instead, I hover.

After what seems an eternity, he takes my hand. His amber eyes glisten. "The bond isn't symbolic. We would always know firsthand how the other feels. Always. We would have access to each other's faelight. The bond is unbreakable. Even if our physical forms perish, we will be one forever."

Well, that's heavy.

Phyr closes his eyes and exhales out of his nose. "We would also be stronger for it."

"I—"

He places a finger on my lips. "My dearest friend, I would like to bond with you. However, you, Gabriel, and I will have to discuss what that would mean beforehand."

I nod, a grateful smile forming. "There's no rush."

"I have to do my weekly check-in with him in the early morning. I shall broach the subject."

"Shouldn't I do that?"

He shakes his head. "That's not how it's done among fae who have a bondmate and a consort. Besides, I don't think you'll put it as delicately as I will. Diplomacy is not your strong suit."

He had me there.

THE NEXT MORNING, I wake to a light tap on my door. The digital clock on my nightstand reads 5:30 in the morning.

I open the door to Phyr. Exhaustion saturates everything about him.

"Gabriel needs time to consider the arrangement I suggested."

I rub my eyes. "Arrangement?"

"Fae queens have several consorts. He understands, but it will take some time to consider."

I'm wide awake now. "What? What did you suggest?"

My head swam with unbidden images of some reverse harem fiction Rhiannon had recommended I read. I balked at the notion of keeping a cadre of lovers.

He laughs deep from his belly. "I enjoy the direction in which your mind veers, Tati, but no. I reminded him you are Oberon's heir, and, as such, have cultural expectations to meet among the fae, as well as physiological ones regarding bonding. We will bond in the fae tradition, but he will be your consort."

I rub my temples, processing.

"We all have much to consider. I'll let you get ready for work." He kisses my forehead, something he does often, as close fae do, and then shuts the door behind him.

3

Still-dark shops and barren trees covered in stringed lights line the street. Windshield wipers rhythmically swipe away the constant winter drizzle. I yawn for the third time since Phyr, Rhiannon, and I got in my car. We usually rotate so that one of us is at the shop with the two assistants I've hired. Today is one of the rare days all three of us are on duty.

In the rear seat, Phyr browses the internet on his phone, chuckling at memes on social media, no doubt. Rhiannon sings "If I Ain't Got You" off-key in the passenger seat as Alicia Keys belts the tune perfectly on the radio. The rock witch gets half the words wrong, inserting her own nonsense words.

Checking my rearview, I catch sight of something white sticking out of my hair and nearly hit the curb. I pull over, turn on the interior lights, flip the visor down, and slide the mirror cover to the side. Not one, but *two* hard protrusions sticking out of my scalp.

"Horns," I gasp.

"Really?" Phyr leans forward, touching the white antennae gently. "Not horns, antler buds."

A shiver of pleasure passes through me at his touch. Our gazes lock in the mirror. His hand suddenly falls away.

Shaking off what passed between us in that moment, I return my eyes to the road. "Ugh. When will these changes end?"

My skin stopped being freckled and pale, turning white with a patina that could rival any pearl. It's creepy, not pretty. A few weeks ago, my roots turned a shade of pink akin to Oberon's. A week ago, my eyes shifted from a fairly human green to a glass bottle green with a preternatural glow. Phyr taught me to weave a glamour most of the time to hide these changes.

"You're coming into your true form. A blessing from Danu." Humor paints Phyr's tone, and there's a twinkle in his eyes. "May your rack grow large."

Rhiannon chortles. "Phrasing!"

"I'm going to have to cast a glamour all the time now," I groan.

"Why?" Rhiannon asks, taking her turn to gingerly touch one of the buds on my head. "Oh, it's harder than I expected, but velvety on the outside."

"Phrasing," Phyr says in the back with an amused snort.

Rhiannon's touch tickles, but it is nothing like my reaction to Phyr. Is his blood already affecting me?

"Mundanes," I say in response to Rhiannon's question. "I don't want to provoke them further."

Phyr's fingers delicately skim over the other antler. "Yes. Very velvety." He makes a sound akin to a purr. This is the Phyr I'm used to. "When they're full-sized, many fae will envy you."

I duck out of their reach. "Okay. Petting zoo time is over."

The drive to the bakery passes without further comments on my appearance. The businesses around Enchanting Treats are still devoid of life. Few people keep bakery hours on the Eastside of Seattle, especially midwinter, when the dark lasts until almost eight in the morning.

I park in the lot behind the bakery. Rhiannon gets out first. Before joining her, Phyr casts a glamour, curling horns disappearing, hair turning a human dark brown, and his skin settling to a shade of light brown. I cast a glamour too. I grab my purse from the trunk, following them.

The brush of magic tickles my skin as I walk through the back door. I've warded the shop against intruders. Nothing harmful like the one I have around the perimeter of my property; only a powerful urge to turn around and run.

We grab our aprons and then mill about, flicking on lights and starting our morning duties.

"Can I leave work early?" Rhiannon asks as she leaves dough to rise on the counter.

I scowl. Rhiannon is a natural at baking, but not always reliable. "We just got here."

"I know. It's work-related, I swear."

"Like going to a bar and starting a fight in the middle of the day was work-related?" The corner of Phyr's mouth quirks as he speaks. When we first reunited a few months ago, my friend rarely showed emotion. Slowly, Phyr has allowed more expressions to play on his handsome features, especially when he's teasing.

"They said that witches are the source of warts, you know where. I was defending our honor," Rhiannon counters.

I chuckle as I take the dough out of the fridge to rise.

She waves a rolling pin. "I got a lead on Baba Yaga's honey cake recipe, brought all the way from the old world to Russia, and now it's here."

I've learned from Rhiannon that witches trade on a supernatural black market for spells leaked from my old coven's library or from grimoires the Archivists haven't gotten their hands on. She'd taught herself Kairska and how to read spells. Rhiannon sometimes displays erratic behaviors, but no one could say the rock witch didn't have brains.

I fire up the ovens. "Not a good idea."

Rhiannon shrugs. "Looking can't hurt."

"Remember when you brought us that parchment with a supposed spell to animate rudimentary machines?" Phyr asks, a grin tugging at the corner of his mouth.

Rhiannon glares and turns her back on him.

I raise my hand. "I do! The enchantment turned out to be an

excerpt from a Soviet Era machine maintenance manual written on cardstock and soaked in sheep's urine."

Phyr cocks a dubious eyebrow. "Sheep's urine?"

Recalling the powerful odor coming off the supposed parchment, I wave my hand. "Let's just say it was sheep's urine, okay?"

Phyr chuckles.

"So, the answer is no?" Rhiannon's expression falls.

"We're saying your quest is a bad idea, but if you want to take personal time, go ahead. Just help us with opening, K?"

"Okay!"

She gleefully delves into her opening duties. She works doubly hard all during the prep work, which is something, considering Rhiannon is a hard worker.

Phyr uses magic to do most of his labor. I roll my eyes at him. I prefer baking with my hands and tools. The work clears my mind and helps me prepare for my day.

Rhiannon finishes off the morning dishes and is out the door before the first customer comes in.

The day passes quickly as I fulfill breakfast orders. Phyr serves drip coffee and takes care of customers as well. We have an excellent system, dancing around each other with ease.

Nearing the end of our business day, an elderly mundane woman enters the shop, followed by a younger woman with blonde hair plaited in a neat French braid. The elder of the two wears a plastic rain bonnet from another decade. Neither wears makeup. Long, plastic rain slickers cover their upper bodies. Shapeless skirts brush the tops of their rubber rain boots. They carry large purses almost as large as briefcases. These women could be from anywhere in Pennsylvania, where I grew up, but are out of place on the Eastside.

From behind smudged wire-rimmed glasses, the elder of the duo eyes the tables and chairs, as well as the glass case, as if any item might bite her.

The younger woman's hands grip the straps of her large purse. She takes everything in wide-eyed.

I smile to ease her nerves. "Welcome to Enchanting Treats."

A smile starts on the younger's face, but she drops it quickly, as if she possesses manners but remembering friendliness is a crime.

The elder woman scowls. She opens her mouth to speak but falls silent when Phyr appears from the back, human-looking glamour in place.

Both women stare. Phyr is that pretty.

"How may I be of service to you, ladies?" He lays the Irish brogue on so thick it's almost comical. His glamoured-brown eyes sparkle along with his white, blunt-toothed smile.

The younger woman blushes deeply.

The older woman clutches her purse close to her body, murmuring under her breath, "Get behind me, Satan."

"The devil has no place here," I assure her, hoping to ease her fears. "I forbid it."

"What?" the younger woman asks, confusion furrowing her brow.

The old woman's mouth gapes. "How did you hear me?"

I stammer, unsure of what she means. She spoke out loud, didn't she?

"We want you to know we are all friends here, is all." Phyr's voice oozes with charm that tickles my ears.

The elder woman scrutinizes us both for a heartbeat before reaching into her purse.

I dip into my witch light and murmur a deflection spell. If she's got a gun, the bullets will bounce off. I don't want to hurt them, but I also don't want to die.

In my periphery I see Phyr sidling closer to me. His hand is at his hip, where the hilt of his invisible sword rests. As always, he has my back but lets me lead.

"My name is Jan, and this is my friend Ella. We're here to bring you the good news." The blond worries her lip as her friend slips a pamphlet on the counter. "This time of tribulation will be brief for those who accept the word of God."

The brochure features an illustration of Jesus, who looks more like Kenny Loggins than the son of a god, with a bunch of children.

Everyone is smiling and happy. I exhale in relief, banishing the spell. They're trying to convert us.

Jan continues, "Would you like to live in paradise where there is no more death, no more sorrow—"

"I hear the Summerlands are boring," Phyr interrupts. His eyes on the blond, he adds, "I prefer to take my pleasures right here where I can still feel."

Her cheeks turn a bright shade of crimson.

"Summerlands? Is that what they call Heaven, where you're from?" Jan asks.

His nose wrinkles. The fae and angels are ancient enemies. "Absolutely not. It's better."

"Well, the paradise I speak of will be right here on Earth," Jan insists. The plastic on her head crinkles as she nods.

"I believe so too," Phyr says, a flirtatious grin returning. This time, it's aimed at Jan.

My head is spinning, trying to keep up with all the nonsense.

"I know so. It says so in the Bible." She pulls out her Bible in case we've never seen one. "We are in the end times. I'm here to tell you that the Creator loves all of you and wants you to repent." She gestures to both of us. "Whatever you two are under those disguises, he'll remake you in his image."

Phyr and I trade looks.

"Huh." I pick up the pamphlet feigning interest, glad they're not hostile like the guy on the soapbox and his companions. "Imagine that."

"I can arrange for you to learn how God can make you clean for the upcoming tribulation by studying the Bible with Ella and me."

"What about me? Am I going to get some time with you and Ella?" Phyr asks, winking.

Jan returns his flirtation with a dour look. "It wouldn't be appropriate. A brother acolyte from the Paradise Center would happily lead you in a Bible study."

Phyr quirks an eyebrow, an amused smile playing upon his lips.

"Why would I want to learn from your sibling when you two can read to me?"

Color flooded the blond's entire face. Her eyes dilate and her respiration speeds up. "Less of a temptation for us to commit forni—"

"Sin," Jan says, putting herself bodily in front of her companion. "There's information on how to contact us or a brother at the Paradise Center on the back of the brochure."

Phyr and I hold back our laughter until the duo rush out the door.

As we load the car after closing the bakery, something troubles me. "How did she know we have illusions covering the way we look?"

Phyr shakes his head and shuts the trunk. Leaning against the rear, he folds his arms across his chest. "She didn't. Unless she had a charm, there's no way a human could see through our glamour."

My eyebrows knit. "Then why would she say that?"

He shrugs. "She made an educated guess."

Realization dawns on me. "The gala?"

He points his fingers like cocked guns, then mock fires, suggesting my suspicion is correct. Since guns weren't around the last time high fae walked the Earth, where he learned to do finger pistols is anyone's guess—a movie he'd watched with Jada, the most likely culprit.

4

Before we head home, I pick up Jada and Roxy at Papillon Academy. Kirsten has grounded Roxy from using her BMW. Again. I didn't ask why because I don't mind resuming my old role driving mom taxi. Usually, good conversations sprouted from the busy teens on these rides. For some reason, they talked more in the car.

Roxy has a new look. Her once long, electric blue hair is now shaved to stubble dyed neon pink. A barber artfully designed wings on each side of her head. Both girls wear heavy makeup highly stylized.

Jada and Roxy buckle up and pull out their respective phones. Both seem flustered, and it's not like them to just zone out.

"Can we listen to one of my playlists?" Jada asks.

"Sure." I hand her my phone. She understands the Bluetooth connection better than I do—a recently remembered childhood spent in a faerie is the likely culprit for my technophobia: pre-industrial revolution era life in a faerie and magic instead of tech.

Music fills the car. The vocals are distorted, and the melody is bizarre.

I lower the volume manually to a nice ambient racket.

"How was senior ball planning?" I ask over my shoulder.

In my rearview, Jada rolls her eyes. "Pfft. Normie mundanes ruined it."

"How so?" Phyr asks, interest piqued.

"We got anti-supe zealots on the committee," Roxy informs. "What's up with your head? Did you get something done?"

Apparently, Roxy can see through my glamour. Good to know.

"I'm growing antlers," I sigh.

"Sick," both girls reply.

"Thanks, I think." Slang changes meaning so often, I'm not sure if it's a compliment anymore.

"It's a good thing, mom. Just keep the glamour on around school. Okay?"

I turn onto the street that leads opposite my house to drop Roxy first. Gabriel lives in a much nicer neighborhood than I do, past the vineyards. Not that the million-dollar houses on my block are anything to sneeze at, but it's expensive to live on the Eastside in general. The archangel has old money and more business than I can recall off the top of my head. I'm living off a trust from my late husband, who had new tech money, and I'm getting a bakery off the ground in a time when supes are the new thing to fear.

"Are these zealots giving you two a hard time?" I ask.

Neither girl responds. In the rearview, I see them glance at each other, shifting nervously.

"Did you two give the *zealots* a hard time?" Phyr asks, a hint of a smile evident in his tone.

Roxy folds her arms across her chest and huffs. "I would have loved to, but dad would kill me."

I meet Jada's gaze in the rearview. "Am I going to get a phone call?"

"Nope."

"Jada—"

She growls in frustration, sounding not quite human when she says, "Some jerks said supes shouldn't be able to come to the dance because magic is technically a weapon, and weapons are not allowed on school property. Then the meeting became this whole debate whether supes should even be able to go to the school. I made them shut up about supes and talk about the dance, okay?"

My stomach dips. My daughter is a demigod. Fae could influence the minds of a small crowd. She could influence the minds of myriads. She's turning eighteen soon and will be on her own at college next fall. I won't be able to temper that power with Mom Authority.

"Jada, we spoke before about asserting your influence over others. What did your father say about it?"

"Pops said I could in self-defense!"

Pops meaning her fae adoptive father, Phyr, not her actual father Rafael, who had ascended to godhood a few years ago. With each year that passes since Raf left, his words matter less and what the adults in her life currently say matters more. I don't regret Phy'rs place in her life, but fae never take the moral high ground when it comes to humans. The fae take exactly what will benefit them.

I glare at Phyr. He knows she hangs on to his every word.

"Did you?"

He shrugs.

"You weren't there," Roxy whines. "They were awful."

"There's no way I can get in trouble for using my gifts—there's no rule against it," Jada protests and then buries her face in her phone, tapping away. "Can we drop it? The meeting was stressful enough."

I pull the car over to the side of the road. Unbuckling, I turn around so I can fully face Jada and Roxy. "No. We cannot drop it. You two were in a position where you could prove that supes were nothing to fear. Instead, you chose to abuse your gifts and do exactly what they fear from us. You used your power to take away their free will. There can be no greater violation than what you did."

Roxy has the sense to cringe.

My daughter, however, has too much of my attitude at seventeen years old. "It's not a big deal. The mundanes have no idea what I did."

"If you challenge a core belief," Phyr says in a mild tone, "cognitive dissonance will break your influential magic and they will know you duped them. Hope they are weak of mind, or—"

"This will come back to haunt you," I finish for him.

The girls are silent for the remainder of the drive, hiding behind their cellphones. Phyr watches a baking competition show on his phone, making verbal commentary here and there about the works of the competitors as if he's been baking his entire life.

I veer off the main road, butterflies in my stomach. I haven't seen Gabriel since I tried to eat him. An ornate, wrought iron gate meets us. Unseen barbs prickle my skin, a magical warning that I'm close to a substance not for me.

Phyr curses under his breath.

This is the first time I'm feeling the sensation. Phyr always has this reaction. Is this also another downside of fae puberty, an aversion to iron?

That's going to suck.

"Want to wait here?" I ask, knowing the full-blooded fae might be in actual pain.

He shakes his head and flashes a rueful smile. He mutters softly, "Thank blessed Danu, wrought iron is too expensive to be a ubiquitous fencing material. It's only the gate. The rest of the fence is likely an aluminum alloy."

I lift an eyebrow.

"The portal of Wikipedia," he replies to my unspoken question.

I don't even want to ask what he was doing on that site.

"Want me to get the gate?" Roxy asks.

"Would you?" Normally, I do, but I don't think I can tolerate pushing the button surrounded by the poisonous metal.

Fortunately, neither of us needs to get out to push the call button. Someone on security detail recognizes my car and triggers the gate remotely.

A winding private road leads up a hill. Evergreens so tall I can't see the tops litter the vast hillside property, accompanied by ferns, brush, and deciduous trees barren of leaves but heavy with moss, the verdant greens of the flora a sharp contrast to the gunmetal gray sky.

Besides indigenous wildlife, the forests of the multi-acre estate are stocked with deer, elk, and moose for the shifters to hunt. So, I keep an eye out for animals and shifters in animal form as I drive.

Gabriel's house atop the hill is a two-story, sprawling mansion with stables and a dairy barn. Shifters love milk, something I hadn't known until I started dating Gabriel.

In my periphery, I catch multiple dark shapes rocketing in my direction and slam on the brakes.

Roxy sniffs the air like a bloodhound and smiles. "The pups are hunting!"

She hops out of the car, tearing off her clothes to shift into wolf form.

Phyr averts his eyes, grumbling about giving warning.

A massive white wolf and several other adult shifters: a giant honey badger, a grizzly, and a few more wolves, along with some wolf pups, all sprint across the road. Roxy, in white wolf form, howls and joins the chase.

Phyr rolls his eyes, muttering something about muzzles.

"Mami, can I?"

Jada pleads with me with her eyes in the rearview. She wants to shift into animal form too. She's not a shifter in the technical sense, as in born to a pack and shifting into one animal, but one of her godly powers passed down from her father, Rafael, is the ability to become any animal she sees. She and Raf preferred to be panthers. Sometimes when she's with Roxy and Gabriel on hunts, she takes on a dark gray wolf form.

I sigh. "I didn't ask Gabriel if he can take you home."

"You know he will if it means seeing you later," she whines.

I don't know if I want to see him. I feel so much shame for the way I acted yesterday, and Danu knows I don't want to talk about consorts and fae bonding. Some time apart would help.

Too late to pull out now. After a few yips toward the hunting pack, the wolf changes directions and heads toward my car.

Crap. Gabriel wants to talk.

Instinct at seeing an apex predator lumbering toward me raises my heart rate. My reasoning brain knows it's Gabriel, so I engage the emergency brake and get out of the car.

The wolf bows his head as he approaches. I stroke his soft fur. He smells of forest and animal, and strangely, a scent I associate with Gabriel's human-ish form—not that he's human at all.

His fur recedes. His body lengthens and stretches. I no longer gag as the snap, crackling, and pop of his body changing shape fill my ears.

A tattoo of wings adorns the smooth brown skin laid over dense muscle. Gabriel pushes to his feet. He's big, but not overly bulky. He isn't just perfectly proportioned; he has won the lottery in the features department: high, prominent cheekbones, a jaw that could cut glass, a cleft chin, and eyes that tilt slightly upward at the outermost corners. His mouth is so damned full and shapely, I'm having a hard time concentrating on anything else.

Well, not the only thing.

Phyr's voice rings in my head. I turn toward the car, but he's not even looking at me. His eyes are on Gabriel too. I don't blame him. The nephil is a delightful sight.

"Hey," Gabriel strokes my cheek and I focus all my attention on him. "You alright?"

I nod. "I should ask you that."

"We need to talk." He takes my hand and leads me behind a tree, just out of sight of the car.

I begin to apologize.

"Phyr explained why you had that reaction. You wanted to mate-bond with me." He smiles, leans in, and kisses me.

I kiss him back for only a second, then break away, afraid of what I might do. "Jada and Phyr are waiting in the car."

Gabriel glances down between us.

Yeah. You're nude, buddy.

Thankfully, understanding registers on his features. He scratches the back of his head. "Sorry. Hunting makes me...and your smell—oh, these are new."

He reaches for my head. A shiver of pleasure washes through me as he gently touches the budding antlers. "Antlers." The word comes out breathier than I intended.

"You're becoming more and more recognizable as Oberon's child," he says, no small amount of consternation filling his face.

"Fantastic," I reply, remembering that my sibling Maeve looked like Oberon as well. I don't want to be mistaken for either of them.

"Phyr said you were changing, that releasing your faelight has set off some sort of fae puberty?"

I swallow hard, not knowing what else Phyr told him. "I feel like the fae part of me wants to take over until there's nothing left of the witch I was," I admit.

"No matter what you look like, you were never simply a witch," Gabriel corrects. His voice is gentle, but the words sting as if being simply a witch is less somehow. "You're a fae witch, and there's nothing wrong with being two things. You can still embrace both, but one will be dominant."

A nephil-shifter would know. I want to ask him if being a shifter or an angel is dominant for him, but I let it go. He'll share if he wants to.

"I wish I had my whole life to adjust to this." I don't add, 'the way you did.'

He gives me a rueful smile. "Not the midlife changes you were expecting?"

I grimace. Changing the subject, I ask, "How many fae do you plan to give visas?"

Gabriel rears his head. "What?"

"It's unseemly for Oberon to discuss the matter ahead of the meeting. I need to relay it to him."

He brushes his fingers through his curls. "I don't know. I don't know how many fae I could handle right now. I have so much going on." His gaze reaches past me. "I should rejoin the rest. The pups can be a handful."

"How's Mama Doe?"

"Physically? She's healed. Mentally—" Worry etches lines into his pretty features as he shakes his head slowly.

Princess, Gabriel's beta, went camping with her Bigfoot girlfriend Aurora a few days after supernaturals came out. They had planned for a three-week getaway but cut the trip short when the two found a shifter deep in the Cascades, pregnant with triplets and her deaf-mute pup whining next to her. Someone had beaten the poor dear within an inch of her life. She would not discuss how she got that way, which pack she came from, nothing. The only word she will utter is "help" in varying degrees of urgency.

I know what that kind of trauma is like firsthand. Raf, Jada's father, had had to nurse me back to health after I'd faked my death to leave Lucifer.

Gabriel sent out word to all the packs. He had a few leads from packs missing shifters. Six times, attempts to ID her led to disappointment for all involved. No packs recognized her.

The shifters among the Northwest Indigenous, who keep their own hierarchy separate from those who align with the angels, couldn't identify her either. It had been heartbreaking to see the hope in the eyes of an elder who thought it might be one of their missing women, only to have that hope die in her eyes when she didn't recognize her.

"Maybe you should report it to the mundane authorities?" I offer, yet again. "There has to be a missing person case somewhere that matches."

He blows out his breath and appears almost ashamed. "No. No pack would admit to an abusive alpha. They *couldn't*. The mundane authorities would use her as an opportunity to vilify all shifters. Supes can't afford that right now."

Unease twists my gut. He hadn't mentioned it could have been an alpha before.

"Do you think the alpha abused his power over her?"

"Maybe," he admits. "If I can get her to accept me as her alpha, I can undo some of the damage, but—"

The woman wouldn't let Gabriel or any other male presenting shifter around her. Her pleas for help would turn into terrified screeching.

"What if Phyr made himself more femme and did a deep dive into her mind to find out what happened?"

Gabriel's eyes flashed gold. "No."

"Just a suggestion." I take a step back, hands in front of me. I'd seen him act this way. "I really should be going."

Emotions war on his face, as if he's going to relent and allow Phyr to help. Finally, he asks, "Perhaps you could, do it?"

"If you don't find answers, I am willing to try, but Phyr—"

"No." He shakes his head adamantly. "I will not let a high fae into the head of a shifter. They're untrustworthy."

Anger flares hot and wild in my chest. "Phyr has been loyal to Jada and me, and has been my most trusted friend my entire life. And in case you forgot, I am high fae."

I spin on my heel. It takes seconds to return to my car. I move with preternatural speed.

Gabriel calls for me to come back, but I'm already putting the car in reverse and backing down the driveway before it even registers.

5

During Pacific Northwest winters, the sun is like a reluctant debutante, making it to the party, but only staying long enough to say she went. The constant drizzle has upped its game to a full downpour as we pull into my cul-de-sac, adding to the gloom of the day.

The pixies who inhabit my gardens follow my car into the garage. They have their shelters within the garden they've built, so this is unusual.

They buzz around my head, a tinny voice cacophony. I glean the low fae word "cu," which means hound or dog. Pixies wouldn't make a big deal about a neighbor's pooch. So, it's safe to assume my little friends want to warn me about a hellhound.

Anger and fear war in my chest. Lucifer's promises usually meant squat, but I thought that he would at least honor our treaty.

"Alright, alright." I motion for the pixies to stop speaking. Then I switch to High Fae. "The child must go inside for her protection before I can do anything about the hellhound."

The agitated fae settles on top of a shelf.

I spin to my daughter, who is squeezing between the Subaru and the Enchanting Treats delivery van. "Jada, get washed up for dinner prep. Phyr, can you help me with the garbage bins?"

Phyr cocks his head, opening his mouth to speak. It isn't trash day tomorrow, and he's likely to inform me so. I level a look that earns his silence.

"What's up with the pixies?" Jada asks, not budging.

Oh, no. No. No. This is not the time for teenage twenty-questions. I smile. "I forgot their cream this morning." My grin falls to a grimace as the pain of the outright lie sears through me like a fiery blade.

Thankfully, Jada's focus remains on the cute pixies, so she doesn't notice me wincing. "I'll set some out back for them."

"Go in with her." I order the pixies in High Fae.

To Jada's back, I say, "I told them to come inside to make amends. Set a bowl out for them in the kitchen, would you?"

As Jada and the flock enter the washroom adjacent to the garage, I pluck one pixie from the air. They're tiny and their wings are delicate, so I'm careful. Once the door closes behind my daughter, I ask the pixie to repeat the story so I can figure out where they saw this hellhound. Phyr listens in, too.

A hellhound is prowling the neighborhood and might still be there.

Phyr asks in low fae to show us where the hellhound was last seen.

They point in the direction of my house.

"In there?"

The pixie shakes their head and says a word that loosely translates "over and through," meaning "behind."

Phyr and I exchange glances. The Johnsons' place is behind my house. Shawn Johnson is an angel fallen from Grace, meaning he's left Heaven and lives without his full angelic powers.

"Do you believe he is a traitor?"

I almost say no. I've known Shawn for ages, but I hesitate. Despite the longevity of our friendship, he didn't break the news that he was a fallen angel until a few months ago. Nothing is off the table. "Let's investigate. Can you take us to the neighbor's house that shares a backyard with the Johnsons?"

Phyr nods, smiling appreciatively. "Here, I thought you would ask to travel straight into danger."

I huff in disbelief as I get my backpack o' tricks from where it hangs in the garage. I also grab Raf's old crossbow and a quiver filled with rowan arrows Phyr had made. If I can't banish the beast, I've gotta kill it. "I know to find out what I'm dealing with before heading into a fight."

Eyes glittering with mischief, his smile widens. "How long did it take you to learn that lesson?"

I roll my eyes and make a haphazard karate chop, imitating the manner in which the planeswalker cuts a shortcut through the fabric of the universe.

He chuckles before slicing through what seems like thin air with his hand. Then he offers his free hand to me. We travel through the cold interstitial space of the multiverse, protected by our faelight, before we step into our neighbor's side-yard.

Phyr's footsteps are soundless. I might as well have been banging a pot with a wooden spoon, for all the noise I make.

We crouch behind a rhododendron, peering between the leaves. The light coming from the Johnsons' kitchen bay window illuminates the backyard where the hellhound circles the kids' play structure.

My pulse quickens at the sight of the monster. The beast is the size of a Shetland pony, likely weighing four or five hundred pounds. Sleek, dark gray fur covers the creature's body. The maw is closed, but I know from experience there are rows of razor-sharp teeth inside. Scarlet glowing eyes illuminate wherever the beast's gaze lands.

The monster is a menace, but what really scares me are the swirling shadows at the hellhound's feet—shadows that contain magic that will suck straight to Hell, where its master awaits, anyone who gets too close.

I clench my fists. Three months. I've had just three months free of looking over my shoulder for Lucifer's minions.

Micah, a fit man in his early forties, wearing a "kiss the chef" apron, sweats, and a pale blue t-shirt, exits the rear of the house, walking stiffly, like a resurrected mummy in an old B movie. His strawberry blond hair is longer than it used to be, and his former baby face has sprouted a ginger beard. If the zombie act isn't enough to lead me to believe Micah's not conscious, his left hand is holding a spatula, ready to flip.

The Johnsons' ten-year-old, Jennifer, joins her father on the deck. "Daddy, are you okay?" Her voice quavers with trepidation.

No. Daddy's not okay. I want her to go back inside, but I dare not think it into action. Wavering with free will versus saving a child from a hellhound was not on the agenda for this evening, yet here I am.

Her gaze moving from her dad to where he's walking, she gasps and asks, "What's wrong with that dog's eyes?"

The beast's maw emits a low growl. The swirling shadows surrounding the hellhound grow. The monster crouches as if to leap.

Without thinking, I launch myself at Jennifer. Our bodies collide, knocking her out of the way. I stay on top of the girl, but my gaze swivels to the action behind me.

Phyr disappears, reappearing between Micah and the hellhound. The hellhound charges, but is no match for a planeswalker, who simply opens a hole in the fabric of space and time for the dog to leap into. He seals the portal with a wave of his hand.

I roll off Jennifer. "You okay, sweetie?"

She doesn't answer. Her arm is bent all the wrong way, and she's out cold.

Hands on her chest, I push my green faelight into her, intending for the bones to mend, and to heal any other injuries. Since the child is an adopted mundane with no magic to counter mine, her body repairs quickly.

Phyr kneels next to her, placing a hand on her cheek. "She shouldn't remember this."

I don't like the idea of manipulating others, but a mind so young would have a tough time recovering from the trauma of witnessing a hellhound about to devour her daddy.

"What in the hell?" Micah gasps, suddenly aware of his surroundings.

"Where in Hell, you mean," Phyr mutters.

"How—" Micah scratches behind his ear. "How did I end up here?"

"We all showed up because Jennifer screamed," I reply, glad Phyr and I kept our human glamours on. Also, I hope Micah didn't peek at the neighbor's rhododendrons where I left the crossbow and quivers. "A loose dog tried to attack her. Phyr scared it off. Guess Jennifer fainted in the commotion?"

The lies are all hot daggers cleaving through me. I grit through the agony, hoping Micah won't notice in the wan light.

My neighbor shakes his head as if waking from a dream. "Yeah. That's what happened. Sorry. I've been losing time lately."

"You have?" Phyr and I ask in unison.

"I'm seeing a neurologist about it." He gestures to his kid. "I better take Jennifer in and check her for a concussion. Thanks for coming so quickly." His voice is off. I don't think he quite trusts my story but can't remember anything to contradict it either.

I smile thinly, watching him scoop up Jennifer. She's limp as a rag doll in his arms. He waves and we wave back before he goes in.

Phyr sidles close to me. "Should you warn the angel about what transpired here?"

I shake my head. "The hellhound most likely was here for me. No need to upset Shawn."

Phyr frowns. "Miriam, I meant you should report this to Gabriel."

I stiffen. No. I don't want to speak to Gabriel right now. "Why should I tell him?"

My friend gives me a curious arch of his eyebrow, as if the answer is obvious. "Lucifer has broken the treaty you negotiated."

"I'll mention it in the next council meeting." I bend to pick up my belongings, the lie searing my insides.

"Tati," Phyr chides, using the diminutive of my fae name. "You can't fight him alone."

Straightening, I challenge Phyr. "It's bad enough you must report to Gabriel like he's your boss. Do you prefer shifters sniffing around this block, watching everything we do? Things are already tense with the mundane neighbors."

As if summoned, the door to the house next to the Johnsons opens. Their neighbor is wearing a nightcap and a fuzzy bathrobe as she steps hesitantly onto her deck. She closes a fist tight around the collar of the robe, eyeing the quiver and crossbow on my back warily. "Can I help you?"

"Coyote snatched my cat," I say, allowing the burning agony of the lie to show on my face. Hopefully, my pain conveys the grief of a pet owner.

Some of the tension leaves her, but she doesn't unclench the bathrobe. "Foul beasts got your P.C., too?"

"Too," I ask, interest piqued. Coyotes snatch up cats now and then, but so do hellhounds.

"Those meanies ate my Whiskers a few weeks back. I found his mangled collar out back." Her lip quivers.

"How devastating," Phyr says with all the sincerity of a disinterested noble.

"I told the HOA we need to do something about the predators roaming our neighborhood." Her gaze shifts to the fae. "There's been a lot more recently."

With the ever-expanding population in this area due to the tech jobs and Californians seeking tax breaks and slightly more affordable housing, it's no wonder displaced animals are foraging in the suburbs.

"Go inside and forget we were here," Phyr commands with a wave of his hand.

His magic brushes against my skin, silky and convincing. If I were a full witch or a mundane, I'd have felt compelled to obey. The woman nods absently, doing as he bid with zombie-like motions.

I glower at Phyr. Taking away someone's memories and free will infuriates me. He knows it. Worse than that, he could be surrendering his right to remain in this territory if Gabriel finds out. The thought makes my chest ache. I lived without my dearest friend for so long and lament the prospect of losing him again.

I jab a finger at him. "You're not supposed to—"

Phyr holds up his hand, interrupting me. "Peace, Miriam. Gabriel has amended his original stipulations, one of which is to erase any memories from humans when they witness occurrences which could potentially cause panic if widely known."

"Oh." Neither had shared with me that the rules have changed. I must admit the lack of disclosure stings. "Damage control."

My friend squeezes my shoulder. "Please know I didn't mean to betray your trust, dearest. The nephil bade me to not tell you about the new stipulations unless necessary. I had to agree."

Because Gabriel called the shots in this territory. Over supes. Over me. My muscles tense. "Interesting."

Gabriel wants the new rules kept secret from me because he knows how I feel about usurping the will of others. I was addicted to Lucifer's angel dust for years, doing his bidding until I faked my death and freed myself of him. It took me even longer to know my own mind. Sometimes I still struggle with what was coven-taught or Lucifer's brainwashing versus what I actually think.

"I will refrain from using my influence on others unless you or Jada are in direct danger," Phyr says, apology in his features.

I gather my things. He's apologizing, but I'm still angry. I'm disappointed in Phyr and Gabriel, but Phyr's betrayal hurts more. "We keep each other's secrets, not keep secrets from each other."

He spreads his hands. "I made the choice that kept us together."

I know. I know. He's helpless. Either he agrees to Gabriel's terms or must leave. Neither of us wants that. "You're doing dishes tonight."

He bows with a flourish. "As you wish."

My heart squeezes despite my annoyance. Phyr has watched *The Princess Bride* with Jada and Rhiannon at least a dozen times.

I love him too.

And that is too messy and complicated to say out loud.

~

WE GO HOME and have dinner, minus the usual company of Rhiannon and Lance. The rock witch has lived here since she helped remove a hex my mother put on my memory. The shapeshifter Lance stays often, but sometimes the couple stays in Lance's room at Gabriel's house, where many of the shifters and their families live.

When I texted Rhi to see if she would be home for dinner, she replied, "Don't wait up, mom!" Followed by a bunch of eggplant and peach emojis.

T.M.I., Rhiannon, T. M. I.

After Jada excuses herself to do homework, Phyr and I start clearing the table.

I pretend not to notice Phyr's pauses and curious glances as I give P.C. his afternoon wet food. The cat loops my legs, marking his territory before beginning his meal. I turn on the news for background noise. My friend wants more details about what happened with Gabriel earlier, but won't pry. The last thing I feel like doing is discussing Gabriel's insult.

Phyr has done nothing but be an excellent friend and an asset to the supe community since his arrival. The only thing he's ever done that Gabriel might a have beef with is when he called the nephil a "baby killer." That was months ago. Gabriel should trust Phyr by now. It rankles me that he doesn't.

Phyr waits until the decided click of Jada's door before saying, "Excepting when I placed your Creuset Dutch oven in the dishwashing automaton, you are rarely cross with me. Even then, you forgave me. Grudge holding is not like you."

This is true. Phyr gave me little reason to be angry or to hold a grudge.

I take a few clean dishes from the dishwasher and put them in the cupboard before replying, "Gabriel says that he doesn't trust high fae."

"Of course, he doesn't," Phyr replies as if I'd said Gabriel doesn't like cheese because he's lactose intolerant. "The fae were his enemy, until recently. Why does this bother you?"

I turn. "I'm high fae."

I didn't think I was lying, but pain racks my body. The onslaught of it is so sudden, I don't have time to manage to grit my teeth and bare it.

As if sensing my distress, P.C. leaves his dinner to rub himself against my legs. Then, being a cat, he returns to his meal satisfied he's cured me.

Phyr's brow furrows in consternation. He gives me a rueful smile, taking my hand. "We're adults, my dearest friend. You don't have to protect me or my feelings anymore. I hate watching you suffer to do so."

My heart clenches. He understands me sometimes better than I understand myself. I am protective of the person who had my back against my siblings and other nasty fae who didn't like a halfling witch, inheriting Oberon's faerie. "I want Gabriel to like you and you to like him. This rivalry from the beginning, tearing at each other when I care for you both, is eating at me."

"Ah, I see." His grin turns playful. "You want us to like each other because you'd like a menage à—"

"Shut up." I push him away, laughing. I sober. "He doesn't trust you to look into the mind of the Mama Doe shifter."

"I will speak with Gabriel," Phyr announces, "to make him understand our friendship has always been an alliance of us against the world."

"I should tell him." I don't want to. I feel like I'm betraying other High Fae somehow. Imagine that. I don't want to make my notoriously murderous siblings look bad to an outsider. Wow. I hadn't realized I had thought that way.

"Let me play arbiter. It will help him trust me if he knows I want to soothe relations between you two, not be the cause of discord. Besides, tonight is my routine check-in with him, anyway."

I shut the cupboard a little too hard.

Phyr had to report to Gabriel as regularly as any shifter who served the nephil. What happened during these debriefings was between them.

Forget our childhood. The fact that Phyr, a prince among high fae, kneels to his enemy to be a part of my life overwhelms me. I don't know how to express my gratitude verbally. Words seem trite. Instead, I throw my arms around Phyr's torso and hug him. He's stiff at first. Fae aren't huggers. Eventually, he relaxes and reciprocates, squeezing me tight.

When I break away to return to unloading the dishwasher, he says, "Sorry to leave you with the rest of the cleanup, but I should go now."

"Aha, this was all a ruse to get out of dishes!" I wag my finger.

"Absolutely." His chuckle fading as he walks into thin air.

I only hope he's not bound by some agreement to tell Gabriel about the hellhound. Gabriel dealing with Lucifer breaking a pact will end with another enemy on our hands, possibly an invasion, without the backing of the Angelic Anocracy. I know how to handle Lucifer, which gives me an idea.

I HISS as I slice my arm with a dagger. I'm standing inside a summoning circle drawn in the loam of my cache—a pocket universe formed by my magic. The ground is a new thing. I believed there was solid ground beneath my feet, and it became so. A sun shines in the distance, illuminating the once dark space. I believed that into existence, too. The chalice at my feet is from home.

Plumes of wispy smoke snake around me, caressing my face, my arms, tracing down my back.

"No touching," I say. An invisible barrier forms.

The smoke coalesces into a towering pyre of black flame.

"There was a time when you would have done anything for my caress," the King of Hell sighs as he solidifies. "Am I so hideous to you now that I repulse you?"

As if.

He knows he's gorgeous. Lucifer is large and muscular in the way an athlete is large, a swimmer's build, not a bodybuilder. His eyes are two pools of black and his sculpted features are of angelic perfection. His hair and wings are black as the void. He extends the latter behind him. The massive wings possess a silvery sheen. That's new. He's dressed in a simple, silken robe that reaches to his feet, also silver in color. The front of the robe opens at the neck, coming to a "v" just below where a navel would be, if he possessed one. Angels were created, not born. The clothes, also new, more like an angel than a fallen angel.

What game is he playing at?

"No. What repulses me is the way you wanted to use me as a battery for a spell to destroy all of humanity."

"I thought we were moving past that." Lucifer sniffs the air, gaze darting about. He cocks his head to the side, nonplussed, as he examines the dirt at his feet. "Tati, couldn't you grow some grass? Perhaps a flower or two. This is the work of a fae with lesser breeding. I know you possess better taste than this."

Is he really criticizing how I decorated the place with a back-handed compliment? How did young me not see Lucifer as the poster boy for toxic exes?

I decide to ignore the criticism and go straight for the jugular. "You spy on me."

"I am your ally. My hounds survey the perimeter of your grounds because I care about your safety." He has the nerve to sound offended. Going so far as to touch his chest, wounded.

I cover my hands over my heart and gasp exaggeratedly, "Oh Lucifer, I'm so touched."

"Mock me if you must, but I don't trust my nephew. He has all the ambition of my youth, but none of the intelligence. I blame the beast my brother had a fling with. Shifters are volatile in nature and slow in reasoning. He will destroy all that you're meant to be because he wants you as his pawn."

Wow. I'd forgotten how arrogant, mean, and prejudiced he could be when he was jealous of someone I found even mildly attractive. "Aw. We both know only you should be entitled to using me until I am utterly destroyed." I smile meanly, bearing my new fangs. "At least you're the only one allowed to attempt it. You'll find I'm not so easily duped as when I was a kid."

Anger flashes across his face, marring his perfect features with something sinister and volatile. The look is there and gone.

I lift my chin. That's right. Remember, you're only as powerful as I let you be in here, asshole.

"After what you did with the grimoires, why do you think your coven allows you to live? They stay their hand at my request."

I shrug. "I can handle witches."

"Do you think they're your only enemy?" Lucifer extends a taloned hand. He counts off on each finger as he tallies, "Witches, your siblings and all the fae who don't want another war with the angels, the Angelic Anocracy's assassins who will come for you soon enough, and humans who feel threatened by your power. Shall I go on?"

I fight the urge to cross my arms over my chest. I keep them loose at my sides, so he doesn't see he is getting to me. "I have allies."

"I am one of them. I haven't sent a single hound or demon into your territory since we treated."

"Except the ones who watch me."

He holds up a taloned finger. "For your protection—an act of an ally."

"So, you don't want anything?"—except to gather information from my neighbor, who has access to a lot of my life.

Lucifer doesn't answer right away. Emotions war on his face as he deliberates what he's going to say. "I want you to live and fill out your full potential."

"Oh."

Look at me, so witty with my replies.

He extends a hand. Face open with a look so vulnerable it would break my heart if I didn't know he's up to something. "That's why I beseech you to come home. Come to Gehenna, live under my protection until you come into your full potential, and you can protect yourself."

I shake my head. "No."

"I know you have a daughter and others whom you care for. I hold no ill will toward the fae lover of yours nor the little rock witch. They could come too. I would welcome your court. Perhaps we could become reacquainted, understand each other's purpose better. Design a future where your loved ones are safe."

"Plot against the Angelic Anocracy?" I chuckle.

He shakes his head mournfully. In a serious, if not plaintiff tone, he says, "I don't want my brethren gone. They're overpowered, and that is not what our creator wanted. They'll see you and the changes you're bringing as a threat. You are not safe."

Part of me believes he's being sincere, but it doesn't matter. His wants don't matter. What I want does. "Lucifer, I have a community of covenless witches whom I look after. I have my duties on the council and a life that I've worked hard to build. I can't just run away because you're afraid for me."

He grins. "A few months ago, you would have done that to escape my wrath. Now that you see that I am not against you, why not run to me instead of away?"

I school my face to not show my surprise. I'd never made a move his spies could have perceived as an attempt to run away. Maybe Velja told him? The thought he heard from them about my plans made me fear for my friend. Velja may have threatened to make me run from Lucifer, discovering I was still alive, but the demon also saved me from him in the first place. He wouldn't have received any information from Velja freely.

Instead of uselessly denying that I wanted to run away, I reply, "I appreciate your offer, but I don't need you anymore." I gesture to the faerie. "I got this."

He doesn't watch my gesture. His head is bent, and he's trembling. "I understood that when you faked your death," he replies, anguish infusing his words.

Lucifer rarely allowed people to see how he truly felt. He was like a theater kid, always performing, seeking the approval of his peers. This, however, didn't feel like one of his performances. It felt like one of those rare moments when we were alone, and he would lament the loss of his angelic brethren over their differences. How he yearned for his youth spent in the light of his creator's love.

I didn't want or need his help but didn't know how to make it clearer. I had a faerie. A freaking pocket universe that I made with my power, but he remained purposefully obtuse on the matter. Lucifer has power, adoration or contempt of many to fuel it; but what he doesn't have is many people close to him. He craved my attention because I knew the raw, naked him and loved him. Too bad he abused that adoration.

"If you will not take my offer of safekeeping, will you at least allow me to give you something so that you may truly protect yourself?"

He extends his arms, hands palm up. Plumes of smoke billow from each hand. The plumes slither horizontally, stretching between his hands. The smoke dissipates as rapidly as it appears. A sword stretches between his palms.

I remember the weapon mounted on a wall in Lucifer's bed chambers. The thing always gave me the creeps. I couldn't explain how, but the sword seemed sentient, watchful. I swear I felt its judgment.

He held the weapon with such reverence. "This was forged before witches came to Earth. Before humans dispersed from their cradle. When my creator asked me to be his executioner, to punish the wicked, he gave me this sword. I owe my continued existence to it, and my kin owe their lives to me not using it in vain. This sword will strike down angels, false gods, anything."

I shook my head. "I can't take something so precious."

He smiles ruefully. Instead of insisting, he asks, "Do you think I loved you because you could power a spell created by such limited beings as witches?"

I don't let the barb sting. He wanted me for my faelight. I knew that. "I thought that you were using me to power the spell and get what you wanted."

"I could not trust you then to know my true plans. It wasn't until you left, you made clear you were worthy of this. I needed you to figure out what bound your power. You wouldn't have ever done it if I didn't push you."

"Your methods of mentorship suck."

He chuckles, gaze lowering to the sword. "I am flawed and corrupt outside of Grace, but the being my creator made, an angel of light, an exactor of justice, still exists. I wanted to restore the balance to the universe, not one up my brothers." He releases a long sigh. "I know I'm no longer what I once was, therefore, I can't do it. I needed someone powerful. Not only powerful, but someone who can bring beings of all kinds together, rather than tear them apart. That is you."

He's right about one thing. In Hell, as a consort with political sway, I would get the fallen angels to settle disputes with the demon population. Even in hiding, I threw myself into community organization through the PTSA.

I cock my head. "What if I had taken you up on your offer to go to Gehenna?"

He smiles. "I would've enjoyed every moment we had until you eventually perished, but I wouldn't have let you touch this sword."

My heart skips a beat. He means it. All of it. The weight of this moment is far too much. I hoped he'd stop with the fascination. Immortal beings seem either fickle or steadfast when it comes to relationships. My own father likely had hundreds of lovers over his long life besides my mother and namesake, Tatiana. Yet, Shawn loved Micah, and only Micah.

"I know what you are and who you are, Tatiana."

I swallow hard at his meaningful look. He all but called me Mórrígan.

"This sword belongs in your hands now. It will never swing false."

I dip into my light and slip into my second sight, the ability to see the color of magic. The sword shines a strong magenta, the color of god's magic, infused with the golden glow of angelic magic.

Something tugs at my center, my core, where I keep my light. It isn't compulsion. More like a draw to do what's right. I step forward. Instead of taking the sword, I cup Lucifer's cheek. My eyes sting. "No."

"No?" The question is barely audible.

I smile ruefully. "This is your sword. Your destiny. Either wield it as you were meant to or return it to the mount and carry on as you have. Your god gave you a task and the free will to decide if you'll perform it. My destiny is not for you to decide. You neither created me nor named me. I am who my goddess made and who I chose to be."

Tears wet my cheeks. I'm not alone in crying. Lucifer weeps silently as I speak.

"You're wrong. It's too late for me."

I snort. "Says who?"

"Those who made me the villain, the devil of the story."

I shrug. "From the moment Danu whispered my true name, people have told me who I am all my life. I choose to be Miriam, PTSA mom, baker, and community organizer. Nothing grand, but I like who I am. Be someone you like."

Lucifer examines the sword in his hands. A hint of the smile curves his pretty mouth. "You don't, how did you put it, 'suck as a mentor.'"

With that, the once angel of light disappears.

6

The next morning, I stop in my tracks on the way to the shower, unable to recognize the woman looking back at me in the mirror. My hair has turned completely pink, save the tips, which remain red. The buds of antlers gained a few inches in height and forked. I open my mouth and examine my sharper canines, touching my lip with clawed hands. I knew my forties would bring changes, but I'd expected hot flashes, gray hairs, wrinkles, and mood swings. After I shower, I create an illusion to appear as I did pre-fae puberty.

I knock on Rhiannon's door and say, "Five minutes."

When nothing stirs on the other side, I knock once more. "Rhi?"

Still no answer.

I try calling her cell phone. The call goes straight to voicemail. The message I leave sounds exactly as annoyed as I feel. The rock witch's behavior could be erratic sometimes, understandably so after what she'd been through, but I still got frustrated with her. Silently, I pray to the witch mother goddess that Rhi's not on the fool's errand she mentioned.

I send a text to one of the two covenless witches new to the area that I've hired, asking her to cover for Rhiannon on my day off tomorrow. I pay my employees well above Washington's minimum wage, but she's a single mother with two school aged witches and it's expensive on the Eastside. The mom needs the money more than Rhiannon does, so I don't feel guilty about giving her Rhi's next shift. As I expected, the witch replies immediately, she's happy to pick up the extra hours.

Downstairs, Phyr is already awake and waiting to leave.

Something floral scents the air. "What's that smell?"

He hands me a cup of coffee prepared as I like it and nods to the dining room. "Something came for you while you were in the shower. I put it in there."

A massive arrangement of roses and calla lilies sits on the dining room table. A pale pink envelope rests among the flowers. My name scrawled in pretty gold ink leaves no doubt the arrangement is for me. I open the card and read the note within.

I'm an alpha-hole, protective of my pack to a fault. You and Phyr are a pack of two. I'm jealous of your closeness. I'm working on it and will try to see him as something other than my competition, since he assures me the only thing in my way of pursuing you is me.
    Yours,
    Gabriel

I send Gabriel a text: *Dinner tonight?*

His reply is instant: *Tell me where and when. I'll be there.*

I name a place which I've never tried before, and he replies: *Perfect. I'm sure there are a few things you need to discuss.*

My stomach bottoms out. Phyr told him about the damned hellhound after I told him not to. That has to be what this is all about. It's not an apology. Gabriel's giving me an opportunity to have a tête-à-tête about Lucifer.

Fuming, I drive Phyr to Enchanting Treats in silence.

To my chagrin, there are picketers with Bible verses on their signs with such catchy phrases as "Thou shalt not suffer a witch to live," "Do not invoke the names of other gods; do not let them be heard on your lips," and my personal favorite, "Mystery, Babylon the Great, the Mother of Prostitutes and Abominations of the Earth," with a picture of me ripped from the bakery's website.

"Ignore them," Phyr murmurs. "Don't let them invoke the power of belief. They are impotent without it."

I pull around back to the lot for business owners. Thankfully, no picketers wait for us there.

Inside the bakery, Phyr and I go about our daily routine. I'm on edge because I want to know what he and Gabriel discussed last night. Unlike when he discussed the bonding ritual, he didn't come to my room afterward. I hate forcing the topic, so I go about my morning. I also can't decide if I can share what transpired between me, Danu, and Lucifer. Phyr has to report to Gabriel what he knows.

The longer the morning goes on without Phyr telling me what transpired, the more anxious I feel.

Phyr has a television he had installed going on in the background. He likes the constant input of information. I rarely mind the background chatter, but today the constant chatter of talking heads on the news has my teeth on edge.

"Can you mute that thing?" I snap.

He looks up from his work, a fondant for a cake. "The remote is located on the shelf under the monitor. There is a button you are quite capable of pushing yourself."

I roll my eyes at his snark. "Now you're the expert on how tech works."

I clutch the remote, not actually knowing how to use the damn thing. "Why are there so many unmarked buttons? They used to label these freaking things."

Phyr halts his progress with the fondant, gently extracting the remote from my hand and muting the TV. "Miriam, are we at odds?"

"That depends if you told Gabriel or not about our run-in with the you-know-what."

He rears his head, visibly affronted. "You asked me not to."

"Then what *did* you discuss?"

"He gave me some terms to negotiate with King Oberon."

My temper flares. "He should have discussed further negotiations with me. I'm the representative of the fae."

More importantly, I'm the Mórrígan, yet to Gabriel I'm just someone to make out with and use to get to Oberon. I don't say that part out loud. It hurts too much.

"He should have, but you're also not discussing matters with him. A lack of trust is the cavern between you two, not me."

I throw up my hands and then sigh. Phyr's right. I don't know what to do about it, though.

"I don't think I trust anyone completely, except you and Jada," I admit. Whoa. That's something I need to unpack. "I know what it's like to be with someone who holds their position in a higher place than the relationship. Lucifer had his fallen and demons. Raf had to ascend to godhood. I think when it comes down to it, Gabriel would pick the pack over me. He did it with his ex-wife, and she's the mother of his children. I wouldn't even blame him. He's their leader." I sigh, then I add, "Logically, I should break it off, but I want him in a way that goes beyond reason."

I sound like an angsty teenager, but in some ways, I haven't ever really been one. Aren't relationships supposed to be easier once you know what you want out of life?

"Not beyond reason. You both exist in a place that is betwixt different worlds," Phyr says, sage as ever. "Like recognizes like even before our minds are conscious of it. You're physically and emotionally attached to him because you relate to his dilemma, and he relates to yours."

"What did he want to negotiate with my father?"

Real smooth way of changing the subject, Miriam.

He sighs heavily. Phyr knows when I won't let something drop. "Gabriel wants the door to swing both ways. Fae with visas may roam freely in his territory in exchange for Oberon's promise to take on any Earthly refugees if the Anocracy declares war on the Pacific Northwest."

I bite my lip. I technically have a place where everyone could go, but so far, there's only some dirt and a star. Not quite refuge material. Besides, I don't want to leave this world. I've built a life here and have contributed to this community far more than angels ever have. I shouldn't have to leave because some Heavenly authority doesn't like my presence.

"I'd rather take a stand."

"You should tell him."

The bell in the front of the bakery rings, alerting us that a patron has entered Enchanting Treats. I wipe off my hands and nod silently in Phyr's direction.

The fae's black horns disappear and his bronze skin settles into a shade more of a human tan. His amber eyes lose their glow.

I throw on a glamour for myself. We work in the back without them because holding illusions takes a lot of faelight.

"I hate how ugly it makes me," Phyr sighs, sidling next to me to glimpse himself in the pot. His glamour takes nothing away from how handsome he is. With a face that is a study of sharp angles, Phyr's looks win him more than a few blushing flirtations from customers.

"We can't let any Angelic Anocracy spies know high fae live here until humans get used to supes." My gut twists as I pat his shoulder, fearing they never would.

I check my apron in the mirror and pass through the door from the rear to the patron space. A glass featuring samples of all our baked goods separates me from the not-patron.

My smile falters.

Rhiannon brandishes an impish grin, appearing almost as feral as when I'd found her. Bits of branches stick out from tangles in her brown hair. Her clothes are torn. At least half a dozen scratches in various stages of severity trigger my healer's need to aid.

Something intangible holds me back from rounding the counter.

In her fingertips, she pinches a piece of what appears to be yellowing parchment. The ragged edge on one side suggests a page torn from a book. Oh, sweet Danu, not again!

"Got the Baba Yaga recipe." Pride in her accomplishment oozes from every word. "And, I have it on the best authority, it's the real deal."

Unease washes over me. A foreign energy, a pulse of magic emanates from Rhiannon's find. "Is that where you've been? I advised you that was a bad idea."

She crinkles her nose as if she smells a fart. "That's the funny thing about free will. I can make all the bad decisions I want. But this is a good one! Can't you feel the magic?"

I nod. I want nothing to do with it.

Phyr is no more impressed than I am. "Did you obtain the recipe by legitimate means?"

Rhiannon beams. "Absolutely. One of her sons sold it to me."

Taking in her disheveled appearance, I find that hard to believe. I cock my head and un-plant one of my hands from my hip to gesture to her general disarray. "Then please explain why you look as if you barely escaped a wolverine attack?"

"Oh!" The rock witch cackles, mischief lighting her dark eyes. "We had a bit of fun. Want the juicy details?" She wiggles her eyebrows.

Ew.

I hold up a hand. "No, thank you. —Wait, I thought you and Lance were a thing." I shake my head. Witches aren't monogamous, but shifters are. "Never mind. None of my business."

As if summoned, the doorbell rings as Lance walks in. He's just as disheveled. Grass stains on his joggers. Dried blood cakes his dark skin from what I assume are healed wounds. Twigs and leave bits embed his long, thin plates.

Eyes darting from Rhiannon to me, then to the floor. He grins sheepishly and lowers his head. "Hey Miriam."

Unease marries with my mirth. He's not ashamed of what he's done—the lowered head while greeting is a shifter-culture sign of submission.

I glance at Phyr, who seems awfully still. He and Gabriel discussed something else last night.

"Lance," I say in as firm a voice as possible. "Look at me, please."

He blows out his breath, exasperated. "It's not a thing I can help. He's claimed you as his mate. The magic is there."

I gape. Gabriel claimed me as his mate to the pack, which means they have to treat me with kid gloves. Why?

"It's for peace and your protection, Miriam. You know how the shifters feel about witches—shifters not like me," his gaze swivels to Rhiannon, who is his girlfriend and a rock witch.

It makes sense for shifters to not trust witches. Witches had aligned themselves with Hell and shifters with Heaven. Also, I'm Oberon's daughter. Crap.

"It is for peace and it's an excellent move," Phyr says behind me. "It puts all allied with the archangel and Miriam in a position of strength, separating his territory, our territory, from the rest."

"Sounds like some Euro-dynasty blending sitch to me," Rhiannon says, waving the parchment.

I want to take it, but there's an energy to the paper that doesn't resonate well with me. Rhiannon might have come across the real deal.

"A marriage for political reasons is not the worst reason to wed," Phyr agrees.

I gape at him. "Marriage?"

Ignoring me, Phyr reaches over the counter and takes the scrap of parchment from Rhiannon. "What is this script, Cyrillic?"

I take the paper, the magic contained within it vibrating against my fingertips. I examine the yellowing parchment. "Similar. Cyrillic derived from Kairska."

"Whoa. Russian is the witch language?" Lance asks, mouth parted in awe.

"Not exactly. Some Slavic languages and the Cyrillic alphabet are derivatives of Kairska like Irish and Scots-Gaelic are derivatives of High Fae. When witches came to this world, we gave mundanes bits of our culture. Some witches and other supernaturals lived as goddesses, priestesses, and oracles around the globe."

Phyr sighs. "Until any faith outside of Christianity was persecuted."

We all shift our gazes past the glass storefront to picketers outside.

The Supernatural Council saw coming out would upset the current order of things, but we also had no choice. Heaven had too much power and Hell wanted it. The only course to take control away from both was to shake up mundane perspectives. In our naïveté, we believed in this modern era people would simply accept that the supernaturals exist, and maybe there was no singular truth. Turns out cognitive dissonance is stronger than living proof.

I identify with how mundanes feel. They have been lied to their whole lives. They're angry and scared. When my memory had a hex on it, my coven convinced me that fae drank witches' blood for strength. When I discovered I was half the monster in my closet, I had a hard time adjusting. With my memories returned, it helped, but I continue to have days where it feels surreal.

"Witch hunts are over now," Lance says. He had the dual heritage of being a Black man in the U.S. and being of the supernatural group that perpetuated a lot of the witch hunting. "All supes have to get along, or the mundanes will discover our weaknesses and exploit them."

Phyr's eyes meet mine. I wonder if he is thinking of the missing shifters.

I look down at the parchment still buzzing between my fingers. I scrunch my brow as I interpret. "Did you read this recipe, Rhiannon?"

She shakes her head. "Nah. We brought it straight here."

"This is a spell. It appears to be torn from a grimoire, not a recipe."

Rhiannon's dusky skin blanches a pale shade of gray.

"What kind of spell?" Phyr asks, likely reading the way I hold utterly still to keep from shaking.

Alone, the spell is nonsense, but combined with thirty-two other pieces, it could destroy a world. Someone wants me to know the spell is still out there, or at least the witches who created the World Eater were still alive and could rewrite it.

I keep my gaze on Rhiannon. "Are you absolutely sure this man was Baba Yaga's son?"

"That's who he said he was."

"No coven would let a man touch a piece of the grimoire. Either this man stole this from a witch and is lying, or this is an invitation to meet a witch, who the rest of the covens thought died long ago." I stare at the spell. "We better return it and find out."

7

Phyr, Rhiannon, and I load the peace offering of all the pastries which haven't sold today into the trunk of my Subaru. Lance has already left to report to Gabriel.

"Are you certain you don't want me to accompany you?" Phyr asks, pulling me aside.

I did. Whoever wrote this spell had powerful magic, and Rhiannon and I facing her alone is likely a bad idea. "Witches have little trust in men."

Phyr rolls his eyes, much like Jada. "I'm masculine because I choose to be."

Full high fae are hermaphroditic, and could shift their appearance, even reshape their bodies, but that is not the point.

"I'm aware. This is something I have to do, witch to witch."

"Are you sure? I am here to be your guard, after all." Judging by the lack of conviction in his tone, my friend is going through some sort of formality Gabriel must have insisted upon.

I grin at his pitiful effort to follow the rules. "I can handle myself. Besides, you need to do the prep work for tomorrow."

"Yes, you can handle yourself. I will not stand in your way. However, I have one simple request." He steps into my personal space, his long, lean body hovering close to mine. Our noses are a breath apart. His face is solemn, as is his tone when he whispers, "Come back to me, Tati."

During our childhood, we were inseparable. First, out of necessity and then because we had grown into the type of friendship that feels like family—perhaps deeper. He has good reason to distrust witches. During our adolescence, my mother hexed my memory and stole me from my father's faerie, from Phyr.

I squeeze his hand. "Always."

Rhiannon pops up behind Phyr and pats his back. "Nothing to worry about. She's got me, buddy."

Phyr sneers over his shoulder at the brown-haired rock witch. He's all high fae princely indignation as he remarks, "Buddy? When have you earned the right to call me that, little brownie?"

"We live in the same house, eat at the same table, and we have each other's back. I call that buddies," Rhiannon retorts with a defiant lift of her chin, but she backs up a step.

The fae prince nods with a glimmer of a grin. "Fair enough."

I kiss Phyr's cheek. "Jada's studying at Roxy's tonight after their senior ball planning, so you'll have all the time you want on the internet."

He touches where I kissed him. His eyes light up. "Oh! This will give me a chance to catch up on 'Ready, Set, Bake!'"

I wiggle my eyebrows. "Maybe you can figure out the secret to getting on the show. I bet if you were a contestant, they'd give you your own show."

Phyr mulls over the possibility with a gleam in his eyes. "Perhaps. A magical bake-off would be the sort of positive representation supes needed." He rubs his sharp chin. "Mundanes could see we're not monsters."

Rhiannon slipped away and got in the car while we spoke. Leaving Phyr inspired, I join her.

"So, did Baba Yaga's son answer your text?" I ask, pulling out of the bakery lot. I glanced in her direction.

Earlier, I healed her minor wounds, made her wash up and

brush out her hair before we loaded up. Also, she is now outfitted in a pair of my clean leggings I had in the back and Enchanting Treats tee from the "merch" section of the bakery—Phyr had insisted upon "expanding our brand" to t-shirts, travel mugs, and key chains.

Rhiannon checks her phone. "Nope. Gimme your phone. I'll enter the address of the diner where I met him, and from there we'll pull up a map. No bars on the cell where we're heading."

"Okay then." I grimace, not liking the idea of going to the forest to find Baba Yaga. "It's in my purse."

Seattle and its Eastside suburbs get a fair amount of rain, but most of it is a misty drizzle, negligible while driving. The fat drops now falling gain traction and will make everyone on their commute home slow down.

I-405 South's bumper-to-bumper nightmare moves at a languid crawl, but the rain lets up after a bit. The clouds clear away, providing us with a view of Mt. Rainier.

"Mountain's out." I declare, as every parent in the Seattle area does out of habit.

Rhiannon grunts. Her phone dings.

I take my gaze off the road long enough to glance her way.

She frowns at the screen, tapping away with her thumbs. She picked up texting fairly quickly for someone who'd grown up on a coven commune without tech.

When she doesn't explain who she's texting furiously with, I ask outright, "Is that him?"

"Nah."

I tighten my grip on the steering wheel. She must be texting with Lance. "Have you checked for messages from him?"

Tap. Tap. Tap.

"Yep. He hasn't responded."

"Check again."

Her dismissive wave breezes by in my peripheral vision. "In a sec."

What could possibly be so important that it's distracting her from our mission? Rhiannon can be impetuous as a teenager at times, but she understands when she has to be serious. I realize something and panic courses through me.

"Did Lance tell Gabriel what we're doing?"

She grits out the words, "Don't. Compel. Me."

My focus is on traffic, but I feel the accompanying daggers she shoots with her eyes.

"What?"

Rhiannon gulps air as if she had held her breath. Settling, she says, "When you spoke, I felt compelled."

I lick my lips, searching for the right words. Guilt tightens my chest. Fae can compel humans, but not brownies. I hadn't meant to compel her and had no idea I could. Had I?

I blow out my breath and clamp down the mental barriers Phyr taught me to set.

"Sorry. It's a new thing for me." One, I will have to keep in check.

"The other high fae tried that. It doesn't work, but I don't like it." Her voice comes out softer, the hurt plain.

When I'd found Rhiannon, she wasn't exactly in good shape, mentally or physically. Phyr had taken a risk allowing a witch into his faerie, claiming her fae because she was one-sixteenth brownie. He didn't go beyond allowing her a place and a door to this world. If he showed her any more interest than a halfling coming home to faerie, Rhiannon would have become a target for his enemies.

"Did Phyr ever try to compel you?"

Rhiannon shook her head in my periphery. "Not at all. He didn't have to. The princey boy provided me with a safe space and asked nothing in return, except a thousand rules while living in his domain. He's so hot and scary, but kind underneath. I did whatever he said, hoping to get a piece, if you know what I mean. Until you came along, and I saw I didn't have a chance. Dude worships the ground you walk on. You're the High Queen of the Fae in his eyes, you know."

I'm at a loss for words. I hold Phyr in high regard, but he earns it each and every day by his actions. I've done nothing to deserve that sort of fealty and hope his friendship with me is out of loyalty to me, not my title.

"Gabriel says to 'be careful and that he trusts you,'" Rhiannon says, saving me from responding.

I glance her way long enough to see Rhiannon roll her eyes at her screen. "He also wants you to contact him as soon as you've made the new ally."

She makes a funky sound. "Oh, I see how it is. Ugh. Why does he have to be such an alphahole?"

"What?" I don't know why I ask. If Gabriel said something jerkish, I don't want to know. This meeting needs to be calm.

"Bird-boy thinks Phyr is with us and has some orders and threats for him."

"Bird-boy?" A chuckle escapes my lips, and I can't help imagining Gabriel in angelic form, wings spread and face disapproving of the nickname.

"You didn't disillusion him of the notion we took our protector?"

"Nope. Just said I'd pass the info along, not when or how."

"Perfect."

We shared a conspiratorial grin.

Exiting I-405 to I-90, we head east toward the Cascades. The sun hangs low in the west behind us, limning the mountains ahead in golden tones. As we drive, the peaks are slowly consumed by the veil of night. It will be full dark by the time we reach Snoqualmie Pass. In the early dark of a winter night is not exactly how I want to meet the legendary Baba Yaga.

I hope it doesn't snow.

～

SOMETIME LATER, white flakes streak the space my headlights illuminate. The windshield wipers rhythmically swipe away the slow but steady snowfall. We've reached Snoqualmie Pass and are no longer on a main road.

I lean forward, driving slowly. The road is clear of snow, but I still need to be cautious of black ice. Snowbanks, possibly two or three stories high, and even taller trees, border the sides of the road.

"GPS signal lost," my phone warns for the fifth time.

"Just turn that thing off, please."

Rhiannon does as I ask, or I assume she does because the phone finally shuts up.

I dip into my faelight, accessing my second sight that allows me to see magic. Like a virtual reality superimposed on magenta light with hints of white and blue streaked through the wall of snow out the driver's side window.

"A ley line is due north. A pretty big one." I frown. Witches from the old world with the proper training could draw on ley lines for power or use them for travel. "What kind of witch is Baba Yaga?"

"I think she's a hedge witch like you."

"Not like me." My witch light isn't as abundant as my faelight and I don't know how to use a ley line.

Baba Yaga is a full witch, maybe having multiple natural abilities as well as ancient knowledge of witchcraft. A grimoire keeper not only transcribes spells, they devise them. We're in over our heads.

Cursing silently under my breath for not bringing Phyr, I grip the steering wheel knuckle-white tight.

"You know, we can turn around. You hid the recipe in a cache. She can't blame us if we don't have it."

I consider going home and trying this again in the daylight, with backup.

My car suddenly halts, jerking my attention back to the road. The engine dies, taking all light and heat with it. The only sounds are the wind whipping around the vehicle and our rapid breaths.

I reach for my phone, but it won't power on. There's no streetlamp out here, no warm glow of lights from a nearby house. The only source of illumination would be the moon, but it's overcast.

Not wanting to use fae magic and reveal all my cards, I pull my witch light from within, whispering an incandescence spell as I trace a pattern on my hand. A white flame springs forth, dancing on my palm.

"Are you alright?" I ask Rhiannon, the hairs on the back of my neck rising.

She shakes her head. Her brown eyes are luminous and filled with fear. "My gut hurts. Nothing good happens when my gut hurts."

She can't see the ley line flicker, but I do.

Something either came into this world or left it, or perhaps Baba Yaga is using the ley line to power a spell that renders vehicles useless.

I take a slow breath and remind myself that I've faced Lucifer, the King of Hell, and met a goddess. Baba Yaga may be a powerful witch, but only a witch. The reminder doesn't take any of the frissons away.

Rhiannon is actively shivering so hard the car vibrates.

I reach into the back, grab a jacket spelled to stay warm, and hand it to Rhiannon.

She hesitates before putting it on. "What will you wear?"

"I enchanted my clothes to keep me warm." I'm glad that since I could now practice magic openly, I can live as a properly trained witch of the Archivist coven.

Witches like Rhiannon possess basic knowledge and fudge their way through, while our skill sets are comparable to someone with a full medical degree and someone with home remedies passed down.

She is a powerful geomancer though—I curse under my breath. Her gift could cause an avalanche that would kill us. Rhiannon's gift would not help us here.

Despite giving Rhiannon the jacket, the car still shakes. My stomach flips when I realize why. The rock witch isn't shivering—not her body, at least. Her nerves are causing her magic to shift the earth below us.

"Rhiannon, I need you to take a deep inhale for a count of four, and then hold it until I tell you to exhale."

We go through the breathing exercise a few times before the quaking stops.

"Okay. We can't stay here."

"We can't walk home from here," she says, voice rising with fear. "We'll die out there."

I force a smile. "I just need a little space. If I can get to my cache, I can get us home."

"What about your car?"

It takes all I have within me to not scream 'the car doesn't matter if we're dead, Rhiannon.' Screaming at a terrified rock witch when you're surrounded by mountains covered in snow isn't the best tactic. Also, it's unkind. I can't yell at someone for being afraid. "We'll come back for it," I say over my shoulder as I get out of the vehicle.

Rhiannon soon joins me in front of the car.

"What witches dare trespass on our coven's land without permission?"

Rhiannon and I turn toward the heavily accented voice.

White witch light glows around the edges of the auras with traces of magenta—gods' magic is in the blood of the three witches in floor-length hooded robes. One gray-haired and hunched over walks at a snail's pace. A middle-aged woman with a streak of gray through her dark hair aids the elderly one with a supportive arm. A young witch, maybe five or six years older than my daughter, walks on the gray-hair's other side. In her palm, bright witch light illuminates all three. The fat flakes of snow don't even touch any of them. It isn't a deflection spell like I have on my clothes.

The snow avoids them.

Shit.

Witches belong to castes according to their abilities. I left the coven, so I'm considered a hedge witch, a solitary witch out in the world. However, my natural ability would be a hearth witch or kitchen witch. I'm good with plants, cooking, healing, making poisons, and the like. Rhiannon is a rock witch or geomancer. These women are water witches of some sort, perhaps bog witches or sea witches. Either way, they can control the snow.

"We didn't come empty handed." I fumble in my pocket, searching for my car fob to open the trunk remotely. The fob doesn't work.

The youngest points accusingly at Rhiannon. "You!"

The rock witch huddles closer to me. The ground beneath us vibrates with her fear.

"You seduced our innocent nephew and convinced him to steal

from my sister's grimoire." The beautiful witch gestures to the thin, elderly woman, who genuinely needs a nap, or a wheelchair, or both.

"Innocent?" Rhiannon laughs. The sound is a little manic. "He taught me and Lance a thing or two."

I cut Rhiannon a glare. Witches can do a lot with a name, and she knows it.

"This is what I say." The middle-aged one says to the eldest in Kairska with a sigh of resignation. "He does anything for sex. I told you to kill that one when he was a baby and feed him to his sisters to make them stronger. No one listens to me."

"Perhaps I eat you," the elderly witch grumbles in Kairska, her voice raspy and papery thin. "Become young, strong."

Rhiannon looks to me to translate, but I don't dare let on I understand them yet.

The middle-aged witch doesn't even flinch at the threat.

The youngest rolls her eyes as if they've had this conversation before. "Really? What if they understand you?" She gestures toward Rhiannon and myself.

"Then we have more problems than a stolen page and the natives of this world," the elderly witch replied. "They might know it's not a recipe."

"It's from a grimoire," I reply in English, and then add in Kairska with a nudge of my head toward Rhiannon. "She did not know what she possessed. She is ignorant of ancient ways. I came here to return what is yours."

The young witch wrinkled her nose. "Ew. Stick to English. Your accent is funny."

"Lies," the elderly Baba Yaga snarls, speaking in Kairska. "I'd smell my blood."

"That's creepy," Rhiannon whispers.

Creepy indeed.

She sniffs the air, raises her arm slowly as if it takes great effort, and points a boney finger at me. "You are Tatiana, no? Daughter of Gracia of the Archivist coven. The Great Betrayer is how you are known among witches."

How was she getting all that from smell?

I shudder involuntarily at the mention of my birth name. It isn't my fae name given by Danu but holds power because it is the name my parents gave me.

"Betrayal depends upon perspective," I reply in Kairska, not giving a care whether the youngest witch liked my accent or not. "From where I stand, I saved everyone by stealing those grimoires. The King of Hell wanted me to use the World Destroyer spell on this world, but I destroyed the spell instead."

The three women exchange the type of glances where no words are necessary. Judging by their expressions, they'd come to some sort of conclusion.

"By ancient decree, you have broken prime law by thieving and destroying the grimoires of other witches. We must try you for your crimes," the middle-aged witch declares in English.

"Did you even listen?" Rhiannon demands, the ground rumbling beneath our feet.

"Control your gift," the young witch commands in a nervous whisper.

Too late.

The walls of snow lining the road tremble, crumbling and sliding down. In a flash, snow rushes at us like a raging river. The car blocks some, protecting Rhiannon and I, but the car will not protect us from the other side's rapid approach.

Desperate, I gather my faelight and open a way into my faerie, pushing Rhiannon in. As I follow her, I glimpse the witches staving off the snow. One of them turns, pointing in our direction as I dive in.

Oh, no you don't!

I slam shut the fabric of reality between us.

8

Rhiannon sits on the ground, eyes wide and mouth gaping. Her gaze swings to me. "Toto, I don't think we're in Kansas anymore."

Out of breath and still wired from the narrow escape, I don't reply right away.

"You good, Miriam?"

First, I nod, and then I shake my head. I catch my breath. Part of me wants to return to see if the witches are alright, but I know they are. I'm right about what caste of witches they are. All three of them have to be water witches for the snow to avoid them, and one was a frost witch to control the snow. They likely got away. Finally, I manage to say, "I don't know. That went so terribly bad."

Rhiannon struggles to her feet, brushing dirt from her backside. "It could have gone worse."

I rear my head, indignant. "How? We could have been crushed!"

"We weren't. Your instincts kicked in and you took us—wherever this is." She spreads her arms, indicating the fledgling faerie. "We're safe. They could have captured and tried you. You're an ex-Archivist. You know what they do to witches who destroy grimoires." She slices a finger across her throat.

"Fair point." Musing, I think out loud, "This is what I know. Baba Yaga is supposedly an immortal hedge witch from the old witch world, living in the forest alone in a cabin with chicken legs. Bog and frost witches, likely. They still speak in Kairska, devise spells, and write grimoires, which should have made them part of the Archivist coven. I don't know which coven they could possibly belong to. I've never seen those women before, and I know all the coven elders."

"Are you sure? Not all covens like the Archivists. Some didn't align with them or Lucifer," Rhiannon provides. "I've met plenty at the Bizarre Market."

The magical black market is called the Bizarre Market, because of course, it is. I rub my forehead. "Do you think someone at this market might know something about the Baba Yaga?"

"Probably." She eyes me warily. "You're a member of the Supernatural Council and the public face of covenless witches. Wouldn't be wise for a goody goody to go there."

I chuckle at the thought of me being a goody two shoes. Then again, that's exactly what I've been for a long time. My laughter dies. Which is the real me? Wicked Tatiana of the Fae, Tati the Ruthless of the Archivist coven, or the hedge witch I've become?

"I lived in Hell and grew up in the court of High King Oberon, Rhi-Rhi. Give me a little credit."

The rock witch scrutinizes me a second time. "I forget you're kind of scary. You do the cookie baking mom act so well. You wanna go now?"

"Not yet. We'll need backup."

WE FIND PHYR WATCHING "READY, SET, BAKE!" in the great room of the house. He has P.C. on his lap, feeding the cat morsels by hand. P.C. stretches lazily and hops off the planeswalker's lap to greet and mark Rhiannon and me.

Phyr turns off the television and pushes to his feet. "All is not well?"

"That's an understatement."

Phyr fixes Rhiannon and me tea, while I briefly fill him in about the confrontation with the three witches.

"Leaving the car will present a future problem."

I wave my hand. "I spelled it to withstand accidents. It's fine."

"Not my point. If the witches could control the snow, they could access the car. Your hair and other personal items are inside. They could use it to track, hex, or summon you."

Points to Phyr for learning about witches over the past few months. However, I wave that off, too. "I have a protection spell against trackers and hexes. I'm going to make a phone call. Get ready to go to the Bizarre Bazaar."

I had to make more than one phone call. The first was to make sure Jada had a ride home from Senior Ball planning. The second was to Lucinda. I brief her on what happened with the witches and then I say, "I need to find out more about them. I'm going to a magical black market. Any chance you'd come?"

"Did you tell Gabriel?"

"Not yet," I hedge.

"You two are dating. I think he'd want to know if his girlfriend is going to do something dangerous."

It would be a courtesy, but since when did he check in with me when he did anything pack or archangel business related?

"No. Gabriel would only want to come, and if I could convince him an archangel wouldn't get far in a black market, he'd want to send a shifter."

Lucinda pauses for so long, I think she's going to say no to coming and push her idea of telling Gabriel what I plan to do. "You're right. However, if I come, it isn't on official council business. I'm coming as your best friend."

Relieved, I exhale, thank her, and hang up.

~

Phyr, Rhiannon, and I are all dressed like something out of an Urban Fantasy movie, waiting for Lucinda to pull up in her minivan. I'm in Jada's leather jacket and combat boots. Rhiannon pulled together a similar outfit. I'm wearing a human glamour for now, but I'm sure once I drop it at the magical market, we won't look as coordinated. Phyr wears his fae armor, complete with sword, under a glamour that makes him look like he's about to go to a goth event.

Lucinda arrives shortly.

Rhiannon calls, "Shotgun!"

With her eyes Lucinda pleads for me to disagree.

"Rhiannon will give directions," I provide.

"I know where to go," Lucinda says as she texts someone, likely one of her kids. She confirms it by saying over her shoulder, "Senior Ball planning carpool got a little complicated, but we figured it out. I guilted Kirsten into picking them up."

I bristle at the thought of Gabriel's ex giving Jada a ride, let alone having her go anywhere near my house. Long story short, a few months ago Kirsten tried to kidnap me. She swore it was only to show me her wolf because she thought I didn't know what I was getting into when I started dating Gabriel. I put an end to her shenanigans and her misbelief I was a mundane with latent powers by drawing witch flame and burning her to free myself. See? Not always a goody two shoes.

I send a quick text to Jada, letting her know I will send Phyr for her if she's uncomfortable riding with Kirsten. My daughter sends me an eye roll emoji. Guess that's a sign she's fine with Roxy's mom.

Phone placed in a clip on her dashboard, Lucinda backed out of my driveway into the cul-de-sac.

Twenty minutes later, we enter the Fremont neighborhood of Seattle. Small independent shops line the narrow streets. We pass the sixteen-foot bronze statue of a man dressed in early twentieth century clothes.

"Who's that guy?" Rhiannon points at the statue.

"Vladimir Lenin," I reply.

"Um, what'd he do to earn a commemorative statue?"

Rhiannon can't help her ignorance. Covens liked to homeschool witches to train them in magic and to keep them from seeking mundane friends.

"He was a Communist Revolutionary," Lucinda replies.

"The Soviet Era wasn't a great time for covens. Many immigrated to western Europe or the Americas around the Bolshevik Revolution."

"How did a statue of a Russian Revolutionary end up in Seattle?" Rhiannon asks.

I knew this one. Jada did a report on the statue in eighth grade. "An Issaquah-born English teacher was living in Eastern Europe post-Soviet Era. He found the statue in a scrapyard ready to be cut up and sold for the value of the bronze. Being an academic with a dream of opening a Slavic restaurant, he wanted to preserve the piece of history and had it shipped to Washington. He died before the rest of his dreams came to fruition."

"So now it sits there? That's weird."

"Yup," Lucinda agrees. "'De Libertas Quirkas.' Fremont is weird. That's why I like it. You should see the naked Solstice Parade they have here every year. It's great."

Three blocks later, Lucinda parks in a neighborhood near Aurora Bridge. "We have to go the rest of the way on foot, or we'll miss it."

The night is chilly, but I don't mind. Phyr walks to my left. Rhiannon and Lucinda, who know where we're going, walk ahead.

"Can you feel it?" Phyr whispers in High Fae.

I nod. The tingle of magic brushes my skin as we walk under Aurora Bridge. My glamour drops of its own volition. I glance at Phyr. His glamour is gone as well. Lucinda is no longer in human form either. Colorful feathers cover her hands, and her face is turned up ten notches of beautiful. Rhiannon is the only one among us that looks remotely human, let alone mundane.

Instead of the stone carving of a one-eyed troll gripping a Volkswagen Beetle covered in concrete, there's an actual giant troll lying under the bridge. A pair of rust color cutoff shorts and an unbuttoned sleeveless flannel shirt provide the only cover for his pale gray flesh, a throwback to Seattle's grunge look, super-sized. His hair, the color and texture of red seaweed, hangs over one eye. A long beard, the same color and texture, sprouts from the lower half of his face. A shiny silver orb spins where an eyeball should be. The scent of the Puget Sound rolls off the troll. He currently uses the Volkswagen Beetle as an armrest.

A glimmering mound of treasure piled up instead of sand and concrete. This wasn't something I knew about trolls, but it made sense if he collected a fee for the passage into a black market. How the heck did Rhiannon get in?

"Rhi, Rhi," the troll bellows. He smiles, revealing conical teeth larger than my head. He has a slight Norwegian accent buried by time and travel.

From what I know about bridge trolls, they all come from Norway and a faerie world before that. They are a type of low fae, born every time someone builds a bridge. The most famous troll among mundanes made it into the story of "The Three Billy Goats Gruff." Most trolls don't have a statue dedicated to them as a cover-up for their existence, but this is Seattle, which was settled by Norwegians. This troll might have sat here for a hundred years before someone thought to capture his likeness.

Rhiannon waved. "Hey Jørgen! I've brought some friends."

The troll one-eyes us and makes a lot of humming noises.

Without my glamour, I look nothing like the witch who went viral for coming out of the supernatural closet. Lucinda, however, revealed her siren form on camera.

The silver gaze lands on Lucinda. "You know the drill. Keep the wings and your song to yourself, Siren."

The siren nods. Judging by her discomfort, Lucinda didn't turn on purpose. Something about the magic that lets this pocket universe exist doesn't allow filters.

His spinning orb of an eye lands on Phyr and me. "Thanks to Rhiannon, you know my name. Who are you?"

"I go by Phyr. I'm a prince of the high court and humble servant of

Princess Tatiana, Daughter of High King Oberon." He bows and gestures toward me with a flourish.

I give my friend a healthy dose of side-eye. So much for going incognito.

Jørgen laughs. "Shit! Royalty! For real? I haven't seen any high fae on this side of the Veil in—" He scratches his seaweed covered head. "My whole life, actually. Usually, you folk have to stick to the other side." He nudges his head backward as if there's another plane of existence behind him. Then again, there very well may be.

I wonder how much a troll, who spent the entirety of his life under a bridge, could possibly see. Given the oddness of Fremont, and that he guards a door to a magical black market, probably a lot. Because I have nothing clever to say, I reply, "Well, now you have."

"Yes, and two royals at once to boot," he agrees heartily.

"All thanks to the angels," Phyr murmurs in High Fae. "This low fae knows no respect. You're due obeisance."

Jørgen's spinning eye lands on Phyr. In perfect High Fae, he says, "I give respect when it's earned, and I bow to know one. You're visiting dignitaries. You lost the right to obeisance when your kind stopped protecting us from the angels."

Phyr goes utterly still, which means he's mortally offended. He fought and saw many friends and kin die in the Fae Wars. The low fae bargained with the angels to stay on Earth, hidden and mere shadows of what they once were, swearing off all allegiance to the high fae courts.

"My friend meant no offense," I say, placing myself bodily between Phyr and Jørgen. I've seen low fae killed for not paying proper respect to my father. "He's new to this world and loyal to me to a fault. A lifetime of courtly manners drilled into his head won't be forgotten so easily."

The troll one-eyes me. "You're not new here. Are you?"

I shake my head, but don't elaborate.

"May we enter the Bizarre Bazaar?" Rhiannon asks, fluttering her eyelashes.

The troll extends a hairless arm. A massive hand hovers palm upright. "Cover fee for four."

Lucinda, apparently expecting this charge, hands over a gold necklace.

Rhiannon grins at Phyr. "Gold coins, please."

Phyr's hand disappears into what I assume is his personal cash. He deposits three gold coins into the troll's awaiting palm. "I trust this should be sufficient."

Jørgen's nostrils flare and shrink as he sniffs the coin. "Faerie gold? My, my! I've never got my hands on this stuff." He twists a torso the size of my Subaru to empty the coins and necklace onto the mound.

A curious expression crosses Phyr's face, there and gone in a heartbeat. I have no time to ponder its meaning. The front hood of the yellow Volkswagen Beetle pops open. Alluring music, the din of a crowd, and a complex bouquet of aromas float out.

Lucinda goes first. Then Rhiannon climbs inside. Phyr gestures for me to go before him. I cut him a look that says, "Don't mess with the troll." He rolls his eyes and makes a shooing motion.

9

A stone staircase spirals down several floors. Above, constellations of stars and distant nebulae I've never seen fill a night sky. Below, the market teems with life and magic.

Because we are up so high, we are provided an aerial view of what appeared to be the exterior of Pike Place Market in downtown Seattle. Or, at least, that's how it appears at first glance. The infamous sign is there. Instead of "Public Market Center," the sign reads "Bizarre Market Center." The buildings lining the street are similar to the mundane original. The glowing signage indicate what's being sold is definitely not fish, produce, and mundane artisanal wares.

Magic pulses like a heartbeat from the churning sea of supes of all kinds wandering stall to stall. I've not been around this many magical beings all at once since my days in Lucifer's Gehenna palace and certainly not this variety of beings.

I dip into my light and settle into my second sight. The colors of magic emanating from the milling throng are a rainbow spectrum.

Lucinda and Rhiannon descend the stairs ahead of me as if they've done this as many times as I've gone to the mundane version.

A hand grips my wrist. When I look back to see why he's grabbed me, Phyr's face could be carved of stone for all the emotion it reveals.

"This is a faerie," Phyr shouts above the noise of the vendors and the milling sea of supes. "Unaligned with any of the high courts."

"I figured that would be the case since a low fae guards it."

He allows me to see a glimmer of frustration. "Your title holds no sway here. Oberon's rule has no hold. The danger presented here outweighs the information you can collect in such a place. We should leave."

I deliberate his assessment. Phyr fought many battles as a planeswalker. He would know if we're entering a place we couldn't fight our way out of, but I disagree.

"I'm here to learn all I can about the Baba Yaga. Any information I can gather is worth the risk."

In turn, my friend considers my reply, eventually sighing and releasing my wrist. "As you wish."

My legs burn with fatigue as we hit the final stair. The four of us stick close together as we navigate the throng. My heart skitters when I notice a four-armed, four-legged demon manning a stall of talismans and other enchanted objects. Horns curve from a protruding forehead. Tusks jut from the demon's prominent under-bite. Bright blue robes mark them as one of Hell's traveling merchant castes—the color, a sharp contrast of their deep, scarlet skin. Their four eyes land on me, but only in passing. A merchant caste demon wouldn't have known me personally.

I bought nothing in Gehenna. I never needed to. Lucifer saw to my every need, lavishing me with gifts. Once, I expressed a desire to visit the market to have a taste of the local color. He immediately forbade it. Soon after, I received choices in my gifts and an assortment of entertainers from the far reaches of Hell and other realms. Lucifer knew how to gild a cage, and line the floor with satin pillows.

Following Rhiannon's lead, we enter the interior of the Bizarre Market Center building. The smell of fried dough makes my stomach rumble, serving as a reminder that I haven't eaten since breakfast.

I'm about to suggest stopping for some food when a person in a brown dress, white apron covered in cherries, and red curled-toe slippers shuffles up to me. They wear a bonnet with a ribbon that matches the apron and shoes. The vendor smiles. Their cheeks are rosy and round as a cherub's, sprayed with freckles.

They remind me of a cartoon from the '80s Raf and I watched with Jada. He told me his cousin had dolls that smelled like the fruit they represented. I wonder if the creators were supes, and the cartoon an homage to what they saw visiting the Bizarre Market.

"Cherry jubilee cakes, milady?" they ask in low fae.

I turn to Phyr, intending to ask him for some of that gold.

"No. Go away," he replies before I can ask.

The erstwhile cartoonishly cute fae hisses, transforming into a hideous creature with blue skin, black fangs, long grass-like hair standing on end, and solid white eyes. Phyr's response meets their satisfaction, and they straighten and resume their sweet, childlike glamour.

"Oh yeah. I forgot to warn you," Rhiannon says, shaking her head. "Don't take anything from the Strawberry Shortcake knockoffs. They're Fomorians in disguise, and they hate high fae."

"Thanks." The singular word drips with sarcasm.

Phyr gave me an "I told you so" look. The Fomorians are ancient enemies of the high fae, specifically my father. Their presence didn't bode well at all.

"Let's move on," I say, not dignifying his taunt with a reply. I learned my lesson. If Phyr says not to go somewhere, don't.

My legs complain as we take another set of stairs down to a level with bookstores that claim to contain rare grimoires, potion shops, and other magical commodities.

We descend yet another set of stairs. My body screams—I haven't gone on my daily predawn run since opening the bakery and my muscles are mad as hell about it. I may be going through fae puberty, but I'm also still very much a middle-aged witch. Fun times all around!

Finally, we come to the seedy part of the already questionable market. A distinct style of music from the thoroughfare above pumps out of the entrance at the far end of the hall, the rhythmic bass associated with nightclubs on Earth. Scantily clad supes line the wall, waiting for a chance for the burly green ogres to let them inside.

Rhiannon skips the line, approaching one of the two ogres. He stands at least nine feet tall. His bristly onyx hair is shaved on one side. Several silver rings pierce his ears, eyebrows, and septum of his snout-like nose. His dark eyes alight with recognition at the rock witch's presence.

"Rhi Rhi," he shouts over the din. She jumps into his open arms. He gives her a big squeeze. Rhiannon has a life outside of my home and the bakery, but I assumed she spent all her free time with Lance. This is not a place I think Gabriel would approve of shifters in his pack going. Then again, when Gabriel's wife cheated on him, this would be the kind of place she would have found an incubus.

The ogre releases Rhiannon and unhitches a rope from a pole to allow her entrance to a club called Twilight Sparkle with a rainbow alicorn. Someone has a sense of humor and is not worried at all about copyright infringement.

"I brought friends, Rambo." She nudges her head in our party's direction.

I bite my lip at the mention of his name. Rambo assesses all of us. His dark eyes land on Lucinda. "No wings or siren song."

She nods.

To Phyr he says, "No weapons."

Phyr slices his hand through the air, removes his belt and sword in its sheath, and places them in a cache. "Done."

The ogre named Rambo grunts and lets us pass.

Inside, the music is louder, laughter and merriment of the patrons more chaotic. Perfumes, smoke, and musks of all flavors of supes cloud the air. The ceiling seems to be endless, and it's too crowded to see what I'm walking on, but there's give with each step that reminds me of moss. Dancers undulate and gyrate to the rhythm beat on floating platforms.

I grab Rhiannon's arm to get her attention. I shout, "How are we going to get any answers here?"

"The witch who hooked me and Lance up with Daystar works here."

With Rhiannon dancing her way in the lead, we navigate our way through the packed club. More than one person stares at Phyr and me. I'd think more eyes would be on Lucinda. She's a beautiful woman. Some take her in, but many of the eyes assess all of us. We've never been here, don't belong here, and it obviously shows.

A tall and slender fae with flowing blue hair with a flower crown, horns and silver white skin, wearing nothing but a strip of cloth to cover the groin area, and a couple of flowers to cover their nipples hops off one of the floating platforms, landing next to Phyr and me. Their fully black eyes shimmer as they cry in High Fae, "Phyr, is that *you*?"

Phyr steps forward. Confusion and something incredibly tragic limns his handsome face. "Fand? I—I thought you died in the war."

They shake their head, ruefully. "No, no. I—"

"Keep up or we'll lose the rock witch," Lucinda says, interrupting. Her compulsion magic doesn't fully pull me, but I am tempted to do as she says.

Beyond Lucinda, Rhiannon still makes her way toward the front. The din drowns my voice when I try to call the rock witch to come back. I turn to Phyr. "If you two need to catch up, you know how to find me."

Conflict wars in his eyes as his gaze passes between me and Fand. He comes to some sort of decision. All his features harden, and his demeanor shifts to that of the lofty prince. "No. My place is at your side, anam cara."

Fand grabs Phyr's arm. "Just give me a little time to explain. You'll understand why I left."

Phyr's voice is impersonal when he says, "I sang a dirge and lit a pyre in your memory myself. I have no time for the dead."

Seeing the pain and helplessness in Fand's face, I waver a second, then decide that Phyr has his reasons, and turn to follow Rhiannon.

"Please, my prince. It was an unwinnable war. Forgive me," Fand calls from behind.

I turn back. The fae falls to their knees, weeping.

Phyr motions for me to keep going, giving me a look that broaches no argument. I think he might cry too if I don't, so I do as he wants. My gut hurts. Fand had fought in what the fae and angels call the Great War, likely under Phyr's command. Maybe even as a member of his own retinue. Fand might be another planeswalker or someone Phyr obviously cared about. How many people has he lost that he never speaks about? How much does he suffer behind his easy manner and light flirtations?

I feel selfish for not prying more. Even when we were children, I had to work on him to open up about the things that bothered him. He would die for me, I know that without a doubt, but I wish he would trust me to tell me these things. Anam cara is a "soul friend," the most cherished relationship between fae. He called me that on purpose, but why now? Why did Fand look like he struck them when he said it?

Rhiannon sits in a VIP booth. Leaning against the booth is a short-haired brunette in a black tank top, ripped and covered with safety pins, and a black thong for bottoms. Black boots laced up to her knees look a lot like a pair of Jada's Demonias. The woman's build is human, not fae. Examining her with my second sight, her magical light glows witch white with a few threads of green. Like me, she's a halfling.

The rock witch motions for us to join her. The strange witch eyes all of us.

My attention diverts to a fae couple in the booth next to Rhiannon. They're making out, hands under the table, doing things people don't do in the open in clubs, at least not reputable ones. No one else bats an eye, and they're not alone in this kind of activity. It's been a long time since I've been in this type of environment and if I don't stop staring, I'm going to get into a fight. Mentally, I shake myself and slide into the booth.

"Hey, Condra," Lucinda greets the witch, sliding in on Rhiannon's other side as Phyr joins me.

"Hey yourself." Then, to me, "You don't look like the type to come here," the witch says. Her gaze shifts to Phyr. "You do, but I haven't seen you before. I'd remember."

This would be the point Phyr normally flirts, but he says nothing. He doesn't even acknowledge her. His gaze scans the crowd.

Condra shrugs it off. "What can I get you?"

"A fizzy flier," Rhiannon says, nudging her head in Phyr's direction. "On him."

Phyr doesn't respond to that either.

"For everyone else?"

"What do you know about the Baba Yaga?" I ask.

Condra eyes me. "How much you got?"

Still aware of the conversation, apparently, Phyr sets four gold coins on the table. "To start."

"Mother, help me, what are you doing?" Condra hisses. "Don't show you got bank like that." The witch swipes the coins off the table and deposits them in her bra, muttering something about how he's going to get her killed. "Any of you able to make an isolation bubble?"

Phyr snaps his fingers. Suddenly, we're enveloped in silence. The party still goes on around us, but we can't hear anything, and more importantly, they can't hear us.

I glance at Phyr. I don't know how he did that. Hopefully, he could teach me.

"Okay. Here's what I know. Baba Yaga isn't a person. It's a coven from the old world. Nomads, who don't mix with the other covens, and don't take part in supe politics. The Baba Yaga are different. They don't give their boys up for adoption like other covens do, for example." She nods at Rhiannon. "Once in a while, they want to add some fresh blood to their fold."

"Good for them. Incest is gross," Rhiannon proclaims.

Condra shrugs as if she has no opinion on the matter, then continues, "So they send Morningstar, Eveningstar, or Nightstar, the eldest sister's sons out into the world to find three covenless hedge witches suitable for making babies. That's four coins' worth of information. Can I get you anything else?"

"How do you know any of this?" I ask.

She glances over her shoulder, forgetting we have an isolation bubble, or fearing someone who could listen through it, perhaps. When the witch's gaze returns, she whispers, "They wanted me to join them."

"Why didn't you?" Rhiannon asks, and I wonder the same.

She sighs. "I'm married to my work."

"A geas keeps you here, doesn't it?" Phyr asks, interest piqued.

A geas is a soul binding agreement. It's rarely done. I had one that bound my faelight by my mother so Lucifer wouldn't be able to use me as a battery for the World Destroyer spell.

She doesn't reply, but her wrinkled brow and nervous look over her shoulder is all the answer we need.

He pulls out a bag and sets it on the table with a clang, giving away the contents. "Does everyone who works here have one?"

She doesn't answer directly. It's quite possible she can't. "We all came from somewhere far worse than this place."

Phyr and I exchange glances. His friend Fand might have made a deal out of desperation. Afraid of an angelic retaliation for the Supernatural Council coming out, shifters fled to here as refuge.

The witch reaches for the bag of fae gold. I place my hand on it.

"Do any shifters work here?"

"No. You must be at least a little bit fae. The owner doesn't like outsiders working for them."

The owner could conscript fae to indentured servitude with a geas. "If I could get the owner to break your geas, would you want to leave?"

"I've said enough." Condra swipes the bag of gold and dissolves into the throng, soon replaced by my half-siblings.

My blood runs cold at the sight of Maeve, who I look more like now than a few months ago, and Nix, whose onyx hair flows and shimmers as if the night sky poured from their scalp.

"Sister, you're almost grown," Maeve begins. "Now isn't the time to be where you are powerless."

"Do you own this place?" I ask, incredulous that my siblings have indentured servants. Oberon, our father, is guilty of many things, but he wouldn't allow it in his faerie.

"I made this place long before you moved to Seattle, little one," Nix replies, voice silk as night. My sibling pronounced Seattle strangely, perhaps the correct way to say the late chief of the Duwamish and Suquamish tribes.

I don't balk at the use of 'little one'. My siblings are millennia old. I am a child in their eyes. Knowing that makes their desire to murder me since I was an actual child even more despicable. "Does our father know?"

Nix shrugs. "Likely. However, he wouldn't admit to the way we know everything about Earth."

"And you," Maeve adds with not just a hint of malice.

Phyr stiffens, but his face is as unreadable as the masks my siblings wear. I suddenly feel like Kate in the movie *French Kiss*, when she has a breakdown about "using the corresponding face to the corresponding emotion."

"Go home, little sister. You're not ready to fight us," Nix says, then adds with a glance in our mutual siblings' direction, as if to remind Maeve. "And we're bound to wait."

I'd like to say I challenged them right then and there to save all the people they held in their faerie. I couldn't, though. The way I could render Lucifer powerless in my faerie, Nix could do the same to me. My siblings couldn't fight me, but they had many fae here who hadn't made the same promise. I had a choice. Go home with my head held high and wait for the day I could release these fae and halflings, or harm people who had no choice but to fight.

On the way to Lucinda's minivan, she wraps an arm around me. "Sometimes being an adult and not an impulsive kid, who will die on any hill because they think it's right, sucks."

"You did the right thing," Phyr agrees.

"We're totally going to fight them when I am ready," I reply.

He nods, face grim. "We won't be fortunate enough to have a choice, anam cara."

IT'S LATE when we get back, later still after I shower the stink of the club off me. I'm drifting off to sleep when there's a knock on my door.

Phyr waits on the other side, in his night sweats. No shirt. Red rims his amber eyes and his lids are puffy. "May I come in?"

I open the door wider and gesture for him to enter.

My mattress sinks with his weight as he sits at the foot.

"Should I make us some tea?"

"No, thank you." His voice cracks and he buries his face in his hands.

I sit next to Phyr. Rubbing circles on his back, comforting him the way I did when we were children, and he was sad but didn't want to talk about it. Most fae could really use a therapist.

"You are a balm to my soul," Phyr says in High Fae–the English translation my mind comes up with is not even close to the poetry of what he truly said.

"Who was Fand to you?"

His amber gaze meets mine. I would do anything to take away the sorrow in his eyes.

"They were my lover, my friend, and a planeswalker who fought by my side. When I told you I never considered bonding with another fae, I lied. There was a time I questioned whether everything I felt, our friendship, or any of our promises, were ever real. It was a time when only the immediate moment and those in it mattered."

I know nothing about war or what it does to a person. "I wouldn't be angry if you had bonded with them. If you still want to, I'll find a way to help Fand out of their geas."

"No." His eyes grow fierce. Anger sharpens his features. "Fand is a coward and a traitor to everyone who fell."

"You know Maeve and Nix," I coax. "My siblings likely tricked them into hurting you."

His shoulders slump. "Fand told me they were frightened the night before the battle and asked to go home to see their mother one last time. I became angry with them and told them a coward could not sleep in the bed of a prince. They left—I presumed to go to their own tent or see their mother, but come back for the battle. I never saw them again until this evening."

All this time he presumed his lover died in battle, and to find them dancing in Nix's club in a faerie, whole and safe, had to have served a blow. He struck back, calling me his anam cara in front of Fand.

"My siblings used that moment against you."

He shakes his head. "I believe a good many things about your siblings, but not that. Maeve and Nix fought in that battle. We needed everyone, especially the planeswalkers, our means for retreat. So many fae died. A good number deserted.

"Nix and Maeve rounded up the traitors afterward, executing them. I think Fand used their planeswalker powers to go home to see their mother. Rather than serving a death sentence for betrayal, they likely made a bargain with Nix. Your siblings may hate us, but they did a merciful thing by offering a jail sentence instead."

The geas still seems wrong to me, but I let it go for now.

"I'm sorry they hurt you."

"I do not mourn my relationship with Fand. The tears I shed now are for all those fae who died because I didn't do the right thing. I should have comforted Fand and bolstered their confidence for the fight."

I squeeze his shoulder. "You could have, and perhaps it would have gone as you think it would have. If they had voiced a desire to go home, there was nothing stopping them from leaving while you slept. No matter how supportive and loving we are, people leave. It's not your fault. What other people do is simply out of our control."

My own sadness over Raf's ascension to godhood creeps in, the hurt blunted by time, but still there.

"You've grown wise in our time apart. I wish you hadn't had to suffer to gain that wisdom. Thank you for providing me solace." He lifts my hand and kisses it, sending electric tingles up my arm. Then he's gone, the door closing behind him.

10

Phyr didn't go to bed after he left my room. I discover this when he knocks on my door at 4 a.m.

"Gabriel is downstairs and would like to speak to you."

I rub my eyes. I'd ask how much he knows, but Gabriel's shifter hearing would likely pick it up. He also had the gift of speaking every language from his namesake father, the angel Gabriel, a.k.a. The Herald, therefore, speaking in High Fae wouldn't afford any privacy.

Phyr moves out of my way, not following me downstairs. Alright then. It's me and Gabriel time. Great.

Gabriel's hair is mussed and there's stubble lining his jaw. He's in his gray sleep joggers and a yellow hoodie with a green logo of the local high school our daughters attend. The hoodie likely belongs to Roxy, tossed on to ward off the cold on the way out the door or through a portal made by Phyr. Somehow, he's still sexier than ninety percent of the men on the cover of magazines, let alone walking down the street.

He watches me descend the stairs. Unlike Phyr, Gabriel doesn't hide his emotions behind a mask of indifference. A war between desire, anger, and fear, wages on his handsome features.

He licks his lips and gestures toward the kitchen/living space down the hall. "Can we talk in private?"

"It's four in the morning, Gabriel," I say, letting all my exhaustion sink into my voice.

"I know. I'm sorry. After the night you've been through, you're tired, but it's a matter of your safety and it's important that we talk now."

I lead the way to the living room and plop on the sofa. He takes a seat next to me. "Why didn't you tell me anything about what you were doing yesterday?"

I shrug. "It was witch business. I'm sure the rest of the council doesn't report to you when they go about their people's business. You don't tell me about all the things you do as an alpha or an archangel. That's why we meet as a group, right?"

He blows out his breath and runs a hand through his curls. "You've done things on your own for a very long time and we've only begun our relationship. I don't expect you to check in with me, but I also don't want to hear second-hand about you risking your life."

"Rhiannon went with me when I spoke to the witches, and Phyr, Lucinda, and Rhiannon came along when I went to gather information about the Baba Yaga coven. I may have gone into a dangerous situation, but I was prepared and had backup."

Gabriel is quiet for a moment, swallowing hard. His eyes are wet. "I know you have friends who you can turn to. As someone who cares for you a great deal, I would hope I could be the person you would rely on sometimes, or at the very least, someone you confide in."

It isn't enough for Gabriel to be my romantic interest. He wants to be my hero.

I take his hand in mine and lace our fingers together. With my free hand, I push his curls out of his eyes. "I don't like you because you're the alpha, or the archangel and a magical badass. I like you because you're a good friend and a decent father. Also, I've seen you naked."

A smile plays upon his shapely mouth. His voice lowers a few octaves when he asks, "Did you like what you saw?"

My face and nether regions flood with heat. I did. Gabriel's beautiful body sent Commander Buzz Feel Good on many missions. "I suddenly can't recall." My oh-so-witty reply comes out breathier than I intended.

Gabriel's nostrils flare as he leans closer. Oh, sweet Danu, what can that shifter nose smell? His gaze is positively feral with desire, triggering some interesting reactions in me. "Perhaps you need a closer inspection?"

"Perhaps," I purr. Purr? Who is this vixen, purring?

"What are you doing here, Mr. Crowfoot? Is everything alright, Mom?" My daughter's questions serve as a cold bucket of water on my head, and let's face it, my lap.

Gabriel adjusts himself, settling back in his spot, but doesn't let go of my hand.

I clear my throat, trying for a modicum of decorum. "Everything is fine. We're having an adult conversation."

"Uh, huh." Jada sees our clasped hands and rolls her eyes as she opens the fridge. After grabbing a water bottle, she closes it with her hip. "In the dark."

"Shifter and fae sight," Gabriel explains with a shrug. "Didn't think of it."

Jada isn't buying it.

"What are you doing up so early?" I ask in my Mom Voice.

Jada waves the water bottle as if that answers the question, leaving us. Enter Rhiannon. The rock witch flicks on the lights, yawning and stretching. "Anyone make coffee yet?"

"No." Gabriel and I reply at the same time with the same level of annoyance.

She throws up her hands. "Okay. Okay! I'll make some. Sounds like you two need it. It's your day off, but you need to drive me to work, Miriam."

"I can drop you on my way home, since Miriam abandoned her car last night," Gabriel says.

I cringe, remembering.

Then, to me, "We need to meet about the Baba Yaga coven's allegations as a council. You may be covenless, but you're not without friends."

He's right. The council needs to know that a coven in this territory wants to try me for destroying the grimoires. We decide to call a meeting tonight and hash it out then.

Before he and Rhiannon leave, he pauses at the door. His green eyes flecked with gold focus on me. I find myself drawn right into his arms. He kisses me sweetly, breaking it off before we turn it into something more. "Between your house and mine, we'll never get a chance to be alone. Let's plan to get away soon."

"THE BABA YAGA is not a single witch. They're a nomadic coven," I explain to the council. We're all sitting around my dining room table, so Lucinda wouldn't have to close her cafe for the meeting. Leilani and Cian brought their dinner. I served the rest of the council tea and scones I made for the meeting. Bad news always digests better with food.

"They want to try me for destroying the grimoires. If I'm found guilty—which you all know that I am — the punishment is death."

Lucinda, who already knows this, sips her tea. The rest of the council gasp or show some form of surprise.

Leilani wipes the corners of her mouth. "How can they try you if they don't represent the coven you come from?"

At the head of the table, Gabriel waves a dismissive hand. "There won't be a trial. We are the law of this territory, not some nomadic witches."

His "we are" feels a whole hell of a lot like "I am."

I clear my throat. "Because Rhiannon started an avalanche, I didn't have time to explain myself to the Baba Yaga. We could work this out with a simple discussion, explaining that I destroyed the grimoires but kept the spells and am in the process of making new grimoires."

"You shouldn't go alone," Princess says over her cup of tea. After taking a sip, she adds, "You don't know how many there are."

"We're going to approach this coven as a council and offer them a place within our community. If they refuse, they must leave my territory," Gabriel agrees.

We vote on a day and a time, which is the next day.

JADA FOLDS her arms across her T-shirt with Black Girl Magic written in glitter, not moving from her seat in Gabriel's SUV.

We're in the car queue in front of the high school. Gabriel and I are in the front. Rhiannon, Phyr, and Jada are in the middle row. The shifters Lance, Princess, and Syd compromise the third row. Roxy, Gabriel's daughter, is in the fourth, pull-down seat in the rear of the vehicle. The rest of the council, Lucinda, Aurora, Cian and Leilani, follow in Lucinda's car as she drops off her teenager behind us.

My daughter is a demigod, likely the most powerful person in the car, but I don't want her facing the Baba Yaga.

"Jada, please get out."

She shakes her head, looking so much like her father when he puts his foot down on a matter.

I sigh. "We've been over why you can't come."

"I'm eighteen in two weeks." She holds up two fingers, in case I've forgotten how to count. Her big brown eyes narrow to slits. "I'm coming."

Gabriel blows out his breath through his nostrils but says nothing. Everyone in the car is annoyed with my kid, including me.

Phyr leans over, whispering to her, "Jada, don't be in a hurry to experience danger. It will come of its own accord soon enough."

She rolls her eyes. "Yeah. Well, I saw vampires shred Mr. Crowfoot to bloody ribbons with their fangs and nails in the street in front of my house. I was part of creating the spell to keep the King of Hell in check. So, I think I'm already initiated in the blood, gore, and bad guys coming after us, gang."

"Fine. You want to come? As archangel, I say you can come." Gabriel puts the SUV in gear. "If your mother is harmed, or if anyone comes to harm defending you, I will also, as the archangel, hold you accountable. Are you ready for that?"

Jada lifts her chin. "Yes."

I glare at Gabriel from the passenger seat. Wrong move, dude. She's the daughter of a halfling witch and demigod, not a shifter readily obedient.

"He may be the archangel and you may also be almost eighteen, but I'm your mother. Get your backside out of this vehicle and go to school, or you will not go to the Senior Ball. Do you understand me?"

Both Roxy and Jada gasp. They'd been planning this ball for a month and planned on going together.

Tears in her eyes, my daughter pushes the door open, barreling into the milling students without closing the door behind her.

I roll down the window. "Hey! Come back here and shut the door."

"Okay, let's keep it moving!" the parent volunteer shouts. When her jaw goes slack, I realize my mistake. Relying on the tinted windows, I hadn't thrown on a glamour.

Phyr slides into Jada's former seat and reaches for the door.

Several students turn to gawk.

"Supe!"

"Holy crap! What is that?"

"Demon!"

Out of all the children staring and shouting, I somehow see the silent one. Jada turns slowly. Teary-eyed, she shakes her head and then turns her back on us.

Gabriel takes off the moment Phyr slams the door.

I roll my window up, hoping Jada will be in a safer place than where we're headed.

TRAFFIC IS ABYSMAL, and the snow is coming down fast in fat flakes, taking us much longer than we intended. When we finally reach where I had the run-in with the Baba Yaga, there are several police and emergency vehicles blocking the road.

A backhoe works on the remains of Rhiannon's avalanche as rescue workers and dogs canvas the area. A uniformed officer holds up his hand, approaching our vehicle.

In the rearview mirror, Lucinda does a k-turn before driving away. Smart. I'd do the same.

"Raise a glamour, Phyr." I dip into my light and throw on an illusion.

Gabriel rolls down the window. "What's going on?"

The officer shakes his head, face grim. Eyes on the scene ahead, he replies, "Avalanche. Need directions for a detour?"

Phyr leans forward. "There are search and rescue animals. Were there victims?"

Magic pulses against my natural defenses.

The mundane cop turns his gaze to Phyr. "Chief thinks monsters caused the avalanche to kill someone, but I'm not supposed to tell you that. Can't cause panic."

Phyr rolls down his window. "Come."

The cop does as the fae bids. He touches the officer's forehead. "Supernaturals were not behind this. It was an earthquake, and no one died. Stop the search and report that to your chief. Pass it on." Phyr trembles, bearing the searing pain all fae feel when we lie.

The officer nods and returns to the rescue workers, touching each as he speaks.

"What did you do?" Gabriel demands as he turns the SUV around.

Phyr grins. "Everyone he touches will believe without a doubt it was an earthquake and no one died."

"What's going to happen when they find Miriam's car?" Princess asks from the back row between Syd and Lance.

Phyr and I exchange glances.

"I could get you inside the car and open a portal between your world and my faerie large enough for you to drive through."

I lift my eyebrows dubiously.

"That sounds risky," Gabriel says. "I don't like it."

"Noted," Phyr replies and then turns to me. "Miriam?"

I don't like it either, but I also don't like the idea of the authorities finding my car buried under all the snow. There's also no proof there was an earthquake, not the natural source, at least. Phyr's lie could be easily disproved.

"We can give it a try. Pull over. I don't want Phyr cracking open the fabric of the multiverse in the car."

"Thanks," Princess says dryly with an eye roll.

"What about them?" Gabriel hikes his thumb toward the rear, meaning the rescue workers we'd left behind.

"I'll cast an illusion. They won't see a thing," Phyr offers.

Gabriel pulls the SUV over, grabbing my arm gently before I can open my door. "It's going to be impossible to get that car out. You're going to have to destroy it."

My stomach sinks. I use that car for so much, especially my business. The only other vehicle I own is the bakery delivery van.

"Claim it stolen so you can get insurance money," Princess offers gently. "You don't want to get into a new car payment because Rhiannon and Lance fucked up."

Lance glares at her, a low growl rumbling from his throat. Princess raises her middle finger in response.

We're all mature adults here.

"Good idea," Gabriel agrees, oblivious to his beta and gamma squabbling. "Use your faelight to burn it."

"No," Princess leans forward. "They'll have specialists investigate the arson. If there's no cause for the fire, they'll know she left it there and then burned it."

The dilemma only increases the tension over facing the Baba Yaga, tying my gut in knots.

Phyr turns to her. "What if I create a portal under the car? Suck it into a faerie?"

"Could work. You'll have to time it so that a ton of snow doesn't come crashing in too."

"Too much supernatural," Gabriel disagrees. "We got them off our trail."

"Just leave the car and claim it stolen," Syd offers, rubbing his short brown, bristly hair. His voice is as rumbly as the grizzly bear he shifts into.

I waver for a few moments until finally deciding. "I suppose I could."

"Do it online on your phone, Miriam," Gabriel agrees. "Later though. You would be at the bakery right now. We should continue on the mission and find the Baba Yaga. Lance, give me the coordinates where you met up with Daystar up here. We'll canvas from there instead."

While Lance talks, I unlock the screen on my phone. "Can't. No bars."

Lucinda pulls up behind where we've pulled over, gets out and approaches the driver's side. Gabriel rolls down his window. She stands on tiptoe to fit her face into view. Lucinda is barely five-two and has the build of a triathlete because she is one, and a siren, and my closest friend.

"New plan?" Lucinda asks, her words are faintly limned with a Spanish accent leftover from her childhood with her human father in Puerto Rico. A former member of Persephone's arm, she's also fluent in Ancient Greek.

"We're going to head back to where Lance met up with Baba Yaga's son."

"There's a strong ley line running through here. I'd guess the coven uses it to mask their location. I'd start right where we're at."

"Good idea, but the snow is too deep."

"Those of us who can sprout wings could fly. Cian can make himself small enough that the snow doesn't break under his feet."

Gabriel rubs his jawline. "We can't leave everyone in these cars or fly. Not with the road crew so close."

"I could create an illusion to hide the vehicles," Phyr suggests.

"I could cast a repulsion spell so that no one approaches the cars," Rhiannon offers.

All of us cringe except Phyr. When I'd first met Rhiannon, she'd been living in Phyr's faerie, hiding the entrance of a nowhere door with a repulsion spell we all experienced. The spell evoked primal fear and nauseated the victim. Some magic you never forget, and that spell is one of them.

Gabriel agrees to allow her to cast the spell.

He, Roxy, Phyr, and Rhiannon get out of the car. Lucinda retrieves Cian, a human-sized leprechaun who can shrink, from the other car. Aurora gets out of Lucinda's car too. A Bigfoot, the snow and woods would be nothing to her, I suppose.

Gabriel and Roxy strip off their shirts and take on their angelic forms, sprouting wings from what look like golden tattoos on their backs. Gabriel is shirtless, but Roxy kept her bra to salvage some modesty.

I grin at the nephil girl with goth makeup and electric blue hair, and then whisper a protection spell. She's a nephil shifter like her father, but the Baba Yaga are nearly god-like with their witch powers. Every bit of protection can only help.

Lucinda transforms into a siren: taloned feet, feather-covered body and wing in rainbow hues. I hope she doesn't have to sing.

Rhiannon returns to the SUV, but Phyr stays outside, watching Gabriel, Roxy, and Lucinda take off. Aurora mounts the wall of snow up and over with ease, hardly upsetting the plowed drift.

"What are you doing?" I ask Phyr, sticking my head out the window. "You can't fly."

Phyr flashes a wicked grin. "I can walk through space and time, anam cara. A little snow is nothing to me."

11

When you prepare for a confrontation and end up sitting in an SUV on the side of the road waiting for others to find the confrontation, time passes slowly. I do little things to amuse myself, like count the visible snowflakes. No cars come through, likely because they've shut down the pass with the inclement weather worsening.

I glance at those who remain in the car. Leilani is reading something pre-downloaded on her phone. Rhiannon is fast asleep, head resting on Lance's shoulder, mouth slack. Lance's eyes are closed, and his head tilted back.

Princess has earbuds in, staring at her phone as if watching something. I wonder what, since there's no data and no Wi-Fi out here.

Syd's gaze meets mine. I think he shares my worry, until he says, "Got any snacks?"

I have, in fact, packed snacks. I clamber out of the SUV and within minutes, have the cooler cracked open, passing out sandwiches and bottles of water. Soon everyone is awake and happily munching away, except me.

Jada is supposed to go straight to LGBTQIA+ Alliance Club after school and get a ride home from her friend Kai, but I hadn't cleared it with Kai's dad and that bothers me. Since she attends a choice high school, accepted based on a lottery, we lived nowhere near the building. Too many variables are up in the air that I can do nothing about.

"I gotta piss," Princess announces, hopping out of the car.

"Uh," Rhiannon holds up a finger.

I'm wearing an amulet that deflects repulsion spells, but Princess is not.

She vomits before we can stop her.

I grab some charcoal from my purse and rush to the pack beta.

Princess doesn't fight me, only looks relieved as I push back her fringe of bangs and draw a ward on her forehead.

"Thanks," she mutters before sprinting off to take care of necessities.

I turn to give her privacy but wait outside the car.

"Do you think we should send a second party to check up on the first?" I ask when she returns.

The pack beta worries her lip, glancing over her shoulder. "Yeah. Good idea."

I gloat internally. It must've taken a lot for Princess to admit that. "Who?"

She brushes a snowflake off her face. "Me and Lance could handle the snow, but Syd and Leilani are kinda on the heavyweight shifter side."

Technically, Leilani is a demigod, but I get Princess's point. She didn't mention Rhiannon or me, and it's clear why—not being water-witches, and without snowshoes, the two witches wouldn't get very far.

"Okay. Let's inform the others."

She inclines her head and gestures for me to go first, a sign of respect.

We return to the SUV and explain our plan.

"I'd like to stay," Lance says, arm firm around Rhiannon.

I understand that he's bonding with the rock witch, so he feels instinctive protectiveness. However, Princess needs backup more than Rhiannon and I do.

"I took on the King of Hell. Leilani is a demigod, Syd can turn into a grizzly, and Rhiannon has created a powerful repulsion spell. I think we'll be fine without you guarding us."

He looks down. "I can't leave you."

After I get over the initial shock of his response, I exchange glances with Princess. From the way her nostrils flare, she's as pissed off as I am.

"Was it a direct order from our alpha?" Princess asks before I can.

Lance smooths his hand over his long plaits. "I can't say."

A dark look passes over the beta's face. There and gone. Her gaze returns to me. She sighs. "He'll be no good to me."

Months ago, I'd learned from my daughter Jada that shifters become physically ill if they don't obey their alpha. The compulsion to obey increases and their bodies shut down until they can't do anything but what their alpha ordered without pain or nausea.

I shudder. I'd felt like that once. Addicted to Lucifer and compelled to do whatever the King of Hell told me.

"I'm good in the snow," Syd offers.

"Too cold, sorry." Leilani, sitting in Gabriel's seat with the heat on her, says. "I'm out of my element here."

Princess smiles. A rare occurrence around me. "No problem. It'll be better if there's just the two of us canvassing the area." She nods at Syd.

They get out of the car, and I join them. I wait until they undress and hum while their bodies make gross squelching and popping noises as they shift to their animal forms.

Princess is a honey badger the size of a large dog and Syd is a grizzly bear. My mind understands they aren't wild animals, but my instincts scream, "Run! Bear!"

After I ward them against repulsion and compulsion spells, I get an idea that might help. "I'm going to place a tracking spell on you two in case something happens."

Princess bobs her furry head, as does Syd. It's kinda creepy there's people in there. Not overly so. Mundanes would find my budding antlers and shimmering skin creepy.

I clip a bit of their fur and put it in a Ziploc baggie. Then I prick my finger, an old spell used to track kids and pets.

Witches don't often use blood magic because blood tells the story of our ancestors and our own life, but I don't want to take any chances. I only wish I'd thought of doing the same for the first party.

I mark behind their ears with some ash from a jar in my bag and then rub my bleeding thumb over the soot.

"Blood and ash bind you to me," I say in Kairska because I don't want to freak them out, dipping into my light and putting intention in my words. "My feet will follow wherever your feet trod. My eyes will see wherever your eyes see. No matter where you wander, I will find you."

The magic settles, tethering them to me. I rub my wrist where an invisible bracelet stings. The feeling goes away and won't come back until I activate the spell to seek them.

Princess sidesteps away, annoyed. Syd shakes his head. My mother had put that spell on me as a child. I didn't like it at first either.

"The sensation of a collar will fade in a few moments."

Princess hisses her displeasure. Syd barrels down the road, likely looking for a low point in the plowed snow. The massive honey badger lopes after him.

I shake my head. This isn't even the top three of my "this is some weird mess" moments.

ANOTHER HOUR PASSES before Phyr appears out of thin air. He staggers forward, a limp Aurora in his arms. Glamour gone, she's in Wookie mode. Dark, wet stains blotch her fur. Not good.

Everyone in the SUV disperses outside. I open the trunk. Meanwhile, Leilani, a doctor and a demigod, assesses Aurora.

"What happened?" I beg Phyr.

Phyr doesn't respond. He takes my hand, pulling me through a hole in time and space with no warning.

It takes me a moment to get my bearings once everything stops spinning. I spelled my clothes against the weather, but a bitter wind whips between us.

A small village of log cabins with ornate etchings dots a heavily wooded area. Some cabins have bright colors. Others are natural wood. Neatly shoveled paths weave between them. Magic thrums in the air like a living thing.

I believed my former coven was the most powerful. We held all the knowledge of the old world, after all. Like much of my childhood, which is also a lie.

"They trapped Gabriel and Lucinda," Phyr says in High Fae. "Aurora escaped, but it cost her. I cannot be trapped, but I also could not save the others. I called for a temporary truce and a parlay with the fae."

I ask Phyr, "Can you get them out?" Them meaning Gabriel and Lucinda.

"The witches' holding spell is as strong as the circles you create to trap demons, perhaps stronger. I cannot break the trap or find a hole in the spell's weave."

"Could you go back to before this happened and stop Gabriel and Lucinda from doing this?"

He shook his head. "Already thought of that. This is a fixed point."

Before I can ask what terms he's agreed to, we're flanked on all sides by witches. Scores of them. They're all in black hooded robes, faces obscured. I dip into my fae light to see the color of their magic. With my second sight in effect, the witches all glow with the same witch light that dwells within me, but stronger. These are as close to the old world as witches these days got, but not quite as powerful as the three I'd met on the highway.

I, for the first time in my life, don't feel I belong among my people. I feel a stronger kinship to Phyr next to me. There's history between the two of us. These witches are strangers.

The snow falls gently but doesn't land on any of the witches, including me. I've spelled my clothes.

"As requested, I've brought you the one known as Miriam, representative of the Covenless in the Supernatural Council of the Pacific Northwest. Tati the Archivist, Daughter of Gracia the Archivist, among the Covens. Tatiana, Heir of High King Oberon, Ruler of All High Fae," Phyr says, with all the pomp of a court crier.

Part of me wants to add Breaker of Chains, Baker of Goodies, Slayer of Forty Vampires, and Secretary of the PTSA.

The sea of witches parts. Three figures emerge. In unison, they remove their hoods, revealing the trio of witches I've encountered previously.

The youngest of the trio extends her hand, palm up. "The grimoire page for a prisoner, halfling." Her disdain for what I am colors the word. She's also speaking in English, not Kairska.

I'm familiar with it. My mother held the same disdain for the fae. She would have never let my father touch her if she hadn't been selectively breeding a fae child for Lucifer.

"Let me see if they are still alive," I reply in Kairska.

Several of the other witches swerve their hoods toward their neighbors. Guess they didn't know I could speak their language.

The three witches, who seem in charge, trade looks. The eldest grunts and waves her hand dismissively at the other two. "As you like."

The witches assembled part.

I follow the eldest Baba Yaga along the paths cleared of snow, with Phyr close behind. We must walk single file. The snow on either side of the path is hip deep.

We come to a clearing where Gabriel and Lucinda remain suspended midair. They're both in flying poses, as if frozen in time.

"Couldn't risk the siren using her voice or that one smiting our village."

"They came in peace. The archangel wanted to ask you to ally with him, have a say on his council."

The elderly woman eyed me. "Is that so?"

I nod.

"He answers to the Angelic Anocracy. They would subjugate us." Her ancient eyes sweep between me and Phyr. "All of us."

"Gabriel is different," I press. "We revealed who we are to the mundanes to take some of the Angelic Anocracy's power away."

The elderly witch shakes her wizened head. "That will come back to haunt you."

Her words echoing mine causes a frisson to dance across my shoulders.

She holds out her hand and demands, "A page for a prisoner. Choose one."

"I want them both."

The witch shrugs. "Maybe we can come to a deal. You renounce your fae titles and allow us to try you as a witch, then I'll let them go."

I roll my eyes. Why are they so obsessed with trying me? "Not. A. Chance. I do have something else you may want."

"What is that?"

I sigh. "Spells taught to me by Lucifer himself. Many spells no witch has ever seen."

This seems to intrigue the elderly witch. The middle-aged witch and the young one take turns whispering in the elder's ear. Finally, the elderly witch bats the other two away.

"I have a new proposition. Tell us how you stole the grimoires from the Archivist Coven, and we'll let your friends go."

THE ELDERLY WITCH'S name is Ezmal. She invites me to her cabin to tell the tale. Phyr is not welcome past where he stands. He doesn't protest when I tell him I'll be fine, which I hope means he knows I will slip into a cache.

I sit at Ezmal's table along with her sisters, Friza and Shirom. We all have a warm cup of tea and some slices of black bread with honey and butter. They filled the cabin with items straight out of a witch's hut in a fairytale. Jars with eyeballs, dead critters, and things I'd rather not think about. Herbs hang to dry. Her table is solid oak and ornately carved, as are the chairs. She has a small wood bed, beautifully painted. Her massive hearth is what I imagine a boyar's hearth would've looked like in medieval Russia.

On yellowed paper and with an actual feather quill, I draw a map of the Archivist's compound as I tell the story of the first time I stole the grimoires, assuming they didn't know about the second theft.

"When I discovered his plan, I knew the only way to stop him was to steal the grimoires. I had a daily trip to the coven library to commit the spell to memory. The Archivist guarding the grimoires had no reason to believe I would steal them. She led me into the vault. I told her to leave—everyone did as I asked in those days. Once she left, I stored the grimoires in a cache and then left reproductions in their place."

"What's a cache?" Shirom, the youngest sister, asks.

"Fae can make little pocket universes in the subspace between realms."

The witches exchanged glances. Witches are students of the multiverse and its mechanics, and have learned to manipulate through formulas and using their light as a catalyst. Fae magic is, well, to witches, weird.

"How did you make reproductions good enough to fool an Archivist? Another fae trick?" Friza asks, disdain for the fae in her tone.

"A complicated illusion I'd learned in Hell." I would not give away that a demon named Velja helped me craft a very specific illusion and put their own magic into it. Lucifer, hopefully, still doesn't know Velja's part in saving my life.

"Did you ever commit the spell to memory?"

Slowly, I shake my head. "I wasn't myself. I would sit in the vault and rage at my enslavement." In reality, I read comics and listened to music on a Walkman that I pilfered and stored in a cache before the whole consort to Lucifer deal, but I wouldn't tell them that.

Ezmal pats my arm. "Sometimes the best we can do to rebel is to not do as we're ordered. Witches weren't meant to be a tool for a corrupt government to use again."

"The Archivist coven broke their duty." Shirom sips her tea, then adds, "They were supposed to preserve our way of life, not use what we had done to free ourselves in order to harm the innocent."

Ezmal nods.

"Your trial would've gone well if you'd told us the truth," Friza adds.

"No. She destroyed the grimoires. We cannot forgive that," Shirom says.

I want to tell them I made copies of the rest of the grimoires, except for the portion with the World Destroyer, but the thought of sharing more than I need to with these witches makes my skull itch.

We aren't friends. We're not even allies. This is a hostage negotiation, I remind myself.

"We could not forgive the crime, unless," Ezmal pauses dramatically, "we found your old coven guilty of betraying the prime order."

"You'd have to renounce them first. Go through the harrowing, and then live here among us, learn our ways." Friza flashes a brilliant smile. "It would be nice to have a witch of your caliber as a sister."

This feels an awful lot like the religious zealots.

"I can renounce my coven, but I cannot join yours. I have a daughter, responsibilities, and a position within my chosen community I cannot abandon," I say.

Suddenly, the table shakes and the walls tremble. The floor vibrates under my soles as I push to my feet.

I rush outside with the three sisters to find Phyr and Rhiannon outside, along with Lance in wolf form, a grizzly and a giant honey badger.

"The planeswalker is a problem," Shirom mutters under her breath in Kairska.

She's too far to be heard by witch ears, but not fae ones.

I signal that I have it under control. The shifters get it, but Rhiannon marches awkwardly forward. The snow is knee deep where the Baba Yaga coven have not cleared paths. Phyr follows the rock witch at a slower pace, likely to make sure she doesn't plummet face forward.

Rhiannon shakes her fist, shouting, "That was just a *taste* of what I can do. Give us our friends back or I'll—"

"Cease your threatening. I shall free your friends," Ezmal says in heavily accented English. The elderly witch crosses the snow without sinking into it, not even leaving a print. She stops in front of the suspended archangel and siren.

She chants and breaks a small bone. Magic, strong and ancient, prickles my skin followed by an audible pop. Gabriel and Lucinda both tumble forward in the sky.

He lands gracefully. Eyes on me. He also crosses the snow without sinking. Barefoot. Gabriel wears only his sweats.

"We came in peace!" He snarls, not sounding peaceful at all.

Lucinda recovers herself in the air and opens her mouth.

"I have it under control," I shout with my hands up.

She nods but doesn't land.

"Nuh-uh. I do!" Rhiannon counters.

Phyr rushes to steady her before she tumbles, as I predicted, face forward.

"The grimoire page," Ezmal says, holding out her hand.

I retrieve it from a cache and hand it to her. Her eyes never leave my hands as I work the uniquely fae magic.

"Those who sit on the edge of a fence never truly enjoy the grass on either side," Ezmal says as I hand her the page.

"I mean to break down the fence," I reply in Kairska. "So that the two sides can be a stronger, better whole."

12

"**I** don't get it. They lured you all the way up there to hear a story?" Gabriel asks, pacing the floor of Lucinda's Café. He pauses a second to look at his sleeping daughter stretched out on one of the oversized sofas.

The cafe sort of reminds me of one from a '90s sitcom. It's a storefront with an assortment of comfy, colorful living suite furniture and coffee tables, rather than formal dining tables and chairs you find at most places.

Lucinda sent the staff home early with a lie that there was a supposed gas leak reported.

The entire council is present except for Aurora and Princess, and the addition of Lance and Rhiannon. Gabriel dropped Syd, Princess, and Aurora at his place beforehand so Aurora could take her girlfriend home. Aurora's injuries were not serious. Like the page from the grimoire, she'd been bait.

I shake my head. "No. I think they wanted me to narc on my coven and join their ranks."

Gabriel stops pacing in front of me. "If you joined their coven, would they join the Supernatural Council?"

We all turn to Gabriel, shocked looks all around.

"They tricked me into coming to them, hurt Aurora—not to mention held you and Lucinda prisoner when you came in peace. What about their behavior would make them an ally, let alone a coven I would join?" I don't even bother mentioning how they wanted me to renounce my fae side, a demand that rankles every time it crosses my mind.

Phyr positions himself behind me.

Gabriel plops down in one of the overstuffed armchairs filling the room. "I've had a summons from Heaven. The Seraphim Order wants to speak to me."

"About?" I ask, voice wary.

"In heaven, the Angelic Anocracy functions as a lumbering bureaucracy like any other, giving us Archangels positioned on Earth leeway to handle our affairs the way we see fit, unless—" He blows out his breath in an exaggerated exhale while working his fingers through his long curls. "Unless the Archangel is derelict in their duties, or if they've formed some alliance with Hell. Then the Archangel is summoned by the Seraphim Order."

"But you haven't done either," Leilani, who'd been silently sipping cocoa next to her fiancé Cian, protests. "We summoned Lucifer after a rash of hellhound sightings."

My stomach flips. I've allied with Hell.

"I summoned Lucifer," I protest, anger coloring my tone. I'm worried for him. For all of us. "I made a bargain with him, not you, and not to collude, but to call a truce. Surely, my fae heritage doesn't bind me by the same rules as you."

"According to the Angelic Code, I should've never allowed you to do it. They're going to question my motives." He looks helpless. His gaze lands on me. "I don't fear for myself, but they may think you influenced me."

My chest tightens. He wants me to have the protection of the Baba Yaga.

"Negotiation rather than war is a damned good reason to summon the devil," Lucinda says, lifting her head. "You have nothing to be ashamed of. The Olympians and Hades treat all the time. King

Zeus and King Aidoneus are not in the least bit friends, yet they see the value of the other. The feud between Heaven and Hell is childish."

"My mother's family has infighting all the time, but nothing like this," Leilani agrees. "Why must the angels and fallen have a no-negotiation stance?"

It's a good question.

Phyr chuckles dryly, his voice mild, as he says, "The Angelic Anocracy needs Lucifer to play the villain just as much as Zeus relies on Aidoneus to rule Hades and keep the Titans locked in Tartarus. Lucifer has a role in the angelic order, despite his rebellion. Treating with him would acknowledge that role. It's ceding only a modicum of power, but the Anocracy won't, will they?"

"Lucifer would use even a modicum against them," Gabriel snaps. "He'd take all glory away from the creator and give it to himself."

"No." I know this to be untrue, at least in a way. "That was never true. Lucifer wants the Anocracy to lose power, but he doesn't want it for himself. The balance of the multiverse is out of sync. Heaven needs to give up a little."

"That was the reason we formed this council," Leilani says. "To give a little power back to those who had it stolen from them."

"Once you oppose Heaven, they will never forgive you," Gabriel admits in a quiet tone. "Not with angels. We're supposed to be perfect."

Technically, Gabriel is a nephil, but I won't split hairs.

"What happens if you don't comply with the summons?" I ask.

His gaze meets mine, emotions churning in the depths of his green eyes. "They send assassins."

We're all quiet for a while, each lost in our own thoughts. If the Angelic Anocracy does anything to Gabriel, all our efforts are lost. Not to mention, I will not let them touch him.

Lucinda speaks next. "If you choose to defect, I will need to speak with my queen." She sighs. "After I check in with my nanny to see if she can round up dinner. It's six o'clock."

Gabriel nods and then clears his throat, replying in an authoritative tone, "Tell your queen, I am not answering the Anocracy's call. Given the recent threats to supernaturals both by Hell and the mundanes, I must stay where I am needed most. They may perceive this as defecting. She may voice any concerns with me or the Council if she agrees with the Council's theoretical perception."

"I will," she says, a rueful smile relaying she understands his meaning.

"Leilani, would you relay the same to your family?"

The demigoddess nods, standing and pushing the dark ringlets that fall to her waist behind her shoulders. "I will. They have your back, friend." She squeezes his shoulder as she passes.

Cian, her fiancé, rises as well. "I know you didn't ask it of me, but I want to say the low fae of this territory have always allied with you, Gabriel. And, we always will." He makes a bow that seems too formal for the construction worker, then leaves with Leilani and Lucinda.

Gabriel swivels to Phyr. "Tell Oberon it's time to meet with me. I'll come to him, if he likes. It might be better."

Phyr furrows his eyebrows. "Now?"

"No. Give me an hour. I'd like to take Roxy home so she can get some rest, and I can check in on Mama Doe and her pups." He looks at me.

"Perhaps Phyr could take me home now, and you could meet us there after you attend to your obligations? I'd like to check in with Jada. This morning was rough."

After the entire ordeal with the Baba Yaga coven, I'd almost forgotten the situation at the school. I check my phone. There are no messages, missed calls, or voicemails.

Gabriel offers, "Of course, that makes sense. I'll take you straight home and have Roxy nap there while I meet with Oberon. I'd like to talk to you about something private."

~

GABRIEL CARRIES Roxy to the SUV. "When the kid's out, she's out," he says with a grin.

I open the door to the rear for him. He settles Roxy in and buckles her up as I get in the passenger seat. The kiddo grumbles a bit but is out cold before Lance and Rhiannon get in the far rear. The rock witch snores soon after Gabriel exits the parking lot.

I send Jada a text, telling her I'll be home soon. Much to my chagrin, she leaves it unread.

"What did you need to tell me?"

"If I keep avoiding the Anocracy, they'll send seraphs to collect me. My pack is loyal, but I don't want any of them hurt." He blows out his breath. "I'll go willingly, but you'll all need to flee."

My turn to exhale a slow and shaky breath. "The whole reason we came out was to stop a fight with Lucifer." Now, I'm not so sure that was Gabriel's intention.

"Usurping their rule. That's how they'll see it. They won't see it as a compromise to prevent a war." His fingers white-knuckle grip the steering wheel.

The windshield wipers' frenzied beat, the steady rain, and the honk and hum of traffic marry into a soundtrack for the rising tension.

"I committed treason. First, when I didn't execute Kirsten, and second, when I agreed to summon Lucifer. Both acts call for my execution."

I swallow hard. "I won't let them hurt you."

He takes my hand in his and squeezes. "The Seraphim assassins won't stop with me. They'll come for my pack and for the ones who they believed corrupted me." His gaze swings briefly to meet mine. "They'll go for the entire council, treaties or no."

"Why didn't you warn the others?" I demand.

Facing me, he replies, "They know what to do. When we started this council we knew, at some point, it might blow up in our faces. The others have a protocol and a safety net. The council all went home, Miriam. Since you won't seek refuge with the Baba Yaga coven, I'm going to ask your father to take in my pack and the low fae, if worse comes to worse."

"Shit," Lance whispers in the back.

Shit indeed.

The song "Eye of the Tiger" begins playing tinny and muffled. "Call from Princess" flashes on the dashboard screen.

Gabriel grimaces as he presses a button on his car's console. "Hey. Aurora okay?"

Princess's voice comes over the stereo speakers, "Yeah. She's fine. We have a problem though. Syd's missing."

My stomach drops. Have the Seraphim started their culling?

"How? I dropped him with you at the house."

Her responding sigh is loud and impatience colors her tone as she explains, "He made it into the house just fine. After I got Aurora set up in my suite, I went downstairs to get something to eat. Nate was in the kitchen and asked me if Syd came back with the package yet."

Nate handles the compound security.

Gabriel scowls. "What package?"

"That's exactly what I asked. A delivery person, I'm assuming a mundane male from the footage, rang at the gate. Syd told Nate that he was expecting some new headphones and went to get it."

"That's not protocol," Gabriel starts.

"I know. It should've been Nate. He knows too. But, Syd was really excited about the noise-canceling headphones. You know the new pups, yipping all the time is a bit much for him."

Gabriel sighs and nods as he turns down the street that leads to my cul-de-sac.

Princess continues, "The security footage shows Syd opening the gate for the delivery person. The driver led Syd to the back of a standard blue delivery van. He's gone."

"How could anyone kidnap a six-foot-five shifter, who probably weighs three times as much as I do?" Gabriel asks through gritted teeth.

"I don't know," she replies, her bewilderment and frustration clear. "There was no scent of magic. I couldn't even get a clear view of the delivery person. They wore a hat and tinted glasses, and a black gaiter over the lower half of their face, nothing out of the ordinary for a driver in uniform this time of the year trying to beat the cold."

"Get our best trackers on it," Gabriel orders, his voice close to a growl as he pulls the SUV into my driveway. Worry lines crease his forehead.

"Already done, alpha. I ordered them to hunt as a pack, no separating."

"Good work, beta. Keep me posted—don't let the pups out until we've got this figured out."

"Yes, alpha." There's a brief pause. "You coming home? We could use you, along with Lance and Roxy, on this."

Of course, they'd want the wolves to track.

"In a bit. I have to take care of the plan we discussed first."

"I don't like that plan."

Gabriel rubs his forehead. "Neither do I, but where else can you go?"

Now it all makes sense why he wanted me to join the Baba Yaga coven. They'd gone under the Anocracy's radar for centuries, if not millennia. My coven knew little about them and we were Archivists. Or perhaps they didn't tell me, so I'd have nowhere to run.

Princess blows out her breath, a long-suffering sound. "You're right. It's just that Aurora—I don't think she could last in a place like faerie long."

"I don't think I want to be there permanently either," I admit, knowing my siblings want me dead.

"It's only a worst-case scenario plan," Gabriel replies, disconnecting the call.

While Rhiannon and I head into the house, Gabriel stays back a second to speak with Lance and Roxy. It's only been twenty minutes since Gabriel told Phyr to give him an hour, so I'm surprised to hear voices wafting down from the great room when we enter the foyer.

Roxy kicks off her boots and heads down the hall first. "Jada! We're back! Whoa! Holy shit! What are you?"

"What a kind greeting, dear," Oberon, High King of the Fae, replies dryly from somewhere in my living room.

Rhiannon wrings her hands. "Can I be excused from, uh, that?" She nods her head in my father's direction. The rock witch may be one-sixteenth brownie, but she's uncomfortable around fae other than Phyr and usually makes herself scarce during my father's visits.

I want to assure her she's safe with me, but I'm not always safe with fae. "You don't want to know what's happening?"

Rhiannon shrugs in contrast with the unease on her features. "I don't think I'll be needed, and I'd like to take a shower and relax."

"Go on." If I had the option, I'd take a shower and relax. My life hasn't gone that way since a hellhound showed up in my neighbor's begonias a few months ago.

In the kitchen, Phyr mans the kettle and tea service. Meanwhile, in the living room, Roxy gapes at Jada sitting with a high fae dressed like he's in an '80s music video replete with a white lace cravat and bright purple, complementing tight-fitting paisley embroidered trousers and vest. A face with bold and excellently carved features lifts to meet mine. His antlers are white and large, sticking out from hair the same shade of bright pink as my roots.

A little fang shows with his smile of greeting. "My dear Tatiana, take that glamour off. I'd like to see you."

Tatiana is the name my father gave me when I was born. I am known as Tati to the rest of the fae because they hate calling me their dead queen's name. When I faked my death to escape Lucifer, and Raf found me wasting away from angel dust withdrawal, we decided I'd be Miriam. Phyr adjusted, but my father refuses to use that name or the pet name the fae gave me.

Doesn't matter. I don't care what I'm called these days, as long as it isn't my true name given to me by the goddess Danu, which is yet another story, and something only privy to myself and Phyr, and of course, the goddess herself.

I'd forgotten I'd fashioned an illusion to make me look human. No wonder the Baba Yaga thought I could just renounce my faeness.

I do as my father bade, removing the glamour.

"Ah."

How could so much pride fit in a single syllable? Oberon's face transforms from mildly amused to absolutely radiant.

"Is this why I have been summoned?"

My gaze flicks to Phyr, who pours tea from an electric kettle into an ornate teapot with his eyes on his duty. The scent of lavender fills the room.

I return my attention to my father. "No. I don't need you for this." I gesture to my hair and the general area where the buds stick out of my head.

"Jada, it's time for your mother and I to have a chat. Why don't you take your companion to your quarters and frolic?" Oberon says.

Jada and Roxy snort and giggle their way upstairs, the word "frolic" a bit too much for teenagers to handle gracefully.

Rather than opting to take Jada's place next to my dear old dad, I take a seat in an overstuffed chair.

My cell phone rings. I dismiss the call and put my phone on vibrate.

Phyr carries the tea service around the other side of the breakfast bar as far from me as possible.

Oberon waits for Phyr to serve him, then he dismisses the prince with the wave of his hand, as if he's a servant. Phyr bows with a flourish, taking his leave.

Once my father and I are alone, his features sharpen. "You must bond with him, and soon."

"Why?"

"Maeve or Nix will kill him if you don't."

Not if I kill them first.

"Is Jada in danger too?" I sometimes wonder at the way I respond to things that are not normal to hear, but my question is important.

He shakes his head. "No. She is Phyr's heir, not mine. She's an asset."

Interpreting my expression, Oberon elaborates. "I can only name my successor. I cannot name yours. Until you do so, Jada is Phyr's heir."

"Do I need to name a successor?"

"No faerie belongs to you to name one."

I vaguely recall from the collection of newly returned memories of my life in faerie the rules of succession. Overly complicated and somewhat nonsensical rules.

"Why me? Why name me heir? Clearly Maeve and Nix want it more."

"Precisely," Oberon replies, mouth slightly curved. "You would never kill me to sit on the throne, so they believe. I named that reason to spare them. I chose you as heir because I saw the greatest potential in you, Tatiana. You are a creature of three worlds: Kairska, Earth, and faerie. If the high fae are to survive in this ever-changing multiverse, we need to change who rules." His smile broadens, showing lots of sharp white teeth. "Eventually. I don't plan on dying anytime soon, or ever actually. Which is also why you need to make your own faerie, so you won't need mine." The smile fades. His voice takes a serious tone. "I love you, dear Tatiana, but I trust no one."

13

Twenty minutes passes and Gabriel still doesn't come in. I go out front to see what's the holdup.

At the end of my driveway, two men in dark suits, each carrying briefcases, face Gabriel and Lance. The strangers are clean shaven and have military-short haircuts. One is a bit older, perhaps in his early sixties, and has the build of a prosperous life. His companion, standing slightly behind him, is younger and lean.

Gabriel and Lance listen, arms folded. I can't see their faces, but I'm sure from their body language they are not pleased with what the strangers have to say.

The situation seems oddly familiar.

"God will remake you in his image," the older man says, reminding me of the zealots who came into the shop.

"I am perfect as I am," Gabriel responds. "You have been misled. There will be no paradise on Earth. This is the only world we have, and we must solve our own problems."

"No," the man shakes his head, face turning red with anger. "The Great Pretender has deceived you!"

Gabriel removes his shirt. His wings unfurl, letting himself be seen, really seen. His angelic beauty is perfect.

The two men gape. Tears wet the cheeks of the younger man.

"I am Gabriel, son of the Archangel Gabriel, who granted me guardianship of the Pacific Northwest. I would like to speak to whomever is leading your organization."

He nods to Lance, who hands a card over to the man who is currently wetting himself.

My nose tickles. I rub it, regretting having done so as soon as I get a whiff of his angel dust. Warmth blooms head to toe, my whole body throbbing with need. The rest that transpires is hazy.

Someone leads me away somewhere cold, and then into my room. It's not Gabriel. Oh, so beautiful, Gabriel with full lips that taste so good and a body that feels so nice. I'm tired of kissing on the mouth, I'd like to—

"Yes, yes," Phyr says, interrupting my thoughts. "I'd like to do that to him, or have that done by him, too. Drink."

I giggle and take the mug offered to me. "Would you like to do that to me?"

Phyr grimaces. "You don't have the parts required. Drink, Miriam."

"You flirt with everyone but me," I pout.

"I would rather cut my tongue out than use it to play with your heart," Phyr replies. "Drink."

"Wait, wait, wait, you used to have a crush on me," I say, confused. "You swore to love me forever."

"You made similar promises, a very long time ago. Drink." He kneels next to where I sit. His face is devoid of expression.

Suddenly, I'm on the chair beside my vanity and don't know how we got here.

His hand guides mine, holding the cup. I feel all sorts of tingles where his skin covers my flesh. I gaze into his eyes.

"We have more than friendly feelings between us."

He cuts me off by tilting the mug, forcing me to gulp down the liquid.

"Tastes like pennies." I say, wiping my mouth. My head clears. A hazy recollection of how I behaved outside and then to Phyr, as he took me inside while under the influence of angel dust, makes me want to curl up under the covers.

"It's my blood. Again," Phyr says, interrupting the embarrassing recollection.

"Bonding would protect you both from his influence," my father says quietly from my door. "The archangel stated his business. I gave my answer. He left to take his youngling home but asked me to return to my home as soon as Tatiana felt more herself. She seems rational. Let's go. You will bond with her upon returning." Oberon wraps an arm around Phyr's shoulders in the fatherly way he had when we were children.

I don't trust it.

Or my father.

I recall Oberon showing affection to doomed courtiers.

He and Phyr disappear before I can stop them.

~

I BREATHE EASIER when Phyr returns unharmed.

He says, "Feeling yourself?"

I nod.

He blows out his breath, relief washing over his features. "You were like another person. Wanton. Lustful. Feral."

I blink. Barely containing my mirth, I ask, "Did you just call me wanton?"

"Yes. I did. I also called you feral." His dark eyebrows gather at my amusement. "Sexually unrestrained is the meaning of wanton. Does it mean something else now?"

"It's sort of an insult, but your definition is still correct."

"Oh." He holds up his hands. "I meant no insult. Your behavior under the influence of angel dust surprised me. Gabriel, too." Phyr tilts his head, eyes lost. "He seemed unsettled as I took you away, although he was the one who sent for me. I don't understand. The whole incident was an accident?"

I took a deep breath. "He was showing off his wings to a mundane, claiming to be an angel, not a nephil-shifter."

Phyr and I share a knowing look.

The difference meant everything.

I shudder.

"What did father say to Gabriel's asylum request?"

Phyr grimaced. "The king stated he would welcome any guests you brought as your retinue. However, the moment you step into the High Court with coming into your fae maturity in evidence, you will be a target for your siblings."

Although they've told me a thousand times, it's still chilling to hear my own flesh and blood want to kill me. "How did Gabriel respond?"

Phyr grins, eyes dancing with mirth. "He said your retinue will make their task difficult."

Remembering that they would make Phyr a target, I ask, "Is there a way I could broker a peace with Maeve and Nyx?"

"No." He rubs his bronze forehead. His eyes latch onto mine. "Any attempt at negotiation will be seen as weak and cowardly."

"Father says we need to bond, or they'll kill you."

"Gabriel has agreed to the bonding, but wants to be present," Phyr provides.

I place a hand over his. "Phyr, you don't have to bond with me at all. Not if you still have something for Fand."

"They are dead to me." His tone brooches no argument.

"Phyr," I begin.

"Surely, you know I will do anything to protect you," he replies, his hand sliding up my arm. Heat bathes me in the wake of his touch. "All the best days of my life have been at your side: as a playmate of my youth, as the first person I kissed, as a simple baker, as your housemate, as a guardian to your child. I want to bond with you so that we will never be apart again, even if our bodies separate. Not even death ends a bonding. I assure you with all my heart and all the light within me, there is no one else I would rather be bound to for eternity than you, anam cara."

I struggle for words.

We both turn our heads to the knock on my door. Phyr backs away and straightens. "It's open."

I'm glad he can speak because I cannot. My heart thunders too loudly in my chest and I cannot turn off the way he did so easily.

Jada opens the door and peeks her head inside. "Mami, there's a police officer at the door."

I DIP INTO MY LIGHT, producing a glamour to make me appear more human. I don't remember everything that transpired outside, but I'm pretty sure I did nothing that warranted someone calling the cops.

Also producing a human glamour, Phyr accompanies me downstairs.

Jada had closed the door to come fetch us. Good girl.

Raf taught her from a young age to invite no one inside, even our friends or the authorities. A wide variety of supes possess the ability to use an illusion spell or literally shift into the form of someone else but couldn't enter a home unless invited. The insidious kind preyed upon children.

I have wards against anyone with ill intent, but you never know. Drawn by the power that resides within me and my daughter, the supe might step on the property out of curiosity and later decide we'd make a tasty meal.

I open the door and plaster on my PTSA smile. "How may I help you?"

The two state troopers in full uniform stood at my doorway. One stepped forward. "Are you Miriam Diaz owner of a—" he describes the make and model of my car.

All the blood drains from my face. I'd forgotten to report the car stolen.

"Yes. I—oh goodness—I was going to report it stolen on the website, but I didn't have a," I ramble a bunch of nonsense that isn't a lie because it's nonsense.

The officers exchange a glance. They're not buying my story, but I can't stop talking.

Phyr puts a hand on my shoulder. "Doesn't matter, love. Did you find her car?"

The officer, who has been quiet, says, "That's an Irish accent."

Phyr nods but gives no further information.

Ignoring both of them, the cop who spoke first asks, "When did you notice your vehicle was missing?"

I swallow hard. I would avoid lying as best I could. "Can't say an exact time."

Another look between the cops.

Shit. Did I run any red lights to get caught on a traffic cam?

"You didn't need the vehicle for your business?"

Oh, they searched my car. We loaded the Subaru with baked goods, and I had business cards in there. "My business was closed today. I had a personal matter to attend to."

"How did you do that without a vehicle, ma'am?"

"We have a van," Phyr says behind me. Not exactly a lie. We had a van we used for catering events, but it took too much gas to use for our small errands.

"People generally report their vehicles stolen right away."

I narrowed my eyes at the way he said 'people' as if he didn't consider me people. "Is it a crime to not report your car stolen?"

"No. No, it's not. We found your vehicle buried under an avalanche in Snoqualmie Pass with no trace of a driver or how they escaped."

They look at me expectantly as if I'm supposed to have some sort of reaction. I only stare, making no reply.

Phyr leans against the door frame. "Fascinating. Was the car damaged?"

"We're having a forensics team examine it," he waits for a response. When we give him none, he continues. "There have been several disappearances in the area. Strange lights and spot earthquakes with no scientific explanation. A remote place like that would be a good place for a witch cult to hide their victims. You said you represented witches at that televised gathering."

"And High Fae," the other officer provides. "Aren't fae known for kidnapping people."

"Now that's a leap," I say, anger flaring. I jab my thumb at my chest. "I'm the victim here. My car was missing and now I'm suspected of, what, exactly, sacrificing people to the devil? You'd think I'd pick a more convenient spot than Snoqualmie Pass in the middle of winter."

"You thrive in winter," the cop hisses. "You cannot change my mind. I have God on my side, Baba Yaga."

At least, that's what I think he said. The officer said it in Russian, which is related enough to Kairska for me to glean his meaning.

"I'm sorry, what?" I ask, feigning confusion. "First you make wild accusations. Now you're not even speaking English. Do I need to call my lawyer?"

"You know what I said. I saw it in your eyes," the officer accuses.

The other cop places a hand on his companion's arm, silencing him. He extends his other hand. In it, he holds out a card.

"Why don't you get some rest? Come to the station and make an official statement about your vehicle. The sooner the better."

I take the card, neither agreeing or disagreeing to doing anything Danu might bind me to do.

"For argument's sake, what if she doesn't show?" Phyr asks.

"It's better optics to cooperate," the cop replies, leading the silently seething cop off my porch.

I shut the door, wiping away the glamour. I suddenly feel a thousand years old.

"Do you think the Baba Yaga coven is kidnapping the missing supes for some sort of ritualistic sacrifice to Lucifer?"

I bark a laugh. "Lucifer might smile at the fervor of their belief if they did it in front of him. However, a few witches and a couple of sacrifices aren't really enough of a magical pick-me-up for him."

Phyr chuckles, moving closer. "See, the fae are superior. We appreciated the small gestures. No genocide in our name needed."

I grin up at him. "It's good to have standards."

"Mine are very high." He leans closer, his breath fanning my face. "I will not let these human authorities take you. Say the word and I will slip into their minds and break them."

Lucifer used to make offers like this. Except he wanted me to want him to demonstrate how powerful he was. There's no cruel joy in Phyr's offer, only a solemn vow of protection.

The officer did seem a bit off, breaking into Russian and assuming I am Baba Yaga was a stretch.

"You didn't do something to them just now?"

He shakes his head. "No. However, I peeked inside. The one who spoke first has a vendetta against all supes, but no proof you're guilty of any crime. He goes to the same place of worship as those people that came to the shop and confronted Gabriel in the driveway. The Paradise Center was heavily on his mind."

"He didn't want to harm me, or he wouldn't have made it past my wards. I think that religion is targeting supes for some sort of brain-washing. This is something Gabriel and the council should know."

Phyr sighs. Planting a hand on each shoulder, he steers me toward the stairs. "In the morning. We need some sleep."

We pause briefly at the top of the stairs as if we're each coming to some decision.

Rhiannon pops her head out her door. "Coast clear?"

For the briefest of moments, I want to lash out at her for the trouble she caused. A younger me would have thought that way and probably would have cruel words for her. I know her role meant nothing. The Baba Yaga coven wanted to lure me, using her as a pawn. No parties were aware that a cop had a serious erection for supes.

"For now. I need to make a statement at the police station tomorrow about my car."

The rock witch swallows hard. "I'll handle the bakery."

Phyr and I exchange a glance. He suggests to Rhiannon, "Maybe you could have Lance there for security?"

She smirks. "You think I need a bodyguard?"

More like a babysitter. "It's just better if no one is alone."

"Okey dokey, smokey. I'll send Lance a text-a-roonie that I need him to be my Kevin Costner." With a salute, she's gone. Through the door I hear her humming Whitney Houston's "I Will Always Love You."

I frown.

Phyr tilts his head. "I thought you wanted him there to protect her?"

"I do. I just can't remember if the bodyguard dies to save the singer in that movie."

Phyr chuckles. "Perhaps we can watch it together and find out?"

I smile at his offer of normalcy, after so little of it as of late. I yearn for movie nights. With all that's happening, it will not be for a while, but the promise that there will be peace again appeals so much it hurts.

"It's a date," I reply.

As we turn to our separate rooms, I glance over my shoulder at Phyr. A smile graces his lips as he enters his bedroom. A genuine smile that makes my heart clench.

14

Gabriel sits at the head of my dining room table with me at his left and Princess at his right. Princess has her elbow propped on the table holding up her head, sipping coffee from a mug that says, "Less talkie more books and coffee." Her girlfriend Aurora seems well despite her former injuries. Bigfoot doesn't touch the muffins and drinks her coffee black. I forgot Aurora is a vegan and topped the muffins with cream cheese frosting.

Next to me Lucinda rips small pieces of her muffin, dipping them in coffee. Leilani is dressed in her professional attire. When she arrived, the demigoddess announced that she didn't have long before she needed to go to her clinic and start seeing patients. Poor Cian had to take the morning off from his construction gig. Fortunately, the leprechaun works for one of the companies Gabriel owns.

We all have jobs to get to, so I try to keep it short and to the point while I relay what happened with the officers.

"Phyr is certain the officer is a member of that church?" Gabriel asks.

I nod.

He grimaces. "Not good. They're no small organization. Paradise Centers are all over the United States. They span into Canada and have a few global missionaries. The organization has been around for almost a hundred years. I don't know why they'd start trouble now."

"We came out of the closet, boss," Princess provides, stretching. Dark circles under her eyes telegraph how late she stayed up searching for Syd.

"How do you know so much about these Paradise Center people?" Lucinda asks.

"Yeah. I've never heard of them before recently," Leilani adds.

Cian nods his ginger head in agreement.

Aurora clears her throat. "Neither had I."

Gabriel puffs his cheeks and puffs his exhale. "The Angelic Anocracy assigned me to monitor the Paradise Centers in my territory. Their practices seemed cultish and a bit on the fanatical end, but no more so than most evangelicals."

"So, these Paradise Centers have the blessing of the Angelic Anocracy?" Lucinda asks.

"Absolutely, which makes it hard for me to go against them in any way."

Leilani, usually the sweetest, bubbliest demigod you'll ever meet, narrows her eyes. At this moment, she seems much, much older than the twenty-six or twenty-seven I'd peg her to be. "Do you personally gain from the Paradise Centers in your territory?"

Gabriel doesn't answer at first. Emotions battle on his face.

"Gabriel," Lucinda urges in the same tone she uses on the PTSA when people deliberate on how to vote for too long. "It's a yes or no question."

Finally, he admits, "Yes. Their belief affects my angelic gifts."

The table is silent for a moment. We all know why the Angelic Anocracy and their archangels here on earth have so much power, but to know that Gabriel directly benefited from a sect with a malicious view towards supernaturals is a bitter pill to swallow.

"These Paradise Center acolytes, or whatever, camp out in front of my clinic every day, preaching Armageddon is nigh nonsense," Leilani says. "I run them off. They're scaring my patients, especially the supes."

Cian clears his throat. "I've had brochures waiting for me on my doorstep. I tossed them with the recycling, thinking nothing of it. Two men in suits came to the worksite looking for me specifically."

Gabriel frowns. "Did they ask for me, too?"

Cian shrugs. "You own the company, but I'm sure they understand the boss man doesn't run the backhoes and such."

"Fair." Gabriel quietly owns two of the largest construction firms in the Pacific Northwest, employing lots of supes. Supes, especially shifters, build most of the new construction that happens in the Seattle area.

"They were in my shop before," I say, digging in my purse and producing the brochure. I don't know why I kept it. "Two women offered me a Bible study. I refused."

"They came in my cafe," Lucinda sighs. "When I asked them to leave my property." She spread her hands. "They started preaching fire and brimstone outside."

"Robby was taking Bible studies from someone," Aurora agrees, nodding fervently. "His cousin said the last time she spoke to Robby, he tried to get her to go to a Paradise Center meeting. Two women have been showing up at his cousin's house and her workplace, offering Bible studies. I also had one show up at my shop."

Princess snickers, "They must have felt out of place really quick."

Aurora owned a new age shop that sold crystals, candles, herbs, incense, etc. The shop regularly hosted guest tarot readers, tasseographers, palm readers, and other types of human diviners with small magics. Not exactly a spot I'd try to proselytize if I were their flavor of Christian.

"I've been looking at it all wrong," Princess says.

We all turn toward her.

She elaborates, "I've been thinking it was the witches in the woods or Lucifer taking the supes. I think the missing supes are getting conned into the free Bible studies these zealots offer and end up —" Her voice trails off. "What if one of these Paradise Centers is where Mama Doe escaped from?"

I shudder.

"Someone outright kidnapped Syd," Gabriel says.

"No evidence of magic. No wolfsbane. Maybe he was going to their church, and they said it's time for Armageddon or some nonsense?" Princess retorts. "We should go into one of those Paradise Centers and see what it's about."

Gabriel argues, "We need harder evidence before we commit crimes like breaking and entering."

Princess gestures to me. "We have a fae right here that could get it from Mama Doe's head."

I blanch. "I barely have any skills at that. I'm still learning, but Phyr—"

"No," Gabriel's answer is so swift, so vehement, that all of us recoil.

His lack of trust of my dearest friend burned.

"Mama Doe doesn't do well with males," Princess says. "She can't stand the smell. Whomever her captors were had to be male."

Cian glances at me before saying, "The high fae, the full-bloods at least, without getting too much into the technicalities aren't exactly, um." He scratches the back of his head, face flushing. "Ah, I don't know how to say it."

"Intersex is the term you're looking for," Leilani squeezes his hand.

"You know better than I would, my love, being a doctor and all," Cian says with no small amount of pride in his tone.

Leilani smiles at him before addressing the table. "What my sweet but shy fiancé is implying is that Phyr won't smell either way except fae."

"Huh," Princess says. "I've never thought about it."

I hate this entire conversation. It left too much up to smells and parts for gender, and gender simply couldn't be defined this way, especially among fae.

"Fine. He can see Mama Doe, but I want you and Miriam present," Gabriel grumbles. "As for the rest of you, I'm going to send a few of my people out to your places of business. Princess, notify other packs that the Paradise Centers aren't to be trusted. We're going to keep an eye on these Paradise Center members."

AFTER EVERYONE LEAVES, Gabriel remains, helping me clear the table and load the dishwasher. We work together in silence. I hadn't expected him to stay to clean up, but I appreciate the help.

"I enjoy doing this with you," he says, wiping his hands on a dishtowel. His button down and slacks don't hide his brawn. His body is muscular without being too bulky, eye-catching as his handsome face. "Feels normal. Right."

I smile and set the dishwasher to run. When Gabriel had first started coming around, I had no one but Jada and I. The small gestures meant so much more. In a few short months, I'd grown accustomed to Phyr tidying and cooking, and Rhiannon taking up some of the cleaning duties. Life is better with a family, found or otherwise.

"I want to woo you. I wish—I wish I had pursued you before."

My face flushes with embarrassment. I had kissed Gabriel once, not long after Raf ascended into godhood. Right after. I'd wanted to drown my grief in Gabriel the way I'd turned to Raf to get over Lucifer.

He braces his hands on the counter. The muscles of his forearms flex. Gabriel's green gaze focuses on my movements from under locks of curly hair. "I'm ashamed to admit it, but I thought about what happened between us a lot."

"I don't think it would have ended well if we pursued anything then. I was too—" I'd spent two months in a bad mental state, barely able to get out of bed.

Gabriel takes my hand, pulling me to him. The other hand brushes a stray hair out of my face. "Perhaps I did the right thing by not pursuing you, but I wish with all my heart I was there for you then. That I had been strong enough to be just your friend. I wanted you too much."

I feel how much he wants me now. The hard length of him pressed against my hip.

He leans forward a bit, whispering, "I always have. I've never stopped."

I breach the distance between us, kissing him. He tastes sweet and his pretty mouth is so soft against mine.

Suddenly, he pulls away. A low growl erupts from his throat. "You could announce your presence."

Phyr shrugs, opening the fridge. "You sent me a message to come here as soon as possible. I thought you'd expect my presence."

He has a point. I deflect, by saying, "Now that you're here. Let's go."

15

Gabriel's house stands three stories tall and sprawls. My suburban McMansion could fit in the structure seven times over. Gray and stone, his house resembles a chateau out of a fairytale more than a house.

There's a dairy barn and stables for horses. Wild game roam the many acres. Greenhouses for growing vegetables year-round cluster to one side of the property optimal for sun. Gabriel took me inside them on tour once. I could have stayed for hours. I am, after all, a hedge and hearth witch. Herbs and green and growing things appeal to me. Perhaps it is also part of my fae nature.

I never really understood the economics of this world, but I know Gabriel has a lot more wealth than I'll ever have. However, the alpha doesn't hoard his wealth, eating alone. His local pack, the shifters he'd consider family, live on the premises. Shifters in human form go about their daily chores, maintaining the fully functioning farm. Shifters in other forms prowl the grounds, hunting.

Princess waits at the front door, letting us in. Despite the size, the house isn't a cold estate with priceless art and expensive furniture.

Small children in human and animal form, too young to attend school, play games in one room. Older shifters past their prime watch the young ones. I don't see Mama Doe's pups among the littles.

Phyr smiles broadly as a little girl about four years old skips out and dances around his legs. Her silky black braids bounce. She has a finger in her mouth as her big brown eyes take him in.

She extracts the finger to point at his head. "You forgot to put your horns away."

Innocent of the world beyond these walls, the girl likely assumes Phyr's dark, curling horns make him an animal shifter of some sort.

His grin takes on a mischievous quality. "Thank you. I like my horns as they are."

"I like my fur. I wish I could wear it all the time. It's soft," the girl replies.

One of the grandparent types, a man in his fifties, sweeps the girl up and takes her with the others. Phyr watches with a wistful look as we walk on.

The look makes my gut knot. He could have a child with Fand.

"Don't fret, dearest friend. Children are so few in faerie. They're a novelty, but I don't want one."

I heard his voice as if in my head.

I check my mental shields. *How?*

He walks as if he didn't hear my attempt at telepathy.

"How?" I ask out loud, soft.

Gabriel and Princess are deep in conversation.

You drank my blood. Once we're bonded, we'll have to focus to keep out of each other's heads.

I nod. Good to know.

We head up winding wooden stairs; the carpet lining the center is worn by extensive use. Thirty or perhaps forty or fifty people live in this mansion/farmhouse.

"Only one staircase in such a large house?" Phyr asks.

"This is one of three," Gabriel says over his shoulder. He stops at the beginning of the hallway where Mama Doe's room lies. "I can't go past here, or she'll smell me," he whispers, making room for Phyr and I to pass.

We follow Princess past rooms with mothers and newborns, the smell of diaper creams and baby powder strong. The nursery wing of the home, a quiet retreat for new shifter mothers to bond with their babies.

"The birthing room is in there," Princess points out a closed door. "Gabriel soundproofed this entire floor, so the whole house doesn't have to hear the screamers. Some guys get real freaked out by childbirth. They shift and become aggressive, especially when it's their mate having a baby." She rolls her eyes.

I wonder what it had to be like being a lesbian and dating outside the shifter pool of eligibles.

Princess seems to read my thoughts. "There's been lesbian alphas. They don't have to mate with a male. They have to get inseminated at some point. Producing the next generation is important in our culture." She blows out her breath. "Wish those m-preg shifter fics were true. Save me a whole lot of 'she's almost forty' whispers."

"I couldn't imagine the pressure you're under," I reply. "I'm sorry."

"You could if you'd stayed in faerie," Phyr grumbles.

Princess eyes him. "You get a lot of shit for having no kids, too, huh?"

Phyr nods. "That's putting it mildly. Procreation is a sacred duty for all high fae, yet a gift our bodies don't oblige us often."

Some kind of understanding passes between them.

"Good thing you got Jada as your heir." Princess sighs. "Wish a honey badger shifter teenager would just fall into my life."

She stops in front of a shut door and knocks. Princess tucks a lock of her dark hair behind her ear. "It's me. I've brought two people who want to help. You want help, right?"

The growling within intensifies.

The small hairs on the back of my neck stand on end, instinct telling me to get away as fast as I can or prepare to fight a wolf. Shifters in their animal form size-up much, much bigger than their full animal counterparts. Knowing the size of Gabriel and Roxy in their wolf forms, I have doubts about the door's capacity to keep

Mama Doe within. Then again, Gabriel had this house custom-built to accommodate shifters.

Even so, I've learned by keeping company with Gabriel and Lance that shape shifters don't shift into their animal forms inside the house past puberty. Mama Doe not only displays poor manners by shifting into animal form inside, but I sense something very wrong on the other side of that door.

"I know they smell strange," Princess soothes. "They're not pack but trusted by us. One is our alpha's future mate. You know Gabriel wouldn't let anyone inside the house that wasn't safe."

Mama Doe snaps her jaws on the other side, the accompanying growl low and menacing. Despite the seemingly aggressive behavior, the shifter's panic emanates from the other side like a foul odor.

"I'd take that as a no," Phyr whispers.

The pack beta shoots us a helpless look, worry wrinkling her usually smooth brow. "She's in wolf form. If we go in, she'll attack you."

"No kidding," I say, not helping. I can't help it. If this shifter goes feral, we're all screwed. We could stop her, but at what cost to her deteriorating mental health?

"I don't need to enter," Phyr assures her.

Normally, I don't like the idea of digging through someone's mind when they don't have the capacity to consent, but she's not even keeping human form within her own room. Functioning on flight or fight mode, the wolf in Mama Doe is choosing to fight.

Princess worries her lip, considering, and then nods. "Okay. Do your thing."

To me, Phyr says in High Fae, "A broken mind is a dangerous place. I want you to accompany me as an anchor." He offers his hand. "Contact helps."

I accept his long, smooth hand—a swordsman without calluses, thanks to fae skin regeneration.

Close your eyes.

I blink, realizing he's talking in my head. Again. Adjusting to this notion, I close my eyes. I see Phyr in my mind as if we're standing in a cache.

"I made a construct so that we could speak without alarming Mama Doe." His voice and body seem so very real. He's in his fae armor instead of pants and a T-shirt from our bakery. We're holding hands in the construct. "No matter what transpires, don't lower your mental shields. Also, if we come into trouble and are separated. Find this path."

A florescent green thread unspools, illuminating a virtual path that seems infinite.

"The light will lead you to the construct," Phyr says, drawing my attention back to him. "No mind can come inside this space, but yours and mine."

"I really wish I'd gone to the Jedi Academy," I murmur.

"Thanks to a movie marathon at Jada's behest, I understood that reference." His grin lights up his face, and I'm pretty sure the fae prince just made a double reference to two pop culture franchises.

"Also, you attended a school of sorts, young Skywalker." He taps his temple near his horn. "Your memories are there, but you're not recalling them all. To recall an entire childhood suppressed for long as yours was hexed is likely impossible. I have a dual purpose for bringing you along on such a perilous mind dig. I'm hoping this exercise inspires connections to your former training. You'll need them for defense once—" He gestures to me in a sweep, indicating all the changes of my second puberty. "—your transformation is complete."

If a mental projection of yourself can shudder in your head, I do. "With all that's transpired, I forgot my siblings want to murder me."

"I haven't. Then again, they want to murder me as well." He shows no more emotion about this than when we were supposed to dine as a family in the Space Needle restaurant, but the reservation was canceled by mistake. A mild annoyance.

I wish I could feel as nonchalant.

"Ah, I think I've found the memories we're looking for," he says. "Mama Doe's name is Carmen Ramirez, by the way."

I arch an eyebrow. "Multitasking?"

Phyr winks. "Always."

I let it sink in that while Phyr is talking to me in the construct; he's also perusing Mama Doe's mind.

He leads me from the construct into a space that is small and dank. Wan light. No furniture in sight. The floor, cold and hard, seeps into my/Carmen's bones. The odor of urine and excrement is overpowering. Water drips somewhere.

Her perspective is from a very low vantage point. Carmen is huddled, conserving heat and energy. Her thoughts superimpose over mine. She's frightened. The new lives within her stir. Last ultrasound showed triplets. All she wants is her kid and to leave. They can't fix her. She's a guardian, angel blessed. Where is the archangel? Why hasn't he come for them? For her?

In my periphery, strings of light offer escape from this place. Escape is not available for Carmen, but for me, Miriam. I want to go. I don't want to be in her head anymore.

Phyr's grip on my hand tightens. "Push her feelings out."

"It's hard."

He squeezes again. "Focus on this."

A metal door creaks. Light floods the tiny space. A tall figure, face unrecognizable to me or Carmen, enters. Male. The scent is male. My/her eyes adjust. He's wearing a suit. Not the type of tailored suit Shawn would wear. Even my untrained eye knows the fabric is cheaper. The jacket is ill-fitting in comparison, like the kind of prêt-à-porter suits salesmen or the evangelists for the Paradise Center wear. He smells strongly of aftershave.

A man similarly dressed stands behind him.

"Time for your study with the sisters."

A low growl emits from Carmen's throat. She snaps at them, not quite shifting to her wolf form. The wolf shifter doesn't want to hurt them. The mama is terrified for the pups in her belly and the pup they took from her, but the tough act will keep them from making her sit through another round of shock and save.

The two men exchange a look. "We're trying to save your immortal soul."

"My soul? I am a servant of the archangel of this territory. Your soul is the one you should be worried about. The Archangel will punish you for this!" The shifter no longer believes her threat, but she says them anyway. Her pack has always kept the peace. Why isn't the Archangel coming?

"An agent of Satan has misled you. Angels inhabit Heaven. The Earth is for man." He holds up his leather-bound Bible. "God has promised man a paradise here on Earth."

"In case you haven't noticed, pendejo. I'm not a man." Her growl turns fierce and inhuman. I can feel her perception shift. She's got to fight.

Phyr pulls me a step back. We're on the green path. "It's ugly from this point, but this is when she escapes a Paradise Center."

We walk through other memories, gleaning more information about Carmen. I learn along the way. I remember what to do. How to see the memory without her emotions overwhelming mine.

YOU COULD FIT my sizable kitchen and family room inside of the pack kitchen. Copper pots hang from the ceiling above a giant oak table. There's a chef's double oven with an indoor grill. Farmhouse stainless steel sinks could fit a couple of mid-sized dogs. The appliances are all state-of-the art and the cabinetry, hand carved and gorgeous. The aroma of cider with orange slices studded with cloves simmering in a large pot fills the room. It feels like home and a bed-and-breakfast at once.

"Carmen is from Southern California. A place called San Pedro, a port city south of Los Angeles. Her mate is the alpha of the San Pedro and Long Beach clans."

I wrap my hands around a cup of steaming cider, grateful for the heat and the heavenly aroma. I wasn't ever in that cold, disgusting cell, but my body had a hard time warming up after what I witnessed.

Gabriel, Phyr, and I all sit around the large kitchen table. Princess leans against the counter. Her features darken as Phyr and I recall what we saw. We were in Carmen's head for seconds, but I feel like I've experienced days in the poor shifter's tortured memories. One thing I gleaned from being in her head is that Carmen stayed strong for her kids. I admire her for that and hope that in time she would heal from what happened to her so she could continue to be strong for her kids and herself.

A muscle feathers in Gabriel's cheek. "Frank Ramirez."

Princess glowers. "Frank is one alpha I called when we found Ma—Carmen. He said there were no missing members of his pack but offered his aid by extending an invitation to take our 'Mama Doe' and her cubs if we were overburdened."

"This doesn't surprise me. Frank is the one who signed the entire pack up to be saved by the True Believers," I reply, rubbing my arms. The kitchen is warm, but I can't shake the chill of Carmen's former cell.

"True Believers is what the people who attend the Paradise Center churches call themselves," Phyr provides.

Gabriel grimaces. "That's new. They've only referred to themselves as Christian before."

"Sounds like the makings of a cult based on a mainstream religion," Princess sighs. "Where's the archangel of the southwest region in all of this?"

"Ariel is based out of Panama," Gabriel says. "They're hands off."

South America, where religion is held a little more tightly than in the states, I think to myself but don't say out loud. Phyr's expression telegraphs he's thinking the same thing.

"Carmen hasn't seen their archangel since she was a little girl, yet she believed Ariel would come." I agitate the cider with a cinnamon stick, still bothered by Carmen's faith in her archangel shattered.

"The alpha has complete control," Phyr says. "The San Pedro pack considers Frank's word the word of the Angelic Anocracy."

"She's the only one who thought her mate wasn't infallible," I agree.

"How did she get so far north?"

"Pacific Crest Trail. She and her cub stayed in wolf form most of the time. She's fought cougars and a lot more to get here." My respect for Carmen in my voice. I could see it in Princess and Gabriel's eyes, too. "Since she believed her own archangel forsake her, she sought the archangel of the Pacific Northwest—you—for asylum. Carmen trusted no other alphas, believing them susceptible to the True Believers or that they might call up her mate since she's not well. The woman had a lot happen to her. She needs professional help."

"I know a therapist trained in trauma," Princess says. "She's in Eastern Washington and mainly deals with veterans."

"Is she a shifter?" Gabriel asks.

Princess shakes her head. "A bigfoot like Aurora. Carmen trusted Aurora." Her gaze flicks to Phyr and me.

"Carmen didn't like our fae scent," I provide. I didn't blame her. Bigfoots are all over. As a Guardian, Carmen likely ran into many. Fae have long been banished from the Earth. "New people with unfamiliar smells about them would frighten her after the ordeal she went through."

Gabriel gives me a grateful smile for understanding why the shifter would be hostile. It's almost apologetic, telegraphing he already thinks of Carmen as one of his pack. To Princess, he says, "Think this therapist will make a house call?"

Princess pulls a cell phone from her jeans pocket. "Only one way to find out."

My phone and Gabriel's cell start ringing at the same time. I would have ignored the call, but that's too odd of a coincidence. The caller ID reads, "Papillon Academy".

"It's the school."

Gabriel nods. "Yeah."

We both answer.

The line clicks, and a prerecorded voice tells me that Jada was marked absent from fifth period. I meet Gabriel's gaze. He nods. "I see," he says into the phone.

Not the same phone call after all.

I hang up and dial the school, reaching the school receptionist. "Hi, this is Miriam Diaz. Jada Diaz's mother. I'm calling be—"

Before I can finish my sentence, the receptionist cuts me off. "Oh, the principal is on the phone with another parent regarding the incident. She will call you next." Leaping to a myriad of parent-panicked thoughts as to why the principal is calling me "next", I sputter, rearing my head in shock when I'm placed on hold without notice.

Gabriel presses the screen of his phone, his mouth flattening in a line.

Uh oh.

Placing myself on mute, I ask, "Do you know what happened?"

He nods, providing no further detail. Judging by his scowl and the way his free hand curls into a fist as he scrolls the phone screen with the other, Gabriel isn't withholding information. He holds a finger up. "Hey, Dave. I need to speak to Kirsten about Roxy. Yeah. Now. It's important."

Shit.

On her phone, Princess plugs her ear with one finger, leaving the room.

Concern limns Phyr's features. What is happening?

Before I can reply, the phone clicks. "This is Principal Smith. Mrs. Diaz?"

"Yes?" I clear my throat. "Yes. Speaking."

"There was an incident during lunch. As you know, we have an open campus policy for students at Papillon Academy. We're small enough to know who is who and usually have no problem with trespassers."

My stomach knots.

Every parent's nightmare unfolds as Principal Smith continues, "We had some trespassers on the campus today. One student engaged with these trespassers. There was an altercation—I have informed their parents of their part in this."

My attention flicks to Gabriel, who is on the phone, speaking in a hushed but hostile tone. He paces the vast kitchen.

"From what I understand, Jada attempted to mitigate the circumstances." The principal pauses. "We can't find her or the student who instigated the altercation, Mrs. Diaz. By the time school authorities were notified of this transpiring, all parties involved disappeared. We've called the police. They're interviewing witnesses and will contact you soon."

She says more, but I don't hear it. My mind is back in that cell where they'd locked Carmen up, but instead of Carmen, I picture Jada cold and hungry, with no way to escape.

"Miriam," Phyr's voice cuts through my panic.

"Jada is missing," I say, as Phyr takes the phone from me. "How do you kidnap a demigod who can control minds?"

He squeezes my hand. "From what I gather, Roxy is missing, as well. Perhaps they're hiding from circumstances, not captured."

"I don't care if she's eighteen, Kirsten." Gabriel thrusts his fingers into his hair, frustration oozing from him. "That's not the point. She could be in danger." He pauses as if listening. Fury sparks in his eyes. His tone flattens and his face takes an eerie calm as he replies, "Well, if that's your take, you should be perfectly fine without my protection, too."

He hangs up and turns to me. I don't know what look I have on my face, but it must encourage him to sweep me into his arms. "We'll find them."

Although he's holding me, it feels as if he's assuring himself.

A HALF HOUR LATER, Gabriel, Phyr, Princess, and my least favorite shifter Nate in all his blue and green-haired glory, and I all sit around a laptop with a pretty large screen. He's here because he's supposedly an excellent tracker. We're all looking at a map of the school and the bordering area.

"They fenced the entire property," Gabriel begins. "Unless the trespassers climbed the chain-link fence, then they entered here or here." He points to the entrance to the parking lot for visitors and where parents unload kids in front of the school, open to the general public, and then to the bus entrance/staff parking lot.

"My bet is on the second," I say, pointing to a patch of green next to the teacher lot. "This is the commons right outside the cafeteria. The students hang out here during lunch and breaks. Roxy and Jada would have been here, not in front of the school, at the time of the altercation."

Gabriel nods in agreement.

I check my phone for the fiftieth time. Still no response from Jada to my texts. No surprise. We'd already exhausted the "find my phone" app. The girls' phones were at the school, which made sense. After the supe coming out event, Papillon Academy announced a policy that all students must keep their phones in their lockers. I heard through the PTSA grapevine pictures or videos of students suspected of being supes surfaced on the internet. The supe vs mundane trend quickly devolved into a whole new form of cyberbullying and shaming kids for either A. Being a supe or B. Being a boring mundane. It's a lose-lose situation for any student who had the misfortune of this happening to them.

Being seventeen, Jada hated the rule, whining incessantly about how it wasn't safe. She even went to the length of saying, "What if they kidnapped me?"

My argument had been that she was a demigod and could handle a human kidnapper. I want to eat my words.

I sigh deeply.

"There's a copse right here separating the school grounds from a neighborhood," Gabriel continues. "I want four trackers in animal form to sniff out the bordering properties. Miriam and I will go to the police station to discover what they know."

"Before you dispatch a hunting party or confer with the authorities, I believe I have a simpler solution to locating the girls," Phyr says, breaking his silence. "If I may have some hair from each of the girls, I could transport you to wherever they are. It would mean exposing that I can walk through time and space, but revealing my abilities would not be the worst-case scenario, do you?"

Gabriel rears his head. "Why didn't you say something before?"

Phyr's lips stretch into a smile that seems more of a bearing of teeth. "You asked me not to use such gifts if it would reveal my abilities to an enemy of yours. I needed more information about the supposed abduction. I'm not convinced the girls were stolen."

Hope blooms in my chest, fragile as a glass rose.

"What do you believe transpired?" Gabriel voices my thoughts.

"The girls did something they weren't supposed to do, so they ran away."

"That's not like Jada," I reply. Taken aback, he'd even suggest she'd do such a thing. "She would own up to doing something wrong."

Phyr's expression changes. "I'm not assuming cowardice, but a strategy. Remember the crown?"

I am known as Miriam now, but I'd once been Tatiana, named after the late High Queen Tatiana—a point of contention with my half-siblings who were her biological children. Nix and Maeve were always more powerful than I was. With Phyr's help, I had stolen my namesakes' crown, hoping it would grant me power over the faerie and protection from all who sought to harm Phyr and me for some political machination or for the pure joy of torturing a halfling witch and her playmate. We'd ran to a forest to escape notice, Phyr under the belief I only wanted to try it on. I'd meant to wear the crown and rule.

"How could I forget?—oh." An uneasy ache settles in my gut. I had forgotten for years while the hex tied to a geas binding my faelight blocked my memories. "We did something foolish, or rather, I talked Phyr into something foolish."

Gabriel and the other shifters present listen closely.

"I'd humiliated my siblings in court in retaliation for a nasty prank Maeve and Nix pulled on Phyr." The 'prank' had been sawing off one of his horns while he slept. His horn would eventually regrow, but it had shamed him in court. "Young high fae pull awful pranks, but this time, Maeve threatened to kill us both in our sleep. I hadn't known at the time Oberon had forbidden them from harming me, so I believed them. Everyone thought we'd run away or had been kidnapped, but in truth, we were hiding because Phyr and I stole Tatiana's crown."

"I believe the girls showed their power and are gathering their wits about them until they can figure out what to do next," Phyr says.

Gabriel rubs the spot between his eyebrows. "I believe you've just added another potential threat. What better way to get at Miriam than to steal her daughter? Forests, even small ones, are riddled with nowhere doors and other gateways the low fae use."

He leaves the obvious unsaid. It's not the low fae we need to worry about.

"It could be my siblings," I say, icy fear slithering around my insides. "They wouldn't hurt them, but there are worse things than hurting them."

"I can track them anywhere in the multiverse," Phyr says. "If they do have the girls, it won't be hard to find them."

Gabriel gestures to me and Phyr. "Okay, we'll try your way. However, the scents go cold fast." He turns to his beta. "Princess, I want you to get four of your best trackers on this stat. Tell them to look for anything nonhuman and follow it. If they sense anything off, tell them to retreat and we'll take it from there."

"What about Syd, alpha? Aren't we using our best trackers for Syd?"

His muscles tense as he glares in his beta's direction. Clearly, Princess is challenging him for placing more importance on Roxy. Surely, she can't blame him for prioritizing his daughter. Goes to show how much I know about shifter politics.

"You've said it yourself. The delivery van made it to the highway." Gabriel's voice is controlled, but his tone brooches no argument. He rises. "I'm going to the police station while Miriam and Phyr try his method. Give him anything he needs."

16

We're standing in my kitchen as Phyr wraps Jada and Roxy's hair we extracted from their brushes around each hand. He lifts his hands zombie style—I hope to open a door between where we stand and wherever the girls are. The strain of concentration sharpens his angular fae features. Tremors rack his body.

As his hand drops to his sides, he closes his eyes and curses in high fae under his breath.

"What's wrong?" I ask.

"The girls are not—" He shakes his head in frustration. "I cannot find them in the present or anywhere in the past or future. Someone blocked my ability to see them at all."

"They could be in a cell like Carmen. Perhaps lined with iron?"

"If they are in an iron cell, I wouldn't be able to access them now, but I could see them at other points in time."

I check my watch. It's late afternoon. I pick up my phone from the counter to call Gabriel. The doorbell rings.

I figure it's likely the police since they have yet to contact me. I still haven't given my statement to the officers who showed up. My behavior looks bad. Very bad.

I open the door to find Princess and three other shifters waiting. No sign of Gabriel.

"Did Phyr's method work?" Her eyes are hopeful. She and Roxy had bad blood in the past, but Princess is loyal and protective of all of her pack.

I shake my head.

She curses on an exhale. "I'm sorry. That wood is saturated with the odors of teenagers. My best trackers couldn't suss out their scent from the others, not for long anyway."

Hope shatters, the shards jagged and sharp with every breath.

My kid, my one piece of normalcy in my entire fucked up existence, gone. It's my fault. If I'd only ran away. If I never exposed supes as real.

Princess places a hand on my arm. "Hey. We'll find them."

I INVITE Princess and the shifters who accompanied her inside. Phyr busies himself with making tea and serving up some muffins Rhiannon and Lance brought home from the bakery. Apparently, Princess called Lance. The couple let the part-time staff close up. Princess sits at the breakfast bar on Jada's usual stool. Rhiannon next to her and Lance on the other side. The rest of the shifters eat in the dining room. They aren't ranked high enough to eat with Princess, apparently. Also, Lance doesn't take a bite or a drink until Princess does.

I know so little about Gabriel's culture. I wonder if he doesn't eat with anyone who doesn't rank worthy in the pack hierarchy. It's super weird. Since I grew up in a faerie and on a coven commune, I have no room to judge.

"I shifted to human form and talked to a couple of kids playing hooky at a nearby park." After taking *ten* cubes of sugar with tiny tongs, the honey badger shifter stirs her tea with a tiny spoon. Her posture and movements are as refined as a fae at court, which is at odds with Princess's whole badass biker vibe. "They said they saw the whole thing."

Everyone served, Phyr stands next to me, arms crossed.

Princess takes a sip of her tea, closing her eyes for a moment to savor the taste. Her gaze focuses on me. "Paradise Center idiots showed up at the school, preaching fire and brimstone. They claimed that six demons possessed all supes."

"Why six?" Rhiannon asks, mouth full of muffin.

Princess shrugs. "No clue."

"Numbers are significant in many religions and superstitions," I reply. "Some superstitions mark six, six, six as supposedly the devil's number and seven, seven, seven as Jehovah's number. They likely wanted to emphasize six to subversively give some deeper meaning to what is otherwise an arbitrary number."

"Huh," Princess and Rhiannon say at the same time.

"They were asking students to point out the supes so they could save them from said possession. Some kid, likely a True Believer, pointed out Jada. Jada headed toward the school. The whole thing would be over if she would have kept going inside," Princess sighs. "Except Roxy taunted the proselytizers. Told them Heaven was for angels and they were going to be nothing but worm food when they died. To emphasize her point, she sprouted wings and talked in her heraldic voice."

I nearly dropped my cup of tea.

"What does that mean?" Rhiannon asks.

"Gabriel is the son of Gabriel, the herald," Princess explains. "When they decree something in a heraldic voice, believers are compelled to obey."

"What did she tell them to do?" I close my eyes, bracing myself—there's no telling what a pissed-off teenager with herald powers would command.

Princess pinches the bridge of her nose. "To shove their heads up their asses."

Rhiannon is the only one who chortles and claps. "Good for her."

I rub my temples.

"The idiots didn't attempt to do so, did they?" Phyr asks, brows furrowed.

I don't have to ask. I know they would be helpless to obey that voice. Lucifer isn't a so-called herald but has that kind of power. I've seen him make much crueler commands to test his subjects' loyalty.

"They did. Jada stretched her hands out and they suddenly stopped, confused and angry. The True Believers went after Roxy. Shot her with a taser. The kids I talked to had no idea what happened next because they ran. All the kids did. Some for the building. Others ran off campus. I doubt the principal who called you got the entire story. I'm not surprised the cops haven't called you. They have their hands full, rounding up students who took off. A patrol car showed up while I was talking to the kids. I took off before they could question me."

Shifters, even in human form, are faster than humans.

Phyr unfolds his arms, alarmed. "Were you seen?"

The honey badger shifter waves her hand dismissively. "Doesn't matter. Unless they got a headcount, the kids I was talking to ran too."

"Why?" I couldn't imagine why students at a school for gifted children would run.

Princess smirks. "They were vaping."

I don't know what expression I made, but Princess chortles. "Didn't think kids that went to that bougie school did drugs?"

"I'll admit. I may have been Lucifer's lover and pawn as a teenager, but I don't know much about what actual mundane teenagers do, bougie school or otherwise."

All humor slides off her face, leaving horror. "You were a teenager?"

"More or less. Fae age differently in faerie, even halflings."

"I'm fifty-six," Rhiannon admits, stirring her tea.

I blink. I assumed she is at least ten years younger than I am. Lance chokes on his muffin. Princess says, "Yeah, right. Good one."

Only Phyr isn't fazed.

Having one of her rare moments of complete lucidity, Rhiannon glares at Princess. Hurt colors her tone as she replies, "I don't have proof, but I'd think I'd know how old I am."

"I meant you look like you're thirty, at most." Princess holds up her hands. "Sorry if I've offended you."

A grin spreads on Rhiannon's lips. "So good of you to respect your elders."

"So," I say, gathering the attention back to the matter at hand. "This is what we know. True Believers held a pack in California captive but by the pack alpha's orders. Carmen originally had gone along with the so-called saving until they put her in a cell. The Archivist coven sent me a letter bomb. The Baba Yaga coven let us go but they don't like that I won't join them."

"Oh! Oh!" Rhiannon raises her hand as if she's the star pupil in class, bursting with enthusiasm to be picked. The lucid moment is gone.

I fight not to roll my eyes. "Yeah, Rhi?"

"Don't forget you siblings want to—" She slices her finger across her throat.

"As Rhiannon has so colorfully illustrated, there are two deadly high fae who want me dead but aren't allowed to kill me yet. They could have low fae spies."

"Lucifer would love to lure you to Gehenna, no doubt," Phyr grumbles. His mood soured since his plan to rescue Jada didn't work.

"Could you do a tracking spell on her?" Rhiannon asks.

I shake my head. We did a ritual a few months back to protect Jada that blocked tracking spells. Since my daughter is of my blood, I didn't want a demon named Velja to come across her. Realization hit me.

I rush to the sliding glass door, ripping it open to run out back. Everyone followed me. In the same space where I performed the ritual with Jada a few months ago, there's evidence of the same ritual performed and left in haste. The ground dropped from beneath my feet as my brain scrambled to understand why Jada would perform this ritual with Roxy.

An arm clamps around my shoulders, pulling me to Phyr.

"She blocked us from tracking them," I announce.

Princess swears and kicks a candle.

Awesome. My daughter and her best friend are missing, and the beta of the pack is throwing a tantrum.

The beta points at Lance, "Track them."

He immediately strips off his clothes, revealing lots of lean, hard muscle. I avert my eyes. Not only do I not want to see Lance naked, but I also don't want to see him shift. I'll never get used to the gross noises that follow or the way bones and sinew shift under once-human skin.

While Lance shifts, another wolf leaps from my backdoor into the yard. The rest follow. Princess must have used some sort of shifter esp. or something to call forth the shifters.

Once they're on a trail, leaping over the fence and sprinting away, she spins to me. In a whisper, she asks, "How long does that leash spell you put on Syd and me last?"

After taking a moment to recall, she's talking about the tracking spell and then another moment to get over how thick I had to be to forget that I had a tracking spell on them this whole time, I say, "It still should work."

"If these guys don't come back with the girls, we're using it."

"Alright," Princess says, to the shifters returning from canvassing the neighborhood. "Report."

"There have been several hellhounds all over this neighborhood," Lance says, gaze flicking to me. "There are no signs of struggle."

A glacial frisson skitters up my spine.

"How old was the scent?" Princess asks, unsurprised.

His attention shifts to me before he replies, "Days old."

"Is that all you scented?" Princess asks, her blue-eyed gaze keen on her gamma.

Lance crosses his arms. "Yeah."

She turns to me. "Looks like the King of Hell is watching you."

17

Princess hands me a bright pink helmet with glittery, rainbow-hued butterfly decals. The thing is huge. Like big enough to accommodate my budding antlers.

I stare at it, considering riding with Lance.

"It fits Aurora sans glamour," Princess explains.

Aurora appears a blonde, gangly hippie mundane to most people, including me. Since I've only seen her without glamour twice, I forget Aurora is a Bigfoot under that illusion.

A whole lot of inappropriate questions about what it's like to date someone furry come to mind. Princess spends half her time as a giant honey badger, so it sorta makes sense it doesn't bother her.

To each her own, I guess.

I settle the helmet on my head, making no comment about the slight musky scent mixed with patchouli. It's not unpleasant but my sense of smell has heightened during fae puberty. The weight of the helmet balancing on my antler buds isn't exactly comfortable, but it's not painful.

Princess helps me with my chinstrap.

"Don't let anyone know what you did," she whispers. "Gabriel will take it as usurping his authority."

"How so?"

She grimaces and emotions war on her face as if she's betrayed her alpha somehow.

"I only want to know if I broke some sort of rule."

She pushes strands of her dark hair away from her forehead and blows out her breath. "You didn't. Syd and I did. We bound ourselves to a powerful entity in a time of crisis rather than trusting our alpha to protect us."

I don't quite understand, but I could see it really bothered her. I smile and say in a teasing tone, "So you admit *I* am a powerful entity? My, my, how far I've risen in your eyes."

Princess snorts and puts on her helmet. She straddles the motor-cycle first and balances it.

To my chagrin, I get on a lot less gracefully.

She starts the engine, revving it. I don't know how we're going to communicate over the noise.

I balance myself with my hands on her shoulders.

Her voice comes over a speaker in my helmet. "Hold onto my waist, not my shoulders."

I wrap my arms around her waist. "Like this?" I ask at a conversa-tional volume, hoping my helmet has a mic too so I don't have to shout.

"Yup. Direct me."

I rub my finger over my wrist, whispering the words to actively seek Syd. At first, the spell wants to let me know I'm right next to Princess. Then finally, my hand points east as if led by a string.

Spells meant for tracking toddlers aren't that great for tracking a shifter while on a motorcycle. We're not on foot searching a coven compound for a lost kid. We're on a motorcycle. An arm stiffly pointing in a single direction like a "this way" sign sucks in suburban neighborhoods where you have to obey things like using roads instead of riding through lawns and fences.

Between that and learning how to be a good passenger on a motorcycle, we figure out a system.

Through a myriad of subdivisions, we leave my little town,

finding ourselves in the bedroom neighborhoods on the outskirts of downtown Kirkland. The houses are slightly older, mid-nineteen hundreds and the communities more established. The spell wrapping burns my wrist as we wait in a line of cars stopped.

Police are directing traffic heading into a megachurch's parking lot. We don't have a lot of churches let alone megachurches in the Seattle suburbs, but this one is newly built and massive.

My blood runs cold when I see a giant sign at the entrance of the parking lot which reads, "Paradise Center." I have visions of Syd locked up in the basement in a silver cage.

"He's there or somewhere really close," I say over the mic.

Princess grunts. "There's no way we can search the premises unnoticed. I think there has to be two or three hundred cars in that lot."

"We could go to church," I suggest, noting the people entering the building.

"Let me signal the others to fall back."

Splitting up never works out in fiction. "No. We should go in as a family."

"What a family, a fae witch and a bunch of shifters." She chuckles. "Well, the Bible says there's more strength in numbers, or something like that."

Princess signals and after waiting in line for a bit more, we're directed into the parking lot. The shifters convene at Princess's bike. I'm happy to leave the butterfly covered helmet and the musk and patchouli scent behind.

The relief is short lived as our family joins the throng entering the building. With a rose-colored, textured concrete exterior at least four stories high, the church has a feel of an indoor arena or a warehouse rather than a holy place.

The interior has durable rose colored carpeting and neutral colors. Unlike older, established churches, there is very little in the way of religious artwork. It could be any event center.

In the hallway, ushers in suits lead families and groups who want to sit together through double doors. A baby is wailing somewhere.

"I feel that kid," Lance whispers.

An usher in his early twenties, who looks strangely familiar approaches us. "How many?"

He doesn't recognize me, but I remember him from my driveway. His eyes are on Princess and on her alone.

"Nine," Princess says, turning on a smile I've never seen her display before. Used to being around her, I forget how really beautiful she is.

The usher nods and leads us through the double doors. "What brings you here?" He asks Princess casually.

Our obvious lack of long skirts for the women and suits for the men gives away we are not members of the church.

"I met some women with brochures. I liked what I heard and thought I'd bring my family to check out the service."

I'm glad he's talking to her, not me. Lying costs fae and the price is pain.

"Usually, we like to conduct Bible studies one on one before urging worldly people to the Paradise Center, but I'm sure glad you came," the usher replies, his cheeks coloring. "I mean the Holy Spirit must have guided you here and I feel fortunate to be a part of God's calling."

I have to bite the inside of my cheek to not scoff at the remark and inform him that my magic led us here. As it is, I want to flee from this charade and search the building for Syd. My wrist is burning, and I have to hold my arm so it doesn't start pointing on its own.

"Mmmhhmm," Princess agrees. "I did feel compelled."

The interior of the building is like the college lecture halls I've seen on television, but so much bigger. All the seating points to a central stage with professional lighting. I imagine a charismatic leader with a manse overlooking Lake Washington and a personal plane docked next to Bill Gates' Gulfstream G650, coming on the large center stage. Instead, I see empty chairs lined-up behind a podium.

We're taken to a section that is obviously all newcomers by the way they dress. We stand out almost as sharply among them as this section in general contrasts with the devotees of the Paradise Center.

"I don't like this place," Lance whispers. "For a *lot* of reasons. Are you certain this is where he is?"

I look around. I'd only noticed the difference in clothing and general appearance. It's mighty white in here. Maybe supes aren't the only people these good Christians don't like.

I rub my burning wrist. When I let my hand go, my arm point's straight down. "Syd's right below us."

The shifters all exchange glances.

"After the service gets going, we'll go to the restroom," Princess whispers on the other side. "That will give us an excuse to snoop around."

"Both of us going won't look suspicious?" I ask.

She shrugs, "Mundane women always go in pairs at big events, for safety."

Raised in faerie, then an isolated coven commune, then Hell, and then living as a pretend mundane, avoiding large social gatherings as much as possible, I have to take her word for it. The thought that mundane women needed to pair up simply to relieve themselves made my stomach knot. My gut is already a pretzel since entering this building. There's something off about the Paradise Center and the attendees that sets me on edge. Knowing Syd is trapped in a basement doesn't help the unease.

The stage lights flicker and the lights above the seating dim. The crowd quiets.

Not long after we're seated, a man in a gray, three-piece suit walks on stage. Unlike the off-the-rack wear throughout the congregation, the pastor's suit is professionally tailored, and his shoes likely cost more than all the ones I own. Tan and blond, he looks to be in his mid-forties with an athletic build of a much younger man. His features seem off, too symmetrical, too chiseled. He also has a presence. Mundane humans normally don't have a presence about them other than a natural charisma. This man radiates confidence and something preternatural. I know someone in possession of magic when I see them.

A hush washes over the crowd. Usually at large gatherings there's at least a baby crying, a restless kid shuffling in their seat, or someone coughing or sneezing. The dead silence raises the hackles on the back of my neck in warning.

I dip into my light, allowing my second sight that allows me to see the color of magic to take over. Weak threads of magenta, the magic I associate with gods and demigods, streak his aura—thin and dim but there, nonetheless. Stronger, but not by much, threads of golden-white angelic magic limn the magenta threads. He's not part angel or a demigod. Jada possessed more light when she was two months old. This isn't magic he was born with. A whole lot of people believe in him as either divine or angelic in nature and therefore he's becoming so.

"Lambs of God, bow your heads for the opening prayer," the preacher says.

Heads of every man, woman, and child present drop at once. Princess and I glance at each other, then bow ours so we won't be conspicuous.

"Heavenly Father, Almighty God Jehovah, please hear your humble servant's prayer and allow the Holy Spirit to descend upon me so I may guide your flock, the True Believers. I ask this in the name of Jesus Christ, amen."

As he speaks, magic pings at my skin like a mosquito bite, annoying but ultimately inconsequential.

A low growl emits from Princess's throat, drawing my gaze. "False prophets are the enemy."

Crap. Shifters serve the angels as Guardians, earthly watch dogs, because they believe.

We draw a few glares.

I cover my mouth and whisper so low I hope she can hear me, "If we want to find Syd, you need to cool off."

She cuts me a look that reminds me she can shift into a honey badger the size of a mastiff with claws longer than my fingers but gives no further indication she's going to do anything more than sit and seethe.

After that, the pastor calls different members of the congregation to stand on stage and testify their stories of conversion from regular Christianity or whatever religion or non-religion to becoming a True Believer. Then they testify how the holy spirit is working through them today by giving the number of converts they've brought to the Paradise Center. Their converts all have to stand and wave. It all seems like an MLM scam selling kitchen utensils or makeup, so many stay-at-home moms and poor people trying to make ends meet get sucked into. Except instead of sales, they're all piling up the power of belief.

The pastor reads a passage from the Bible about John the Baptist giving Jesus a dunk. He talks about sin, Adam and Eve, and Abel and Cain. Honestly, I pay little attention. I want to know what was the big draw for tonight.

"I have someone special I want you to meet," the pastor announces. He holds up his hands. "Now, don't be alarmed, but he bears the mark of Cain."

"What is a mark of Cain," I whisper in a voice so low only a shifter could hear.

"No such thing. Literalist nonsense," Princess replies. She sinks a lot of derision in the word "literalist".

I assume she means people who interpret their religion by the literal word of the text rather than a metaphorical representation.

A familiar face walks onto the stage. I can't place where I know him from. So many people walk into the bakery on a daily basis, the faces meld. The man looks to be in his early thirties, white with mouse brown hair and dark eyes almost too large for his face. Unlike the pastor in Armani and the congregation in discount warehouse suits and dresses, the newcomer onstage wears a sweater vest, over a button down and slacks. His shoes are nowhere near the price range of the pastor's patent leather. He looks small and average next to the pastor, but not marked by anything.

"Robby," Princess gasps.

Ah, that's where I know him from. Robby is a moth-person cryptid. His family reported him missing. He doesn't look like he's been in a conversion cell like Carmen all this time, but maybe he fared better since joining the True Believers seems to be his idea.

Robby seems confident, but his hands shake as the pastor interviews him. "I was reluctant to learn the truth at first, but then it all made sense. My family are all heathens. We live as we please because we have the money and freedom to do so, but living as we pleased never brought me any sense of pleasure. I hate the way I look without an illusion, if man was made in God's image, I certainly wasn't, but I sought the wrong source to change my appearance." He holds his head low.

The pastor lays a comforting hand on Robby's shoulder. "Whom did you seek?"

"A crossroads demon."

The congregation gasps collectively.

"Now, brothers and sisters, we must remember that our Robert was a worldly person and had not yet received the word or God in his life," the pastor admonishes. "The good lord saw something in Robby to allow him to see the way, the truth, and the light. That's why he's here today."

"I want to be made perfect in the new system," Robby agrees. "I want to remove the mark of Cain."

"He wants to be something he's not," Princess mutters.

I've also had enough of Robby's testimony. I tap Princess's leg and nudge my head toward the doors. "Bathroom."

An usher rushes to us. "We ask that you stay until the end of the service, or at least the intermission."

"When you're a woman my age, there's no holding it," I say.

He grimaces, eyes me like I'm going to pee on the floor and whispers a code into a walkie-talkie. After an affirmation, he nods and stands aside.

"I'm going too." Princess announces. "I'm on my period."

The usher takes a step back as she passes, as if she might make him unclean.

When we enter the hall, there's no sneaking around. They have men in suits posted every few feet. They're a bit larger and more menacing in appearance than the usher.

The usher leads us to the restroom that's downstairs from the main entrance. The hall has the same pink carpet and neutral-color decor and fake plants. Unless they want to bore their kidnapping victims to death, the place doesn't have a torture basement feel.

Yet—My wrist burns, and my arm stiffly points downward.

He smiles and opens the door to the restroom. "I'll wait here so you don't get lost."

It smells like cheap hand soap and heavy-duty disinfectants inside. Princess heads straight to the last stall. There we find a vent over the toilet.

"I wish we'd brought Phyr."

She pulls a set of keys with a Swiss Army knife and grins. "I'm no planeswalker, but I've seen an episode or two of MacGyver."

I eye the vent and grimace. There is no way I'm going to stuff my plus-sized butt in that hole. "I can't fit in there."

Princess gives me an assessing once over and then again, lingering in places as if *noticing* me for the first time. "You have some banging curves, but yeah, you're too thick to fit."

I touch my chest in mock astonishment. "'Banging curves' Did you—did you just compliment me?"

She rolls her eyes. "Don't make me regret it."

Princess steps up on the toilet and starts working on the screws.

I sneak over to the door and listen for our apparent guard.

He's still outside the door, accompanied by the static and squawk of a walkie-talkie. I get down on my hands and knees and press my ear to the door to listen to the chatter.

A toilet flushes.

"Hey, do you have any tampons?" Princess calls. "Aunt Flo went on a bender and she's a bloody mess."

I scramble to my feet, rushing back to the stall. "Yeah. Here you go," I call.

"Pretend to be done and wash your hands," she whispers.

My gaze lifts to the vent. Right. It will probably make some noise when she pulls the cover off.

I leave her stall and open and shut the next stall's door.

"Hey, wait for me, will ya?" she calls.

"Will do! Hurry up. I don't want to miss any of the show." *The show?* Can I make it more obvious that I've never been to church?

I turn on a faucet and wave my hand that isn't leashed by the spell under it to pretend I'm washing my hands. When I turn on the hand dryer, Princess tugs.

I rush over to her stall and take the grate from her.

"I don't know how long they will give us, but stall as long as you can," she whispers in that ever so quiet voice.

I thread my fingers and offer my joined hands for her to step on.

Princess refuses my hands as a step, pulling herself up and into the vent without aid.

I gape for a few seconds at the strength and skill it takes for her to do that and *silently.*

A few minutes pass, I think. It feels like hours.

The usher knocks on the door. "Everything okay in there, friends?"

I turn on the faucet again and pump the soap. "Period blood. It's going to take a minute to clean it up or there'll be stains."

The usher makes some choking sounds. "Uh, I—should I get a sister acolyte to bring you clean, er, underthings and a baggie for the soiled—uh—linens?"

I almost decline the offer, but then realize his suggestions will give us a while longer and possibly get him to leave the area so I can do some snooping, too. "Oh, we don't want to be a bother."

"Uh, no bother. I'll just radio one of the sister acolytes."

So much for getting him to leave his post. Still, waiting for someone else would give us more time. I pretend to have a whispered conversation with Princess.

"Sure. Go ahead."

I listen to him speak over the two-way radio with a woman with a singsong voice. They talk in a calm code, so I figure they have a system worked out for these sorts of accidents. Gotta love the hate for something natural so deep that they have a complete plan for the unclean blood. At least they're buying it, and in turn, buying Princess time.

A thought occurs. I call through the door, "She'll need some pants too. We got a real mess here."

"We'll get you everything you need," the usher assures through the door. "Don't be embarrassed, ma'am. This just means the good lord has made you fruitful. Okay?"

Crap. He's talking to Princess.

"Okay ma'am?"

I clear my throat as I scramble for what to say. "She's too embarrassed to speak."

The man doesn't reply, but I hear his walkie-talkie squawk.

The door flies open. Something hot bites my chest and neck. Suddenly, all my nerves light up with pain. My body trembles uncontrollably and it's hard to remain standing, but I manage. I make my way toward the usher, reaching for him.

If I can get to him, I can stop this.

The usher's eyes bulge as he takes a step back. He's holding something, but I can't make it out, vision blurring with my trembling.

"This should knock you out. What are you?"

I can't answer. I can't protect myself with magic. My teeth are chattering too hard to invoke spells. I fall to my knees. I lose consciousness for a second, I think, as I come to lying prone on the floor. I flop like a beached fish as more electricity flows through me.

"Lord save us!" a woman cries.

I reach a jerking hand, attempting to escape to my faerie.

"My goodness! Did you see that, Elder John? Her hand disappeared!"

I can't keep control of my muscles long enough to keep the door open between this and my pocket realm. Pain roars in my body as what my addled brain perceives as electricity jolts through me, but I've hurt this bad before, perhaps worse, when I was trying to break the geas on my light and when Lucifer tried to bind me to his sword. I keep awake despite my body begging to give in to the overwhelming urge to lose myself to the darkness again.

"See why I won't turn it off? She won't stay out!" The usher sounds like he's pleading.

"Turn it up."

I recognize the clipped voice, but I'm in too much agony to make the connection

"What if I kill her?" There's genuine concern in the usher's voice. Even in my addled state, I doubt it's for me. He's afraid of the consequences.

"No human could stay conscious with that much juice pumping in them." The statement drips with disdain.

The acolyte turns a knob with a shaky hand.

I rip my gaze from the acolyte to the speaker. He's in a suit, but I recognize the face. The officer that came to my door about my car.

"Behold!" The pastor from earlier in the evening exclaims, "The Lord God has revealed her true form!"

I cry out as what feels like a myriad of stinging bees crawl over my body. Losing the battle to stay in the light, I sink into darkness.

18

The stench of urine and feces assault my nostrils. I awaken curled in a ball, lying on my side on a cold, hard floor. When I fully come to, I experience no moment of disorientation. I know exactly what happened and why I'm here. My aching muscles serve as a reminder of the torture I endured.

My head throbs, mouth is dry, and my eyeballs ache too much to open, but I force myself to lift my lids. Little good opening my eyes does me, since it's pitch black wherever they put me. Even with my improved eyesight, I can't see without any light.

I recall this moment as if it happened before. Then I realize that I'm in a cell just like Carmen. We'd gotten so distracted by the girls going missing, that we didn't consider these people might be dangerous even to supes.

It takes a lot of effort, but I push to my feet. I murmur a spell that provides a ball of light in my hand. I'm in a concrete cell approximately six feet long by four feet wide. There's a drain in the middle of the floor, which is where the stench comes from. The metal door doesn't possess an interior handle.

I try to touch it, hissing when it burns my hand. Iron.

"Who's there?"

"Hello?" I say as loud as my raw throat can muster.

"Miriam, is that you?" Princess shouts.

"Yeah."

"Dammit. I hoped you'd gotten away. Why didn't you make a cache or something?"

Now why didn't I think of that? Oh, right. I did. I keep my snark to myself. "I tried. They tasered me."

"You guys are here too? Shit."

"Syd?" Princess calls.

"Yeah. It's me," the grizzly shifter replies. "I was hoping you didn't try to rescue me. They're organized and know too damned much about supes. I think they're an army."

"Mami?" The pitiful sound is weak, but I recognize my daughter's voice.

"Yes, Jada. I'm here. Are you alright?"

"They tased us, caught us by surprise. I couldn't use my magic. They have Roxy somewhere else and threatened to hurt her if I hurt anyone or tried to escape." Her voice cracks.

They likely told Roxy the same thing wherever they held her.

"You can leave this place, but you cannot escape from the eyes of the lord," a high, insect-like voice suggests. "Concentrate on repenting for your sins and then, in the new paradise, he'll wash away Cain's mark."

Great. We had a convert in our midst.

"Shut up, bootlicker. No one wants to hear it," Jada shouts.

I'm glad they haven't had her long enough to completely break her spirit.

"Don't call me names, heathen!"

"Suck my fat shifter dick, numb nuts," Syd grumbles.

"Do not use foul language in the house of the lord!"

I recognize Numb Nuts' voice. "Mothman, this is Miriam. I found you in the faerie. Did they kidnap you?" What were the odds someone had kidnapped him twice in the same year?

"That was my *curse,* not my name, heathen," he snaps.

"Here he goes with the heathen nonsense again," Syd says, sighing. "Piss right off with sanctimonious bullshit, or I'll tear your fucking wings off and floss my teeth with them."

"If you want to wallow in that state, suit yourself," the mothman replies, imperiously. After a brief pause, he says, "To answer your question, Miriam, no. I came to the Paradise Center willingly. I've been studying the Bible with a brother acolyte for a month now and was granted the esteemed privilege of sin cleansing and accommodations here at the center. Once I am free from sin, I will shuck this deformed shell and emerge in perfect, godly form."

I roll my eyes. *Great.* The two zealots who came into my bakery had been recruiting supes to brainwash.

"How many supes have you seen turn into whatever you think is perfect, godly form?" Princess asks in a dry tone.

"The lord will make me a new, perfect body in the new system after Armageddon," Mothman, numb nuts, or whatever his name is, retorts. "Repent all you sinners. Armageddon is nigh!"

"I don't care if they tase me for it. I will bust through this fucking door and rip out your spine if you tell me to repent one more time," Syd growls, his voice barely human.

"Do you have any idea how long we've been here, Princess?" I ask, changing the subject.

"Nope. I woke up a while ago, but there's no telling time in this darkness." I need to know how long the shifters have been without food.

The mothman sniffs. "You'll get light and food as soon as you deserve it."

I roll my eyes. "I have light."

"I don't think anyone is down here because I heard someone come in and leave since I woke. Judging by the smell, they came to feed the idiot and left. Can you conjure something to open our doors?"

Sure, I'll just say open sesame, and we'll all be free. I sigh. "Let me think for a moment."

The exposure to iron up close and all the darn tasing had my head spinning.

"If you can get us out of here, I can bust down the door."

"Why leave? The world outside will perish. We're in the final days."

"It's safe in here?" I ask, trying to buy us some time to think.

Even if our cells aren't guarded, the brainwashed fool might have the ability to call the zealots on us. I did *not* want to escape this cell only to get tased and thrown back in again.

I could simply create a cache and find my way to Phyr's breadcrumb threads that he's left me in the null, but I don't want to leave the others.

The problem with this plan is that I would have to leave my friends in the faerie until I could get Phyr to transport them back to this world. I'd also leave myself a target for my siblings, but that would be a problem I'd deal with later.

Despite the plan being problematic, the chilling words reverberate in my mind, *"It isn't a sin to kill a monster."*

Our lives held no value to these people. Even the mothman, who bought their tripe, means nothing to them if they keep him in the same sort of cell as the kidnapped.

A memory deeply buried emerges...

I'm a small child in faerie, sitting on my father Oberon's lap. Two fae warriors bring a person who has skin like my mother's. I can feel his weakness, his humanness. His thoughts are open and so easy to see.

"Make him dance," Oberon bids.

I want to please my father, so I say to the human, "Dance." It is no ordinary command. I pour my faelight into my voice as my father taught me.

The man's face twists in confusion as his arms and legs move to the beat of a song no one can hear but me. The tune plays in my head.

Phyr, at our feet, laughs.

My stomach flutters at the sound. My friend laughs so rarely.

Nix, who is standing among the courtiers, remarks, "It's so ungraceful. Balters are fun for only a moment. Make it graceful, Tati."

I delight that my sibling, who normally only sneers at me, wants to be part of my lesson. I control the man's limbs with my imagination, making his movements more elegant, more fae.

Beads of sweat form on the man's face, rolling down in fat droplets. He doesn't want to do this. It's making him tired. I know because I'm in his head.

I think I should stop and consider asking father permission.

Maeve, seated at my father's side, claps their hands. "Well done! Make it do it faster!"

Maeve, who could be so cruel, likes my game too. I want Maeve to like me, so I do.

The man dances and dances. I make him do all the moves I'd seen from all the fae balls I'd ever attended. There were many. Everyone delights in the game except him. Still, I would not make him stop. He's human. He's nothing.

My mother walks into the court. Her presence was silent and humble.

I look at her for approval. Surely, she'll love my game too? I see only fear in her eyes.

To everyone's disappointment, I let go of the man's mind. I am no monster.

"So, what are you going to do, Miriam?" Princess asks,

No matter what the jerk who ordered me to be tased said, only my actions can make me a monster, not how I look or how powerful I am. I decide then and there I must save them all by any means necessary.

"I have a plan. Since we're in mixed company, I have to keep it to myself for now," I say, and hope that it works.

MY HEART SKITTERS at the sound of the acolyte's footsteps and the flick of a light switch. I rise to my feet on wobbly legs. I'm in poor condition, but it's now or never.

The mental walls Phyr taught me to put up to keep my thoughts private from mind readers and to keep out of other people's heads slide down faster than an electric window.

The acolyte's mind reveals itself among the tortured and desperate. A nasty place. So much hatred swims inside his puny brain.

The man hates the stench. Hates us. He thinks feeding and

converting the mothman wastes precious time meant for preaching the good word to 'actual humans.' He prays for patience with the annoying creature.

Like slipping on a glove, I see through his eyes and feel with his body. He's carrying a book under his arm. In his hands, he carries a sandwich wrapped in cellophane and a bottled water.

I take the wheel, so to speak, controlling the acolyte like a marionette. He fights back, but I slap him away like an insect. He veers from the mothman's door, dropping the sandwich and water on the floor.

"Neal? Is that you," the mothman asks. "Is it time for spiritual and worldly food? I'm hungry for both."

"Shut up," I say through the acolyte's lips as I dig through his pockets. I'm clumsy with this big body. Finally, I remove a set of keys from his pocket.

"Open my door."

I shudder at the thought that they built this place with a prison underneath. Who did they keep here before supes? I shake my head. Not my problem.

My door swings open. "You will protect me and the others with your life," I say.

"What?" mothman shrieks. "Guards! The witch is doing something fishy!"

"Shut up," I hiss, grabbing his mind. It's different from a human's and I don't like it there. Instead of hatred for others, he loathes himself. I block from letting his emotions drip into my head and poison my thoughts.

I step outside the door with Neal at my side. My stomach drops as I see a long hall of doors to cells.

"How many prisoners are there?" I ask Neal.

"Twelve."

"Are they all supernaturals?"

"No. Wayward members of the flock spend time here to repent." The man's voice is robotic, as if his body is answering, though his mind is not there.

Despite it being my doing, it's creepy as hell.

"What do you mean by 'wayward flock'?"

"Anyone who the prophet thinks might speak against him or break our code of conduct."

A chill snakes through me. This cult has a prophet. Jada's father, Raf, was a demigod. He told me prophets can be regular humans but gain power through belief. The more people who believed in them, the easier they could hold sway over others.

Shit.

A prophet is a one-trick pony, but supes are up against a human who had the power of persuasion.

"Release all the prisoners."

I wait.

Bursting through his door, Syd lifts the acolyte by the throat, growling. I hurriedly grab the mothman's food off the floor.

"Syd, want a snack?"

He drops the acolyte, who robotically goes back to opening doors as if shifter didn't just almost eat him.

Syd devours the sandwich.

A low growl comes from behind him. "Gimme that," Princess commands.

Oh gods. She's hungry too.

"If you do exactly as I say, I will provide you a feast."

Syd's head swings in my direction. Princess's gaze locks on me too.

Double shit.

They're not wolf shifters, but I'm feeling a lot like Red Riding Hood right now. Oh, what big thighs I have.

"I mean, I will cook a feast for you."

"Be quick, Miriam," Princess warns, voice not very human. "Some of these supes haven't eaten in days."

Jada runs to me. I cut our embrace short, checking her over for wounds. "You okay?"

She nods. "They didn't hurt me. They have Roxy somewhere else."

I want to lecture her about the spell, but now is not the time. Hungry shifters surround us, and I have another kid to find.

The mothman is among the supes, let out of the cells. He glares at me but doesn't say a word. I realize he can't until I say he can. Good.

"Do as I say," I say to him, throwing my faelight into the command.

Everyone gathered nods.

Triple shit.

"Mami, are you controlling them?"

I glance at Jada, relieved she's unaffected.

"They're hungry and desperate and might be a danger to us and themselves. Now, do you know where they might have taken Roxy?"

"No clue."

Not knowing what I must face to find Roxy, I need to get Jada to my faerie, but I don't want to call it what it is in front of everyone. "I'm going to take you to my cache. I want you to stay there until Phyr or I come to get you, okay?"

I make a door to my faerie. Jada hesitates for a moment, then gets a look of resolve that for once resembles me, not her ascended father.

The acolyte Neal stands motionless next to the last opened cell; his face devoid of emotion like a powered down android awaiting a command.

I swallow down my guilt, reasoning this man would kill me or let me starve and have no qualms with it. Who wouldn't want to stop a harmful person?

With the minds of the rest in my grip, I order, "Take us to the nearest exit." The plan is to get the shifters outside where they can find their way home and then use Neal to find Roxy.

He turns on his heel and starts walking. The memory of my mother's disappointed look haunts me. I push it aside. She gave me to the devil and tried to have me killed for not going through with her plan. Who cares what she thinks of me?

To the group, I say, "Follow me."

I don't know what we look like walking down the dimly lit halls and try not to think about how each step echoes my own as we climb the stairwell.

I have thirteen people under my control, and I'm doing everything in my power not to think about the consequences of my actions. Who will remember and who they will tell? I can't consider it. Right now, I just want to survive.

We come to the top of the stairs. Armed guards patrol in the hall, drawing guns or tasers at our sudden arrival.

"Don't shoot." Throwing more of my faelight into the command, I grip their minds.

They lower their weapons, all expression wiped from their faces.

Hands trembling, I draw more light and limn my voice with power. "You will escort us to the exit, protecting us from anyone who tries to do us harm."

The guards enter the fold, doing as I command.

Fifteen people.

Do I have a limit?

I shudder, afraid of how powerful I am, but don't lose focus. We make it to the main double doors. The place where we entered. There are no people there now. No throngs of zealots to witness what I'm doing, to share it on the news. I smell coffee.

"Halt!" a guard orders.

He's joined by several more, aiming weapons at us.

"Let us pass," I order, power in every syllable.

The guards, five total, move aside.

Changing my mind, I say, "Escort us out. Protect us."

This is what Lucifer had wanted from me, why he wanted to bind me with the sword of justice—his justice. This is what he wanted me to do. He wanted an army completely under his control to go against his brethren, and he would have if I hadn't made my faerie.

We make it to the outside of the building. I blink against the dull, dishwater gray light of a PNW winter. Police cars, at least five of them, are in the lot. Lights on.

A tall man, blond and tan, and dressed in an Armani suit, is speaking with local police officers. They seem enthralled by his every word. The pastor from the stage the night before.

One looks up and the rest all look in our direction. Among the uniformed cops is that freakin' officer that had come to my house. The one who called me a monster and didn't care if I died.

The guards under my control raise their weapons at the perceived threat. I did command them to protect me. The officers raise their weapons in turn.

"Drop your weapons!" an officer shouts.

Heart racing, I grab the minds of the guards like a puppeteer and force them to obey. They lower their weapons to the ground and straighten with their hands in the air in unison. It's creepy as heck, but I can't help it. I don't know how to control them individually and hold onto all of the supes.

"Forget how you got here," I command into their minds, pushing my light into my words. Then I release my grip on the minds of the guards, while still holding the supes. I can feel the hunger and the rage of the latter. Letting the shifters go now would only cause the tense scene to erupt in violence.

The pastor points in my direction. "The trespassers we had to subdue, officers. Thank you for escorting them outside, acolytes. You may return to your posts." The tingle of the minor magic of persuasion brushes my skin.

The guards all walk back to the building, expressions dazed. No wonder they were so easy to control. This man usurped their free will regularly. It made me sick, but right now I didn't have the moral high ground.

"That man ordered an assault and held us against our will," I retort.

"I wasn't held against my will. I'm here to be cleansed for the coming paradise," the mothman whines, surprising me. Apparently whatever brainwashing they did to him is stronger than my influence. "I let them lock me up. I have the mark of Cain and I'm a danger to the Lambs of God."

A couple of the officers exchange worried glances. A few eye the mothman, finding Robby's diminutive body no threat and his rantings amusing. The officer who called me a monster and had harassed me about my car doesn't share in their mirth. His expression telegraphs utter hatred for me.

The pastor also glares. The look lasts only a moment before he plasters on a smile. "He's a charity case we've taken in. Mentally ill and homeless."

"I'm not," the mothman protests, hurt limning his features. "I was in my cell, waiting for my Bible study and midday meal, when this heathen witch put a spell on me!"

I gasp, hand flying to my chest. "I am an upstanding member of the community, a business owner, and a member of the PTSA. I came to see the Paradise Center after two sister acolytes visited me at my business, inviting me here. I have the brochure in my purse as proof. Without provocation, I was assaulted in the ladies' room and taken against my will to a cell until those guards came and released me."

I don't even need to push my light into my words. The officers take on a different posture as I speak. One of those trained to observe. I have scrapes on my face and hands, and my hair and clothes are disheveled. My appearance tells a different story than whatever lies the pastor told. I hope the other cops aren't associated with the Paradise Center and that they trust their training and instincts.

I let the shifters go at that moment. They all told similar stories. So many voices.

"Alright, alright." A police officer in uniform approaches hands up. "That's exactly why we are here. Someone reported their friends coming here and not leaving. We need you all to come to the station for statements."

Relief washes through me. There needn't be a fight. I can let the human authorities deal with this terrible human and his organization.

The man in the suit blanches. "Officers, officers, I won't press charges for trespassing if these people will agree to let this go too."

I shake my head slowly. I've been the lackey of someone with too much ambition before. This man may not be Lucifer, but he won't let this go so easily. He'll come after me or Jada and I can't let him do that.

"There's still a young girl in there. Her name is Roxanne Crowfoot."

"Not true. My daughter Roxy is home, thanks to the reverend." Gabriel interrupts stepping out of seemingly nowhere. "You should take Reverend Orwell's offer. Keep the peace."

It's not just me who didn't see his approach. Even the officers do a double take.

All eyes turn to the archangel. He's in a dress shirt and slacks, his public attire. The local wealthy businessman is here, not the sweats the nephil-shifter wears on missions. My heart sinks. If Roxy is home, he's in on this somehow.

"It's time to go home," he says in a tone that broaches no argument. The pulse of his alpha magic beats against my skin.

I gape.

The supes present all obey him. Even the woman I know is the low fae Cian's friend reported missing. Princess gives me an assessing look as she passes and turns her back on me, not offering me a ride home as she heads toward her motorcycle still in the lot.

"Better join your friends," Reverend Orwell says, false kindness in his tone. His eyes tell another story. Hatred and fear war there. "We can chalk this whole thing up to a misunderstanding."

I stare, allowing his tiny magic to pelt my skin like gnats at a picnic, annoying but harmless. For several breaths, I don't move. His eyes flare with surprise. He has no command over me, but I can take his people. Take him.

Unease settles in his features. This is a person unused to anyone resisting. No one has ever stood against him.

I smile. I could obliterate this man. I could control his mind and make him wish he never started this cult, make him wish he was never born. Doing so would free everyone under his control. I could destroy all Paradise Centers through this man. Taking so much power from the angels is so tempting.

Gabriel watches me, arms crossed. He says nothing, doesn't even acknowledge my wounds. He knows he can't compel me, and it pisses him off. I could compel him. Controlling one alpha would control the pack. So much easier than controlling them all.

I give myself a mental shake. No. I would not be the monster any of them wanted me to be.

I walk past the reverend and police in no particular direction but away. This isn't over. It's far from over.

I take a look back. They're all staring, waiting for something to happen. I smile, open a door to my faerie, and walk through.

19

My faerie is not how I left it last. A garden similar to the one in my backyard is full of green and growing things, and the pixies who followed me for years. Jada sits on a throne of branches in the center of the garden. A brownie offers her a platter of assorted fruits. Dryads stand watch. Another brownie pours a tea service. Pixies fly about Jada. Some tend the garden. Some dance and twirl in the air like entertainers of a tiny fae court.

"Looks like a party," I comment.

The fae all bow in deference at my presence. I gave no invite to these fae, hadn't been back to the faerie since my confrontation with Lucifer, but the faerie and its inhabitants prospered despite my absence.

"I didn't want to be alone. I told the pixies, and they brought these fae," Jada explains, as if all of this was part of her childhood like it was mine. "It feels good to be around them."

Because faerie-born low fae worship high fae as gods. Their adoration serves as a balm. I bask in the warmth of their belief.

"Did you find Roxy?" Jada asks, pulling me out of my reverie. "Is she okay?"

"She's with her father. I assume she's safe." Used for some sort of deal between Gabriel and the pastor, but I don't share that. Jada doesn't need to be caught in the middle of this any more than she already is.

"When is Phyr coming?"

As if summoned by his name, the fae prince appears in the faerie. Jada runs to him, and he embraces her. She doesn't notice he's in full armor, sword at the ready, but I do.

He checks her over, assessing with his eyes before embracing her again.

"Are you injured?" He asks over Jada's shoulder.

He is the only person who has asked about my well-being. I want to break down and cry, but I don't.

"Minor stuff." Physically. Emotionally, I'm holding it together for Jada's sake.

"Gabriel says that your glamour was off. They saw the real you, Tati."

I blink. Then I laugh, loud and manic. "Good. I'm tired of hiding what I am and what I can do."

A smile touches his lips, there and gone, as he opens a door between worlds. "That is how I feel. However, I am not free to do the same." He offers me his hand.

I take it.

After a brief moment of disorientation, the three of us are home.

Jada gives us both one more hug and begs to go to bed. Phyr and I sit with her for a bit because she asks us to. When her breathing evens out, Phyr takes my hand. He pulls me through time and space to my bedroom.

I didn't want to disturb her.

His voice is in my head.

Not letting go of my hand, he leads me to my bathroom. He shuts the door behind him. Bronze skin, amber eyes, and his beautiful, curved horns, the familiar fae of my childhood, but older, wiser, yet loyal to the bone. It's so good to be with someone I feel completely safe with again.

"Are you sure you're uninjured?" He inquires again, really looking me over. Concern colors his features.

My cheeks are hot and wet. It takes me a moment to realize I'm crying. I'm suddenly in his arms. Burying my face in Phyr's neck, soundless tears tumble into great heaving sobs. He holds me, making soothing sounds.

I know he knows, but the story of what happened pours out. "They shocked me and locked me in a cell with an iron door. I had to use influence on a guard. The shifters were all hungry and were seconds from going clawed and furry. I had to put them under my control. They would have gone feral and torn each other apart."

"I would have come for you, but he wanted to be the rescuer," he whispers in my hair as his hand strokes my back comfortingly.

"Ah, is that what he was doing?" I wipe my nose with the back of my hand. "Could have fooled me."

"I don't think he was expecting you to save yourself." A smile touches his lips. "I never doubted you could."

Lifting my head, I meet Phyr's gaze. There's unfettered adoration in his amber eyes. He looks at me the way the rest of the low fae did. It's almost too much to bear.

"I will suffer any abasement. Wear any mask to be at your side. I would give Gabriel my faerie and all my riches for the time we've shared since our reunion. Surely you know I am not here for your protection. You don't need any and never have. I am here because Oberon granted me a kindness. He knows I am yours, my dearest friend. There is no one I love more than you besides our precious Jada, of course." He smiles, tears wet his face.

I don't deliberate what it means or how things will change by my next actions. I reach for his cheek, tracing the sharp line of his jaw. When my fingertips reach his chin, it takes only the barest of gestures to lead his mouth to mine.

Tingling warmth passes from Phyr to me, his embrace and kiss deepening. All the minor bodily hurts cease. The big hurts of the evening diminish in our embrace.

Just when I think I want to lose myself in him, give him all of me and take all of him, Phyr breaks off the kiss. We both catch our breath, staring at each other. I've had a lot of good kisses, but wow. That one was—

"Feeling better?" He asks, eyes scanning my face. "You look better."

I glimpse myself in the mirror. I'm still disheveled, but the scrapes and bruises have disappeared.

"How?"

"Intimacy between fae who've shared blood has regenerative properties," he explains with a small shake of his head. Smiling, he adds, "A gift from Danu."

"Oh, neat."

My elegant reply, folks.

The stench of urine hits my nostrils and sweet Danu knows what else. How the heck did Phyr bear to kiss me? "I—uh—should shower."

The corner of his mouth quirks. "You should."

He releases me slowly and disappears.

~

SHOWERED and dressed in comfy pajamas, I lie in my bed. I threw up my mental shields a while ago. Phyr doesn't need me to keep him up.

I consider closing the bakery. I consider pulling Jada out of school and having her finish senior year online. I consider running to my faerie and never coming back. I consider a lot of things that are reminiscent of how I felt a few months ago after I banished a hellhound.

My life seems to be on another pivot. I didn't know which direction it would lead.

What I do know is that I am disappointed in Gabriel.

My phone vibrates. I check it in case it's Jada wanting to come into my room.

On the council's group chat, Gabriel calls for a mandatory meeting tomorrow night at seven. He's sent the message in a mode that we must RSVP whether we're going or not. I'm the first to respond.

Oh, hell yeah, I'm going. I cannot wait to give that nephil-shifter a piece of my mind. Then, I check our personal thread between just Gabriel and me. There's nothing there since 5am this morning.

I set my phone on the nightstand, angry all over again.

He saw the condition I was in and *knew* what they had done to me. He'd acted as if I were a stranger, nobody of importance to him, not the woman he set big future plans with.

Maybe I assumed wrong when I believed Gabriel truly cared for me beyond what I could do for him?

Are his emotions conditional upon my complete obedience?

Kirsten, his ex-wife, had said he left her, not because she cheated, but because she put his position in jeopardy. He didn't care for his position as a true archangel. That much is obvious. Had she meant his position as alpha or the head of the supernatural council? Maybe she'd meant the position he'd been gearing up for all along.

He could see the true me through glamour. Had he always known I wasn't merely a latent? Had he seen the potential within me, once locked by geas and thought I would strengthen his position and be what he needed to break free of the Angelic Anocracy?

From the beginning, I had trusted Gabriel so easily because of our long acquaintance. I'm beginning to think I was wrong to do so.

20

It's the wee morning hours when my cell rings. The caller ID lights up, identifying the call from the Washington State Police.

I almost let it go to voicemail, then I remember my Subaru. So much had happened, I still hadn't gone to the station.

"Miriam Diaz speaking." My voice is soft and as sleepy as I feel.

"Sorry to wake you, Ms. Diaz, but we've recovered a vehicle registered to you from Snoqualmie Pass. I'm calling for you to come and claim it."

Before I reply, my sleepy mind struggles how to reply since they'd already sent someone. Didn't they? Someone on the site had said that their superior suspected foul magical play and then the officer obviously in league with the Paradise Center showed up asking me questions. I assumed he was the one out to prove it, but I remembered from the cards he and his partner were local cops, not state police. Was this a trap or overlapping departments not communicating?

"I thought you sent an officer to tell me," I finally manage. "Isn't there an ongoing investigation?"

There's a long pause. Then I'm placed on hold replete with country music as a placeholder. The cop returns to the call. "Ma'am, I don't see any records showing that we sent an officer out, or any investigation surrounding the vehicle. We get abandoned snow-ins all the time. We do, however, need you to come to the impound and claim your vehicle, or the state will start charging storage."

"Can I do it in the morning?"

"My superior would like to ask you a few questions regarding the visit you received. I know it's late, but this is important."

I exhale through my nose, knowing I'm not going to get out of this. Maybe I can have someone side with me against the local cop in the pastor's pocket. I jot down the station's address.

"Thank you for your cooperation," the officer says before disconnecting.

After dressing wearily, I check in on Jada. She's fast asleep. I knock on Rhiannon's door. She answers, wiping sleep from her eyes.

"Sorry to bother you—are you alone?"

She nods.

I explain that I need to pick my car up from the compound and that she can have the assistants we've hired help her open the bakery. "I'll keep an ear out for Jada and will let her know where you went," she promises.

Next knock on Phyr's door.

Yawning and stretching, he plants his hands on the top of the frame, displaying a magazine cover worthy torso. A grin curves his lips.

"How may I serve you?" he asks, wearing only a pair of black briefs that leave little to the imagination. I notice after I get an eyeful of smooth bronze skin covered in tattoos. My cheeks flush. I hadn't meant to ogle him like a piece of meat, but fae bodies are works of art in their beauty and, unlike shifters who go naked all the time, fae cover all that pretty. Sweet Danu. Why am I here?

I shake my head. I'm not a hormonal teenager but tell me you wouldn't be distracted with that greeting and that body on offer. Clearing my throat, I reply, "I need you in armor and armed."

He snaps his fingers, and he's in full armor, sword in sheath at his side. "Who are we fighting?"

"Hopefully, no one." I relay the phone call from the state police.

Lines mar the smooth bronze skin of Phyr's forehead as his ebony eyebrows draw together. When I finish, he agrees, "It does sound like a trap. You should alert someone on the council of where we are going."

I find it interesting that he doesn't say Gabriel as a default contact. After last night, I don't feel like speaking to the archangel much. It still burns that he didn't come to my side and reeks of secrets. Not that I haven't kept some of my own. Coming to a decision, I say, "I'll call Lucinda."

After giving my siren bestie a rundown of what transpired over the last twenty-four hours, she replies, "I'm glad Jada and Roxy are safe and I don't like how Gabriel handled it much, but I think he has his reasons."

There's rustling in the background. I look at the time on my watch. It's five in the morning. Lucinda swims around this time every morning regardless of weather or temperature. I used to think she was some sort of fitness freak for swimming in Lake Washington mid-December rather than a heated indoor pool, but that was before I learned my bestie had a siren secret of her own.

She lowers her voice as she adds, "About the conflict regarding the dirty cop and the officer who called, I can't say what I suspect, but I believe wholeheartedly whoever wants to speak to you isn't the typical police."

"If you know something, spill."

She sighs softly. "Your world is about to expand. Again. I'm glad you called me, but the sea calls, nena. I must answer. Cuidate."

"You take care, too." I end the call, turning my gaze to Phyr. "Council member notified."

"Duty fulfilled," he replies, extending his hand.

A warm ripple of pleasure passes from where my skin meets his. I have no time to analyze how I feel about that. Phyr pulls me through the fabric of reality to a wintery lot where my car is among a number of destroyed or incapacitated vehicles. The officer on the phone didn't lie. My car, spelled to avoid accidents, also avoided the damage of the crushing weight of winter snows. I am both proud of my spell work and afraid of what it might cost me.

How valuable to a law enforcement agency would this sort of magic be?

Would they consider me a threat?

I nod to the parking lot in the front of the building to a copse of trees near it and whisper, "Over there."

Phyr takes my hand once again.

It takes a minute to get over the initial vertigo brought on by moving through the fabric of reality, twice. I may be able to make doors to my faerie, but I am not a planeswalker, evidenced by the way Phyr shows no sign of being any worse for the dual crossing. After making a mental note to ask him how many crossings it would take to tire him out, I straighten.

"Glamour yourself," I whisper. I could look fae because I had a long standing as a member of my community. Phyr's newish fake citizenship didn't account for his bronze skin, magical tattoos, armor, sword, or his horns.

Phyr nods, weaving his Irish immigrant named Brendan illusion.

He's right. Brendan is handsome, but wholly human, not my fae childhood friend. I've learned to accept this appearance as a facet of Phyr, even though he hates it.

We traverse the lot, entering the single-story concrete building. Inside two officers in Washington state dress blues chat at a desk, coffee mugs in hand. They lift their heads and home their gazes on us. Me, actually.

I didn't glamour my appearance.

Plastering on my PTSA fundraiser smile, I introduce myself, "Hi! I'm Miriam Diaz. I'm here for my car."

THE OFFICERS WASTE no time setting me and Phyr up in a room straight out of Law and Order replete with a formica table, uncomfortable plastic and metal chairs, and coffee too scalding hot to drink in my hands. Phyr, ever the foodie snob, declines the questionable brew and gives me side eye as I stir in powdered cream and sugar. I'd only accepted the coffee because my past week was catching up to me.

His eyes on the mirror we face, he says in High Fae, "That mirror must be spelled. I feel as if I'm being observed by a sentient mind."

I explain what a two-way mirror is and that there are probably human minds

Moments after my explanation, he waves at the mirror. "The persons on the other side will be in shortly."

I gape in his direction. He had an express agreement with Gabriel to not influence humans unless the archangel wanted something covered up.

He lifts one shoulder and lets it drop dramatically. "I only peeked in their head. I didn't enthrall them."

I don't have time to respond.

A petite woman with her hair in a neat, chin-length bob and a tall man with his hair in a long plait enter the room. She wears muted makeup and has flawless, youthful skin. Her companion possesses striking rather than traditionally handsome features: high cheekbones, strong jaw, distinct nose. His skin has suffered severe acne at some point, evidenced by some scarring. They wear dark suit jackets and slacks with black button-down shirts and black ties. Both emote about as much as Phyr in my father's faerie court. No magic emanates from them and when I observe them with my second sight; I see no light.

I wait for one to pull out a brain zapper, or whatever it's called in that Will Smith and Tommy Lee Jones movie. Instead of erasing our memories like the agents in Men in Black, they take chairs opposite me and Phyr. The woman opens a fat case on the table facing her. The man pulls a laptop out of a case and hangs the strap of the bag on the back of his chair.

"Miriam Diaz, Brendan O'Connor, I'm Agent Tan," the woman says in a thick Bostonian accent, "and this is my partner, Agent Roanhorse."

Agent Roanhorse has all the warmth of an autopsy table, making his "nice to meet you, finally" sound vaguely threatening.

A now-remembered childhood in faerie and time spent in Hell has taught me to say very little when entering a hostile situation. I did need to clarify one thing though. "Agents of what?"

"We are from the U.N.M.U," Agent Tan provides.

"The U.N. has Peacekeepers. I wasn't aware of a law enforcement department." I'm trying to draw out more information and doing a terrible job of it.

"U. N. M. U. is an acronym for United Nations Monster Unit," Agent Roanhorse clarifies. "We are one of the few government organizations free of supernatural influence."

I bite my lip from laughing at the irony. "Do you find something amusing about that?"

Oh, yeah. A secret international monster hunter agency ran by the biggest monsters on this planet. Mundane humans have caused more atrocities on a grand scale than any so-called monsters, and human belief has more power than any supernatural species. However, I don't want to get on this organization's bad side right away.

"I'm having a hard time because I was called here to reclaim my car. Now I'm being interrogated—" I make a sweeping gesture indicating our surroundings. "—by agents who work for an organization that hunts *monsters*. This is either a hilarious prank or I should be deeply insulted."

"The agency was formed a long time ago. You've never heard of us because we are classified as what you supes call mundanes outside the agency," Agent Tan explains further. "And we like to keep our noses out of supes' lives, if they abide by the law."

"Am I under arrest?"

The agents exchange glances. "No," Agent Tan replies. "We know by the spell work on your car that you're a witch. We'd like to discuss with you what you know about the Baba Yaga coven and their part in disappearances of several supernatural beings."

Ah, of course the witches took them and boiled them in a cauldron. This is what always happens to nomadic, reclusive groups. Something goes wrong and they get the blame. It could never be your neighbor, Joe. It had to be the outsiders with the accents and different beliefs.

"Funny you should think they're involved," I say. "I rescued at least twenty shifters from the Paradise Center near Kirkland last night. My daughter being one of their victims."

Instead of showing any sign of surprise, Agent Roanhorse reaches under the table and digs in his pocket, pulling out a twenty-dollar bill and handing it to Agent Tan. The latter smirks and stuffs the bill into her jacket pocket.

Phyr and I take our turn at exchanging glances. Maybe these two aren't on an Eastside witch hunt after all.

"Did you notify mundane authorities?" Agent Tan asks.

"They were present after the rescue. The pastor of the so-called church has the small magic of influence and claimed I was trespassing. With his magic so clearly taking over the officers' minds. I agreed to drop charges to avoid further conflict."

Agent Roanhorse scowls. "The small magic of persuasion? What is that?"

"Humans aren't non-magical, as you'd like to think," I reply. "All beings have one magic or another. They're simply unaware. Think of it like how some people are unaware of annoying personality traits that are obvious to others."

The agents exchange glances. Agent Roanhorse starts typing away. Agent Tan clears her throat. "This is something we haven't heard of before. Mundane human influencers actually possess a type of magic that makes them popular?"

"Something like that." I teeter on the precipice of the pain of a lie. It's the influencer's popularity that gives them the magic of persuasion, not the other way around. If these agents truly have never heard of this, I am not going to give the agency more information they could weaponize against me or my kind.

"Do you possess this sort of magic?"

My stomach lurches. I possess something much, much worse.

"Nothing so common," I reply with a dismissive flick of the wrist. How very fae of me.

Agent Roanhorse types the entire time. He pauses to say, "We have an ongoing investigation regarding the Paradise Centers." He glances at Agent Tan.

Agent Tan nods. After typing for a few moments, he turns his laptop around. On the screen is a picture of Carmen Ramirez, aka Mama Doe. "Wanted: armed and dangerous" is in bright red text at the top of the screen.

"Was this woman one of the people you rescued from the Paradise Center?"

I lean forward, examining the picture closely. It's probably a few years old. Carmen is well put together with designer sunglasses, expensive clothes and heels. She appears confident and poised, as any Southern California elite. An alpha in her own right by the pride in her stance. Hardly the shifter in mental shambles we'd been calling Mama Doe, staying in the pack's nursery.

I lean back in my chair and shake my head. "No."

Technically, I'm not lying. She isn't a person I'd rescued from the Paradise Center, so I don't suffer any pain.

"This is Carmen Ramirez. If you run across her, steer clear and report her whereabouts to me immediately. Ramirez is wanted by both mundane authorities and the U.N.M.U. "

In genuine shock, I rear my head. Knowing what was done to Carmen, having experienced a mild taste of it myself, I don't blame her for escaping any way she could to save herself and her children.

"What for? She looks like any mom on the PTSA."

I don't know what my reaction told the agents, but Roanhorse nods to Tan when she raises an eyebrow in his direction. Roanhorse clicks a button and the screen fills with numerous murder scenes. There are no bodies, thank sweet Danu, but the taped outlines of floors drenched in dark stains. Crimson and chunks of the gods knew what spatters the walls. Not one a swift kill I know shifters capable of.

I cover my mouth, horrified.

Phyr's hand rests on my shoulder. He shows no emotion. Of

course he doesn't. He's seen much, much worse than crime scenes in the Angel and Fae wars.

"She murdered humans and shifters, members of her own pack, brutally mauling their bodies and dismembering them," Tan explains. "She knows she's guilty because she's fought every authority who has tried to bring her to justice, to a fair trial, not a guaranteed execution her pack is calling for. She fights and murders them. Not only that, we have reason to believe her children are witnessing their mother's murders. She abducted her son and was pregnant with triplets when she ran from her pack's authorities. Those kids deserve better. They have a very worried father as well as extended family, who would like them back."

I swallow hard, unsure of what to say, so I say nothing at all. In Carmen's head, her husband betrayed everyone. However, he himself hadn't hurt anyone. I can see fighting the Paradise Center, maybe pack, but the human cops? If she did fight cops and kill pack members, why did she finally trust Princess? Why did her husband not tell Gabriel she was on the run? None of this added up. None of it would be my business if I hadn't tried to help. Even if any of this is true, the Paradise Center broke her. I saw it. I lived it as if it happened to me.

"Mrs. Diaz, we know you've lived a quiet life here in Washington for the past nineteen years. You volunteer for the PTSA. You own a bakery. A model supernatural citizen." Agent Tan smiles in a way that seems more threatening than friendly. "We have no reason to prosecute you for whatever beef you had on the pass with the Baba Yaga coven, but if you hide a known fugitive, we will have to charge you with aiding and abetting a criminal."

They would arrest me and take me from Jada, my life. Phyr, the fae and witches relying on me, my friends all gone to cover for a woman I didn't know who murdered so many people. I could call it self-defense given what happened in the Paradise Center, knowing first-hand what they thought of supes and how little value our lives meant to them, but she'd only proven that we are dangerous. Instead of trying to seek the archangel she'd believed in, she sought another.

Traversed many miles. It seems suspect that she ended up here by accident. I felt bad for Carmen's plight, a mother going to great lengths to protect her cubs, but I didn't know her. My community, Roxy, Princess, Lance, Syd, and all those little shifters shouldn't be in the same house as a murderous shifter.

"Gabriel Crowfoot has her in his custody," I offer.

"Custody? Am I to assume the shifters are taking care of this?" Agent Tan asks, gaze flicking briefly to Agent Roanhorse. Not surprisingly, she doesn't ask me to clarify who Gabriel is, which makes sense. If they have a file on me, they likely have a whole shelf of files on the archangel of the Pacific Northwest and the alpha of the greater Seattle area pack.

"They didn't know who she was." I pause, taking a deep breath. "The pack found her in a state of shock and have been caring for her. They're setting her up with a therapist, who handles deep trauma. Whatever she's done, she did it under extreme mental duress."

Agent Tan takes in what I say, her expression giving away no reaction. "According to those who knew her, she's a cunning and manipulative person. Her husband said she came from another pack. He took her in. Slowly gained her trust. Carmen claimed her alpha abused her, but refused to disclose which pack she came from. He'd already fallen in love. His pack paid for his trust in her. It seems she's forming a pattern, feigning trauma to gain Crowfoot's protection. I wouldn't be surprised if there's a speedy recovery and during that, she seeks this alpha as a new mate."

"Maybe even convincing him to challenge her old mate," Agent Roanhorse adds. "We don't interfere in pack matters if they don't involve humans."

"Let the filthy beasts kill each other off?" Phyr asks with a chuckle, speaking for the first time. He appears amused, but I know my friend better. This isn't his normal teasing. He's taking their moral measure.

"More like we like to avoid getting killed when they're doing something we can't stop anyway," the big man replies, a small grin on his lips and a gleam in his eye. "You should know a fool's errand,

Trickster." Roanhorse's gaze on Phyr is intense and scrutinizing, as if the agent wants to catch an incriminating reaction.

All fae are considered tricksters, so he gets none.

"I'm not of your pantheon," Phyr says with a casual shrug, understanding something I didn't. "But, I've met Raven and Coyote."

"The point is," Agent Tan says, clearing her throat to get her now-fascinated partner's attention. "Gabriel Crowfoot is well-regarded among shifters. Many who want to split from the Angelic Anocracy are seeking him out as an ally, powerful supes, who either hold political or financial clout. He's going to run for office soon. The coming out from behind the veil was only the first step. Carmen Diaz may have been involved in a situation beyond her control, but if she's in Crowfoot's care, she meant to be there. "

Which made me wonder a few things. "Why are you telling me this?"

"For your safety, Mrs. Diaz." Agent Tan straightens as if I've insulted her integrity. "Until we can speak to Crowfoot, you should steer clear of his home. Carmen Ramirez is not going to like his involvement with you, and she might rid herself of the competition."

Agent Roanhorse pulls a card from his pocket and places it on the table. "This is our number. If you are threatened by the Paradise Center in any way, please let us know."

"We will be investigating what transpired. A small magic, as you call it, makes Pastor Orwell our business."

Not the imprisonment and kidnapping of supes, I think bitterly.

"I think we have enough." Agent Roanhorse closes his laptop and rises.

Agent Tan takes her time, allowing her partner to slip through the door without her. When the door closes, she rises and extends her hand.

I spy another card in her palm.

Our gazes meet. I take the card.

"Thank you for your cooperation."

Her gratitude ripples through me in a binding way. I don't know how to stop her debt of a favor to me, but I can feel it bound in my very marrow. That's new.

I wait until she leaves to examine the card. It's the business card for Jenna Jones, a famous actress turned investigative reporter who does exposés on religious cults, after her own falling out with a Hollywood celebrity cult. On the back of the card, there's two words written in pen.

"Expose them."

21

"**D**o you find any truth in their assessment of Carmen?" Phyr asks.

We're on the highway home. We decided driving would be better than using his ability to make nowhere doors, figuring driving a car through a bridge through the space-time continuum is much more threatening to mundanes than two magical beings appearing out of thin air.

"I don't know." I really don't. After pausing to gather my thoughts, I say, "There was what I saw in her head, but what I saw was limited to her experience at the Paradise Center. We know nothing about who she was leading up to the Paradise Center. I was under the assumption that she was a good person who had a bad thing happen to her, driven to violence."

"Sometimes bad people create their own chaos. She came a great distance. Why north? Why not east?" Phyr asks.

"That area of the country is a desert. She'd have a harder time surviving. Following the mountains was a good choice as far as survival goes. What makes little sense is that she attacked shifters, but not Princess or Aurora. If Gabriel is famous, then his beta is, too."

"You were all on viral videos and your pictures made newspapers."

A knot forms in my stomach. All Carmen had to do was access a newspaper. Easy enough, even for a shifter on the run. I just didn't want to believe a woman would do this, especially a mother.

"If women can be heroes, they can be villains too," Phyr says softly.

He's right. I just don't know enough to condemn Carmen. "Should I warn Gabriel about what I know?"

Phyr glances at me. "Do you still trust him enough to tell him you gave someone in his care up?"

I gave up a wanted criminal. However, Phyr has a point. That's how Gabriel might see it. I weigh out the consequences and the precarious place I stood with the archangel at the moment. By the time we reach home, I still don't have a clue if what I did was right and how he would react, but I do know Roxy and the other children of the pack are living with a killer.

JADA STANDS on the front porch as we pull up, fully dressed. I exchange a glance with Phyr and then check the time. It's about the time Roxy would pick her up for school.

Rather than park in the garage, I park in the driveway. Phyr and I exit the vehicle.

The pixies fly about my daughter, but she's immersed in her tablet. The tablet could double as a phone.

A spark of fury courses through me. The True Believers took her phone and still had it. They stole my property. They captured and detained my daughter.

"Your eyes are glowing, Miriam," Phyr warns.

I don't care. I take large strides until I reach Jada, hugging her.

She lets me for a bit and then says, "Mami, I'm fine. They didn't do anything but bore me to death. You're messing up my aesthetic."

I pull back. "Are you going to school?"

"Yeah." She chews her bottom lip pensively. "They want to scare me from living my life. I'm not about to let them do that."

I'm happy Raf and I raised such a resilient person. Her strength will come in handy in the years to come. "Need a ride?"

She shakes her head. "Nah. Roxy has her mom's old car again."

At first, I don't know how I feel about Jada riding with Roxy after what Gabriel pulled. I decide to not let what the father has done cast a shadow on my feelings about the daughter. Besides, Roxy's appearance will give me an opportunity to chat with the teen when she pulls up. I'd like to know what happened on Gabriel's end while I was sitting in a cell.

Roxy gets out of the car, running to hug Jada. "You were so brave."

"So were you," Jada says, hugging her friend back.

"How did you manage to escape them, Roxy?" I ask, gentle in tone.

"Two goons said that my dad negotiated my release. They brought me home. Dad was there with a shady as fuck cop. That dude was definitely one of those True Believers. Dad said they'd come to some understanding." She shrugs. "Then Lance comes home with a wild story about going to a Paradise Center with you because you had some sort of magical tracker to find Syd. He said you and Princess went to the bathroom and never came back. Dad freaked out. Apparently, you guys broke the deal he had. They were going to release everyone they took, including Jada, as long as he didn't make a big deal about it in the news or with the rest of the authorities. The thing is, Lance went to the cops before he came home. He figured the police would check the Paradise Center and handle the mundanes."

I nod, digesting the information. "Is Lance in trouble?"

"Loads. Dad is super pissed you all made moves without telling him."

I'm super pissed he made a deal with the True Believers and didn't tell the council, but I put on a smile. "Well, the important thing is that everyone is safe."

Jada hugs me quickly. "Bye!"

Roxy even says, "Thanks for looking for us," before giving me a quick one-armed hug.

"Of course—How is Carmen doing?" I ask.

"Oh, yeah. Funny thing. After the therapist came, Carmen started talking. Not much and refuses to talk about her old pack or what happened to her, but she let Dad come near her last night. He was super happy about that after all the stress, you know. "

I swallow down my feelings about the stress. That was a conversation for Gabriel and I to have. "You know the story of Little Red Riding Hood, right?"

She eyes me. "It's a metaphor about predators."

"Yes. It's also a metaphor for deception to lower someone's guard. She's killed people to escape her captors, Roxy. There's no easily bouncing back from that kind of trauma."

Seeming to grasp what I'm saying, Roxy nods. "I'll keep an eye on her."

I wave as the girls pull out of the cul-de-sac, feeling guilty for creating suspicion based on mundane monster hunter information. If Carmen does nothing to create more suspicion, she'll eventually gain Roxy's trust.

I'M late to the mandatory meeting set up by Gabriel. The message said council only, so I left Rhiannon and Phyr at home, watching television. After the past few days I've had, I want to stay home too.

All eyes turn to me as Lucinda lets me into her cafe. Worry creases her brow as she gives me a once over. "Are you okay?"

"As I will ever be," I reply.

Over a decade of friendship and sitting on the PTSA board together allows a silent conversation between us. She lets me know I'm walking into hostile territory, which I already figured, but Lucinda has my back, which means so much.

Gabriel stands. Fury twists his handsome features.

That's fine. I have a lot of anger of my own. I bolster myself to get an earful for talking to U.N.M.U. about Mama Doe.

"Explain why Princess and Syd can't recall leaving the Paradise Center," he demands in lieu of greeting.

"They looked at me like I was dinner," I shoot back. With a glance in Princess's direction, I add, "They were under duress. I needed them calm and human so we could escape without incident."

Gabriel's jaw drops. "So you admit manipulating their minds?"

"I needed them calm so that we could escape without incident," I repeat. Then I grin, showing a little fang. For the first time in a long time, I feel oh so Oberon's daughter, the child of faerie I'd once been. "Just like you used your alpha call."

He scrambles for a retort. Did he expect me to cry and say I didn't mean to? Who did he think stood before him? A helpless latent? I am a princess of faerie, a coven raised witch, and Lucifer's ex-mistress. I've done bad shit. I'm capable of bad shit. However, I'd used my influence to diffuse a scary situation, and I'd do it again.

Although I'm furious, I continue in a tone less perturbed than I felt. "I love how your first question is about what I did to help so many people escape a madman and not to ask if I'm alright. Those assholes shocked and shocked me because I wouldn't go down easy. They didn't care if I died as long as they caught their monster. I did nothing to provoke violence but look for our daughters, for Syd."

Gabriel runs a shaky hand through his hair. At least he's showing some emotion regarding what happened to me. I'm not quite sure if it's for me, or for how tense I made it between him and the mundanes he made a bargain with. "You should have come to me when you knew Syd's location for certain. Instead, you went in there with no plan and put yourself and others in danger."

"I don't think you care that I was in danger. You're mad I didn't ask for your permission to look for my child."

He crosses the room. "Damn right I'm angry. This is my territory, my council, and my pack were at stake."

The entire council rear their heads, including Princess.

"I was following your orders to find the kids. I made the call for Miriam to come," Princess says, pushing to her feet.

After what I did, Princess is the last person I'd expect to come to my aid.

Neither did Gabriel, because pure fury mars his handsome features as he pivots to her. His voice is a low growl when he asks, "Did you know Miriam could control the minds of at least fifteen people when you made that call?"

"No," she says, cowering, but not slinking back to her chair. She rallies her courage to add, "But I'm glad she was there to keep everyone calm. You know there is a point that you cannot push shifters past before we lose our human reasoning. The shifters could have lost their shit and mauled the mundanes."

The Paradise Center had pushed Carmen past that point. I believed that more than I believe the stories her alpha told the U.N.M.U. He'd lied to Gabriel. That is not a man who wants his wife and kids back. He was covering for the Paradise Center.

Shifters could be pushed past the point of reasoning, but they had reasoning in most situations. Gabriel strategized all the time.

"Did you?" I ask in a quiet voice. A stupid traitorous tear slides down my face. "You want me to come to you, but did you come to me when you were making deals regarding my daughter? Trust goes both ways."

Gabriel doesn't answer.

"You said they shocked you. Did you two receive any injuries?" Leilani asks.

"Minor cuts and bruises, but Phyr healed me."

A blush floods Cian's freckled cheeks. "Ah. Danu's blessing to the High Fae."

"You were hurt?" Gabriel asks, his tone softening. Did he not hear me earlier? "You seemed fine. I assumed—" He stammers for a moment, struggling with his words as if he'd had a core belief challenged. "I assumed you'd been captured on purpose to get to Jada. I didn't think they could harm you."

I stare, unbelieving. Did he not see me last night?

"Modern weapons are a great equalizer," Cian replies.

His mournful tone reminds me of when Phyr once murmured, *"The fae will have a difficult time being gods in this world of steel and technology."*

"Electricity will put anything with a nervous system down," Leilani adds, fear in her dark eyes. "Even halflings and demigods. It would take a lot more electricity than it would for a human, and it wouldn't kill us, but it would hurt."

"That makes sense. He had to crank up the wattage to knock me out." I rub my arms, the memory of the intense muscle cramps as I flailed on the ground all too fresh.

"They got me on the first try," Princess says. "I'm sorry, Miriam. That had to be painful."

I nod, grateful someone cared.

"They said they didn't harm anyone," Gabriel protests.

"Why did you bargain with them without consulting the council," Lucinda asks, then she turns to me. "And you, why did you go to a hostile place without calling your friends? First when you confronted the Baba Yaga and now these zealots." She gestures to the entire room. "What's the point of this, if we're not communicating and acting as a team?"

All the faces turn to Gabriel and me. Gabriel grips the back of the chair as if controlling his temper or his emotions, I don't know.

Guilt ties barbed knots in my stomach. Tears sting my eyes. I wouldn't have even told Lucinda about going to the cops if Phyr hadn't made me.

"I'm sorry," I say. "This council has done nothing but support me. I should have come to all of you when I found the page from the Baba Yaga's grimoire. I should have definitely come to you when I was searching for my daughter. It was dangerous and I don't intend to do it again."

Gabriel sucked in his breath and then released in a slow exhale. "I should have texted you when the Pastor's goons brought Roxy home. I was only thinking of getting the rest."

After dealing with mundanes for so long, I forget he isn't a mundane and wasn't raised like one. Gabriel isn't even a typical nephil. He's the son of the archangel Gabriel, the head of the Angelic Anocracy, who raised his son to lead in a way that required complete obedience. The same went for being an alpha. Gabriel had to shoulder the pack's problems, to rule in absolute authority. His admission shows growth beyond what's expected of him.

He continues, "It's no excuse. I formed this council to be different, to share in power and responsibility, to step away from the Angelic Anocracy's way and form a more egalitarian way of governing."

His gaze lands on me. "I owe you the biggest apology, Miriam. In my ambition, in my pride, when you protected yourself and took care of my people, I took offense. I felt like you did the job I should have done instead of negotiating with them. I should have taken back my people."

"You were afraid of optics," Princess says.

He lowers his head, ashamed. "I was. My kid publicly antagonized a protest. The school and the authorities were involved. I'm clinging to my position as an archangel by a thread. I wanted it over before news spread further than the incident. We all have to be careful of our public image right now. "

"That leaves the True Believers with the notion they can indoctrinate more supes," Lucinda argues.

"They'll do what they did to Syd, to some other unsuspecting shifter," Aurora says. "It will not stop unless we stand up to them."

"They're going to get their hands on the wrong supe. One not concerned with optics. There will be blood," Cian agrees.

"What can we do?" Gabriel says.

I pull out the card Agent Tan gave me. "I have an idea."

22

Two weeks later, Gabriel, Carmen, and I, drive to Jenna Jones' Vancouver, British Columbia studio. I'm nervous about leaving the country with a wanted criminal, but Gabriel's passport has some extras on it that got us through without much ado. Planning to drive back the same night, we go straight to the studio. I had no idea that the show was shot there. That was the point. Jenna Jones gave the illusion she was still in Hollywood, exposing Hollywood cults, but she was in Canada, where they are a little kinder and her former church has no reach.

We're all whisked to separate dressing rooms. I don't mind, but Gabriel doesn't like us separated. I've already had a stylist dress me in a plus-sized powder blue gown that is a lot more flowy and glamorous than my usual Pacific Northwest winter gear, consisting of leggings, boots, and a sweater.

The hair and makeup artist screws their mouth as they take me in. I'm not wearing a glamour so I'm in all my freakish fae glory: pearlescent skin, glowing green eyes, antlers and natural pink hair—my ears have grown a bit, pointy on the ends, and my features have sharpened.

"I—uh—your skin is great for your age. Like, you're really, really pretty. Either we can dig into the otherness and make you look like a cosplayer, or we leave it understated and just give your hair a bit of styling." Their eyes slide up my antlers. "Those aren't sensitive, are they?"

"I get ticklish."

They nod. "Okay. We can work with that."

Twenty minutes later, my hair falls in soft waves, my pointed ears sticking out ever so slightly.

"Usually there's a seven month wait list," the woman assigned to shove me here and there tells me as my hair and makeup person spins me in her direction. "Jenna has wanted something on the Paradise Center for a long-time. All the True Believers are tight-lipped. When she heard about the cells and the supernatural conversion process, she put you on the very next spot."

I don't know what to say, so I plaster on my PTSA smile. The assistant flinches. She's a tall woman, and the reaction is dramatic.

Crap. I forgot my fangs scare mundanes. I sigh inwardly. Outwardly, I say, "I don't bite."

"Sure," the assistant replies, gripping her tablet. Then she looks at her watch. "Okay. I'll take you to the green room to wait with the others until it's showtime."

I follow her from the dressing room, down a hall with people hurriedly passing to and fro to some unknown, imperative destination, to a room filled with sofas and a table laid out with food. Gabriel is there.

"No te preocupes, Carmen. Está bien," he says in a comforting tone to Carmen.

My chest burns when I see his hand clutching the shifter's we'd been calling Mama Doe. I don't like the feeling. I'm unused to it and it's unfair. He's being a good alpha and we are in a weird place. I have no right to jealousy, yet here it is, burning away.

Carmen has been through so much; working with a therapist to overcome her trauma seemed as hard as reliving it. Jada had her own sessions with the shifter therapist, and I've seen her a few times myself to talk about my experience—it's led to some interesting talks about my past that I don't want to focus on at the moment. Healing picks off scabs that haven't formed correctly, and I'd rather not have open wounds in front of a camera.

When Carmen heard we were going to be interviewed for the exposé on the Paradise Center, she volunteered to come, even if it meant dealing with the repercussions the human authorities might throw at her.

She notices me before Gabriel does, her dark eyes sliding over my clothes. "You look so pretty, Miriam."

I smile. "So do you." I mean it.

Carmen is drop dead gorgeous with long black hair and warm brown skin, flawless and youthful. She has the lithe muscle of an athlete, a beautiful killing machine like all shifters. She's more like Gabriel's ex Kirsten than I'll ever be, and she's a ferocious fighter, who loves her children dearly.

Push down this stupid feeling. Witches and fae don't settle for one person. Why should I feel jealous?

"I'll be back when Jenna needs you," the assistant says, leaving us three alone.

Gabriel clears his throat, his hand dropping as he rises to greet me. His hand touches my hair as his eyes take me in. For the first time, I notice now that the way Gabriel looks at me is not the way he looks at anyone else, even beautiful Carmen. There's desire, yes, but something more. He's always looked at me like that, if perhaps more subdued before Raf ascended. Gabriel regarded me like I'm his dream come true and I'm not quite sure how to feel about that either. I'm only a person, not an object to be put on a pedestal. His Creepiness had done that. He never saw me, even when he handed me his most prized possession, the Flaming Sword of Justice, it was to own me. I'd never be the object of someone's infatuation again, or at least not reciprocate genuine feelings for infatuation.

I suddenly found myself wishing Phyr was here. My dearest friend would guide me through this quagmire of feelings.

"This, this is a different look for you. I'm almost afraid to touch you in fear I'll ruin your perfection with my imperfect hands."

Ha. The man is half angel, and you can't get more perfect than that. He looks damn good in his button down and slacks. Not a single wrinkle.

We do look pretty together in the wall mirror.

I wrinkle my nose. "I look like a fairy princess."

A deep chuckle rumbles from his chest. "You are a fairy princess."

"Really?" Carmen's excited inquiry, a reminder she's still in the room. "Like are you a halfling with some fae mom or dad back in faerie?"

Gabriel shakes his head as if he'd forgotten too. Then he grins at me. "You wanna tell her?"

"My given name is Tatiana, Heir of Oberon, High King of the Fae."

"So, you're not earthborn? Like, do you have a castle somewhere in another realm?" She waves her hand as if alluding to some lofty place.

I swallow hard. She's delving into territory I'm not comfortable discussing with a stranger that has no idea what fae are like. The council was different. Cian is a low fae, and well, shifters historically tended to kill High fae and ask questions why they were here later. Besides, Gabriel and Oberon, with me as their go-between, are still in discussions about how many fae the archangel would allow in this territory.

"Please tell her a bit about your father's faerie. It will distract her from what she's about to do," Gabriel croons in perfect High Fae.

I'd forgotten he speaks High Fae—every language actually, his father's gift to him.

"I was born to an earthborn American witch named Gracia and Oberon in a castle that would seem impossible to someone who has only lived on earth. There were balls and feasts. It was all very glamorous and magical."

"Heaven had the best parties," Gabriel says, nostalgia in his voice. "I miss them. The extravagance and pageantry, there's just nothing like it here."

There's definitely stars in Carmen's eyes when she casts a dreamy gaze at Gabriel. "I forget you're half angel. You seem so—so, one of us."

"He is one of you," I say a little too sharply, knowing oh too well the way a simple statement like that could burn.

Gabriel gives me a look that tells me all I need to know about why he feels so strongly about me. No one else knows what it's like to teeter on the edge of two worlds. We're surrounded by one-magical-line shifters, angels, fae, sirens, and cryptids, and the demigods have powers, but they grew up on earth because the gods' realms are pure energy. Even Rhiannon, who is one-sixteenth brownie, has lived in Phyr's faerie, but she didn't grow up there.

"The True Believers wouldn't be able to hold either of you. You just snapped your fingers and poof you were out of there. You didn't have to murder to save your daughter from those fiends," she says, tears streaming down her cheeks.

I rush for the tissues and Gabriel returns to Carmen's side. I catch her brief grin when he wraps an arm around her shoulder. "Shhh. You did what you had to. There's no use comparing."

I hand Carmen tissues, wishing I had something encouraging to say. This may be partly a ploy to regain Gabriel's attention, but she honestly needs it right now. I feel guilty for snapping at her and hope it came from protectiveness of him and not from a petty place.

"I'm sorry I spoke harshly. You're right. We have magical advantages shifters simply don't."

Gabriel glances at me gratefully. "You never have a harsh word for anyone, Miriam. It's probably just that fae awakening. You were being protective of your mate."

I do not mistake the glare she gives me. Then she takes a stab with a shifter expectation Princess had lamented before. "Mate? Will you two even be able to have kids?"

"One kid is enough for me," Gabriel says with a light laugh. There's something in his posture, a tension that isn't as easy as his words.

"Roxy is a great kid and grown already. You're a nephil and will live a long time. You should have more. More cubs add strength to the pack, especially from an alpha with angelic blood. It could give us the advantage we need if we open up our borders to other possibilities."

I quirk an eyebrow. Carmen is good. It's back to us versus them. I know it's because she's indoctrinated in the shifter culture of finding the strongest mate to protect her kids, but I don't like it. It seems more than mate seeking. She's talking about opening the door to fae and creating doubt in him about it. I've seen this level of manipulation before. In Hell.

I wait to see if Gabriel catches it. His arm slides off her. "As a new member of the greater Seattle pack, I hear your concern about the welfare of the pack and am honored you show such loyalty. However, I will ask you to respect my decision on the matter."

Carmen lowers her gaze and head in submission. "Yes, alpha."

I hadn't known that she'd swore allegiance to Gabriel. Then again, I concern myself very little with pack politics.

The assistant chose that moment to bustle in. "Okay, Miriam. You're on first."

"We are going into the interview together," Gabriel demands.

"You and your girlfriend together because your stories are related, and the one who fought the True Believers by themself."

"Miriam's my girlfriend," he nods to me.

The assistant's gaze sweeps over our positions. Gabriel sits next to Carmen in close contact. I'm still standing next to the table. Yeah. At a glance, her assessment was correct.

"Sorry. Okay. Miriam and Gabriel, please follow me."

"I'm going to be alone?" Carmen asks in a small voice.

Gabriel waivers for a second. A battle wages on his handsome features. His loyalty to his pack member and her vulnerable moment, and his desire to be there to support me. I hate that she's putting him in this position, that I'm coming between him and his pack.

"You will remain here."

The magic of his alpha obedience compulsion pings my skin.

He adds belatedly, "You're safe here."

For a split-second, there's defiance in Carmen's eyes. She must think better of it and lowers her head in submission. "I trust you, alpha."

I don't think it's a good idea for Gabriel to compel Carmen into calm, but I couldn't say anything after what I did at the Paradise Center, especially in front of the assistant ushering us through a maze of halls. The last thing we needed is for the media to get their hands on supes possessing magical compulsion.

STAGE LIGHTS ILLUMINATED A GRAY DAIS. On the dais sat two plush beige chairs facing a pastel pink chair that possessed more girth and height—Jenna Jones' throne.

"It's good to be the queen," I murmured.

A low standing, neutral-toned coffee table divided the chairs. The singular box of tissues didn't escape my notice.

I would not be crying. I'd gotten all my tears out in the therapist's office. We even played pretend at the interview, running me through questions that Jenna might throw at me or Gabriel to seem unbiased, but were really for the views.

Jenna Jones herself waits for us. She's a petite woman with dark, shiny hair, professionally coiffed. Several shades of purple cover the lids of her light brown eyes, not quite the amber of Phyr's, but close. Her lipstick is perfect as she smiles, revealing straight white teeth.

Funny. Mundanes, even attractive ones, don't have the same allure.

Gabriel's hand slid to the small of my back, walking with me onto the dais. I think it's more for his own comfort than it is for mine. For the second time, he's rebelled against the Angelic Anocracy's rule without raising a sword.

Still, I like the feel of his hand and the way our bodies fit.

"Wow, you two are the hottest couple to walk on this set. You two look ready for the red carpet in Hollywood or a film festival in Cannes." She rises, offering her hand. "Jenna Jones, nice to meet you."

I appreciate the way she's trying to hype us up to feel comfortable, so I offer her a smile while we shake hands, careful not to reveal fang. Look at me! Good job not scaring the talk-show host, Miriam!

She hardly glances at Gabriel. Her focus seems to be on me. Of course, the fae freak gets more attention from someone used to hot men on set.

"My gosh, I can't get over your skin!"

"Being half fae has its perks. No Botox necessary," I reply, grinning. "At least for another couple hundred years, that is. If I were full fae, I could say never."

She laughs, but it's mirthless. "Hollywood is going to beat down fae doors to get actors that don't age."

Nice going, insulting the host, Miriam. I think fast. "I think producers will find they prefer humans who age over those who have lived a long time and easily bore."

"Pull pranks, do they?"

I feel a twinge of guilt for betraying my kind. Having centuries to perfect the art, fae actors are superb at it. I don't want to project the wrong image either and lull mundanes into thinking of fae as innocent pranksters. "Imagine a grandmother, who has lost her give-a-fuck factor ages ago but looks like a twenty-seven-year-old."

"Ah, yeah. Not very moldable," she replies, the relief on her face visible.

"Exactly."

"Speaking of showbiz. Have a seat and we can get into it."

Two GRUELING hours and many hard-hitting questions later, the interview is over. We exit the stage the same way we approached, together with Gabriel's hand on the small of my back. I take comfort in it this time and lean into him.

He kisses my temple.

Carmen is waiting for us next to the assistant as we step offstage. She clutches her pretty dress in her balled fists. Tears stream down her face, ruining the makeup. The assistant is speaking to the shifter in a soothing tone.

"How did we do?" I ask to take her mind off her turn coming up.

Ignoring me, she blurts, "He's here."

"Who?" Gabriel asks, arm slipping from my side to wrap the trembling Carmen in an embrace. A low growl emits from his throat.

I scan the studio, spotting Reverend Orwell, Robby, and Carmen's ex waiting in the wings. What the fuck are they doing here?

"Come here right now, Carmen!" The alpha compulsion is strong, but it doesn't work.

Gabriel turns. There's murder in his eyes. Both of the shifters look as if they're about to go furry.

"Carmen is now part of the Greater Seattle pack." Gabriel's voice is calm.

"She's my mate and the mother of my cubs. That supersedes pack allegiance."

The Reverend watches with grim amusement. His gaze meets mine. He mouths, "Animals."

"Have you broken the mate-bond?" Gabriel whispers.

Carmen shakes her head.

He swears under his breath.

Now would be a great time to do it so he can't track her or know her feelings, but I will not push her.

"I don't give a flying fart about pack order," I say, putting myself bodily between Carmen and Frank Ramirez. "My friend came with me and she's leaving with me."

Frank growls, "Whore of Babylon."

Gabriel growls back. This time it's different from the general warning growl he made earlier. Look at me. Interpreting growls. I could write a best-seller: Is He being a Protective Alpha or is He into You? Shifter growls and Their Meanings 101.

I hold up my hand, hoping against hope he'll let me negotiate. It's our only chance of this ending without a challenge. "Well, that's a new one. Does it bother me?" I pause. "Nope. Not a little bit."

In my periphery, security sweeps Jenna offstage. Awesome. Damage control is handling the wrong person. This feels wrong.

"Code red," the assistant shouts behind me. "The counter side wasn't supposed to come out now, you idiots!"

"How do we know you haven't bent her to your will, demon?" Reverend Orwell says, his small magic pelting my skin.

"First, I'm a fae witch, not a demon. Demons have red skin, four arms, and legs, four eyes, and would scare the shit out of you. Second, if I were going to do that, don't you think I'd bend you all to my will?" I retort. "Or do you think I enjoy being called Whore of Bologna?"

Gabriel chuckles behind me.

I grin in his direction. Thanks for the vote of confidence, sweetie.

"Babylon. It's Whore of Babylon," Frank corrects.

"Bologna is a city in Italy," Robby the mothman offers. So helpful, that Robby.

"Whatever. You're trying to get a rile out of us and it won't work. Go back to your green room and have a snack. You're all cranky and could use it."

Finally, the security team did its job and warned the group they wouldn't get in their rebuttal statements if they didn't return to the green room immediately.

I turn to Carmen. "You okay?"

She flies from Gabriel, tearfully embracing me. In that moment, I realize in all the memories I've gleaned from her head, no one has ever stood up for her.

"You don't have to do it," I say. "You don't have to admit to anything. We can walk away. I have somewhere safe for you and your cubs where no one can find you."

She pulls back, shaking her head. The inner resolve that pushed her to traverse a mountain range pregnant and with a cub in tow limns her features. "I'm going to do it. My cubs deserve to live free of these people."

23

Agents Roanhorse and Tan await us on the U.S. border. Handcuffs in Agent Tan's grip gleam in the customs station light.

Gabriel glances to the rear. "Looks like they're here for you."

Carmen sighs. "Figures they wouldn't let me say goodbye to my cubs."

Not getting that this was planned, I spin in my seat as much as my seatbelt would allow me to. "You don't have to go to jail. I could take you to my faerie."

"I made a plea bargain," Carmen says, unbuckling.

I turn to Gabriel. "You're okay with this? What about her kids?"

"Part of the bargain," Carmen says. "They get adopted by a lesbian supe couple, and Frank goes to jail."

"She promises to bring them for visits," Gabriel assures Carmen.

Finally, I grok that the couple are Princess and Aurora. The kids will stay exactly where they need to be, and Princess contributes to the pack by adopting. Still, I watch Carmen led away by the agents with a heavy heart.

"It feels incredibly unfair that Carmen is going to jail for escaping the Paradise Center."

"She brutally murdered everyone in her path, Miriam," Gabriel replies, voice soft. "She was too weak to harm Princess and Aurora, but she tried. Princess had to subdue her." He blows out his breath. "Carmen has a lot to work out. In the meantime, I can't have her endangering the pack. She'll get the help she needs where she's going. It isn't a human jail."

We're quiet for a while, lost in our own thoughts.

About an hour later, Gabriel exits the highway to a smaller arterial road. Figuring he needs gas, I think nothing of it. When he turns down a dirt road bordered by snow covered evergreens, I give him side-eye. "What's happening?"

He grins. "I have a surprise for you."

We pull up to a cabin with a glass front. It's all lit within, so I can see it's something out of a ski holiday brochure.

"Er—uh—Again. What's happening?"

"You'll see." Gabriel exits the SUV, rounding the vehicle and opening my door with preternatural speed. He offers me his hand.

With no small amount of trepidation, I take it. My heart thunders in my chest as he leads me up the path to the cabin.

On the door, there's a modern lock pad with a coded entry. Inside is all exposed wood beams and sturdy furniture. It's not a family-oriented place since there's a sofa for two, a table for two and one bedroom.

It's not a rental. The place smells of Gabriel's woodsy scent—something I wouldn't have been able to sniff out pre-fae puberty.

I blink. "Uh."

"I come here to think, to get away from being an archangel or an alpha. I used to take Kirsten and Roxy here."

"This doesn't look too family oriented."

He points to a loft I hadn't noticed. "We spent most of our time outdoors, running through the woods."

Since I don't get furry, I doubt that's what he planned for us to do.

Gabriel senses my hesitance. "I'm happy for you to take the main bedroom and to sleep up there tonight, but I would like to have one night alone with you."

I pull out my phone. No bars. "I can't. Jada—"

He cuts me off with a finger to my lips. "Phyr, Jada, and Rhiannon know. They expect us tomorrow."

When he takes his finger away, I protest, "I don't think it's good for us to be alone before I bond with Phyr."

Gabriel brushes a stray hair away from my face. "He left you some of his blood. It's in the fridge, in case you need it."

Well, that explains who started the fireplace and set the table. I scent the air, finding traces of Phyr still here.

"He helped me plan." Gabriel nods to the fridge. "There's a note with the blood."

I went to the fridge to see what Phyr had to say about this. After I broke the fancy wax seal from the envelope, I removed the note inside.

In Phyr's perfect High Fae scrawl, he wrote:

Anam Cara,

Now is the time to rebuild trust between you two. Relax. I would not offer the blood of my body if I didn't approve.

Forever yours,

Phyr

I close the note and my eyes, the love I have for my friend welling in my chest. "There are some things I need to tell you."

Gabriel turns from the counter with two glasses of red wine, handing me one. "Go ahead. I'm all yours."

Well, that makes two of you, apparently. I keep the thought to myself, and start off my building of trust with a doozy. "Lucifer offered me the Sword of Justice given to him by the angels' Creator."

His green eyes flared with surprise. "When?"

I eyed the table. "Maybe we should eat and talk."

Gabriel agreed. We sat at the table. He listened. I talked. We both ate. It told him everything, all the things I held back and my reasons for holding back.

"I don't blame you. I want this egalitarian council, yet I keep making decisions as if they're only mine to make, even negotiating for your daughter."

"I should have told you about going to the Paradise Center."

He shakes his head. "Kirsten wasn't the only problem in my marriage. I get so bent on the role of leader, I don't know how to be a partner. I should know better." He blows his breath out and runs his fingers through his curls.

"You let me handle the True Believers today."

"I had to. I was so close to challenging Ramirez over it." He spread his hands. "It would have given Carmen false hope." He chuckles, but there's no amusement in it. "The poor thing is so strong, so ferocious, but she thinks she has to attach herself to an alpha to be safe."

"It's an age-old thing among many human cultures. Find the man who can provide. I'd done it. I'd relied financially on Rafael to hide from my coven. I should have faced the consequences a long time ago. Running never solves anything."

"I don't think the True Believers are going to be the last group that will come for supes."

"Me either." Gabriel sighs. "I'm worried about my father. It's the reason I bargained with Reverend Orwell before."

"Oh, is he a darling of Heaven?"

He rubs the stem of his glass. "The Angelic Anocracy is leaving me alone for now at my father's behest, no doubt. Once the U.N.M.U. arrests Reverend Orwell and shuts down the Paradise Centers, my father will send an archangel to challenge me for my position."

I rear my head. "I didn't know archangels got their positions that way."

Gabriel smiles bitterly. "I could let them take my Grace. I would become less of an angel and more shifter."

"Just like my mother attempted to take my faeness away from me by taking away my memories. No one should be able to take away who or what we are." I give his free hand a gentle squeeze.

"You understand me so completely." He scoops my hand in his and brings it to his lips. With his eyes on mine, he kisses each finger.

Warmth courses through me. My skin tingles and I clench tight in intimate places. We both rise at the same time, drawn to each other. I'm in Gabriel's arms, his hard, lean body pressed firmly against my softness, leaving no doubt how much he wants me. Cupping my cheek, he lowers his lips to mine.

The kiss starts slow and sweet, building into something hotter and richer. Our bodies sway and move against each other, miming what we both want. His hand slides over my shoulder, stopping to cup my breast. With a thumb, he flicks the sensitive nipple, waiting for his touch.

I want him. I want all of him. Body, soul, and light. Feeling the urge I now know is the claiming fae feel, I break off the kiss. "I need the blood, or we need to cool off."

He nods, rushing to pour some in a clean wine glass and offering the cup to me like a sacred chalice. The shy grin on that sinful mouth does something for me.

I accept the glass and drink it, my link to Phyr strengthening with every gulp. I set the glass down. "You know this isn't a permanent solution, right?"

His chest heaves with his breath. "I think we have a complicated connection, the three of us. Learning you'd spent a childhood protecting each other has changed my mind about him. I'm endeavoring to gain his trust with our check-ins, and he's gained mine. I'm willing to make it work in whatever way you need."

"The bonding ritual involves sex."

"I know. Phyr told me. He also suggested I could be included."

My eyebrows shoot upward at that. "I bet he did. How did you respond?"

"Can we talk about that later?" He asks, blushing. "I know that you're not all mine once we leave here, but I'm all yours, and I'd like it to be reciprocal the first time we're together or whenever we're here. No more talking about your friend, okay?"

I drape my arms around him, humming softly. "That can be arranged."

24

Three months later...

They say that April showers bring May flowers. The spring in the Seattle suburbs brought many things, rain, rain, more rain, spring blossoms, and the episode of "Corrupt: Paradise Center or Hellish Prison?" hosted by famous actress and former cult member, Jenna Jones.

The supernatural council of the Pacific Northwest all gathered at my house to watch the episode to air or livestream or whatever episodes do now. Phyr and I serve snacks, while the council chats.

Princess stands by a window, watching Carmen's cubs play outside in the garden. They chase pixies in their wolf form. I hand her a glass of wine.

Gabriel excuses himself to take a phone call, patting my backside on the way out the door.

I yelp, almost dropping my tray.

Phyr whistles and laughs, kissing my flushed cheek as he passes with the celebratory champagne.

"Gross," Roxy says wrinkling her nose.

"Hey. I thought you were sex positive," Jada says, taking the tray from my hands.

Roxy rolls her eyes, swiping a canapé. "Not when it's my dad and your pops and mom. Ew."

Rhiannon walks through the door Gabriel just departed. She has Lance, and a tall, handsome ash blond in tow. The latter has pale skin, Slavic features and sparkling blue eyes. His magic is so strong it rolls off him in waves.

Curious, I dip into my light. Putting on my second sight, I see his magic. White witchlight with slender threads of magenta. Baba Yaga's son.

"Miriam of the High Fae, the Covenless One, mamushka asked me to bring you this gift as a sign of friendship," he says in heavily accented English.

It's a tin of cookies. Treats from Baba Yaga, not creepy at all. I smile and accept the tin to not be rude, thank him in Kairska, which delights him. When they're all getting comfy in the living room, I whisk the tin away to the kitchen to open later.

Just as we all settle down to watch the show, Gabriel rushes in. He's gorgeous the way he's all flushed with excitement, but I'm biased. I think he's gorgeous all the time.

"Got something to share?" Lucinda asks.

Gabriel swallows and nods. "The U.N.M.U is raiding Paradise Centers across the country. Reverend Orwell and several law enforcement members under his payroll are already in custody."

We release a collective sigh of relief.

The episode of Corrupted went viral within hours of airing. It might have made a few talking points if the media everywhere hadn't covered the raids. The U.N.M.U. got rebranded as the International Supernatural Enforcement Agency.

Quietly, Gabriel began processing fae through the I.S.E.A. to have travel visas within his territory, excluding my father and siblings. Oberon was quite content to stay ruling his faerie. Maeve and Nix wanted nothing to do with the mortal world, thank goodness. My cousin Niamh and their dragon took up residence in the Sammamish River. Niamh may need to live in water, but they have an open invitation to my home. Their dragon Dragan does not.

Jada and Roxy got accepted to the University of Washington and would start in the fall, living on campus. I heard they were petitioning for a supe dormitory. I also heard the mundane students were all for it. Not my battle. Jada would now have to fight plenty of her own. I trust that I've raised her well enough to do so.

And, a new battle for The Mórrígan would come soon enough. Likely the coven elders will make an in-person attempt at collecting my plump ass or my siblings will finally follow through with their threats to kill me, but for now, I am happy.

Miriam's story continues in
Eastside Mórrígan (Midlife Supernaturals #3)

MIDLIFE SUPERNATURALS #3
Eastside
Mórrigan
T. J. DESCHAMPS

EASTSIDE MÓRRÍGAN (MIDLIFE SUPERNATURALS #3)

BY T.J. DESCHAMPS

PROLOGUE

Sparks of electricity spiral down the length of my body, blooming at my core. Gabriel's mouth and tongue blaze a trail along the back of my neck and shoulder. His firm hand grips my thigh from behind, lifting my leg. We both gasp as he slides home.

He whispers, "This never gets old."

It really doesn't.

One year. It's been over a year since the first time we did this in a secluded cabin in the woods. It's *so* good. Every. Single. Time. Probably because the two of us making love without me bonding with Phyr can't last.

My faelight has grown.

Trouble will come.

For now, I relish his large body pressed into mine, the grip of his hand on my thigh, his breath hot in my ear, the friction of his length inside me lighting up every sensitive nerve. The ripples of pleasure build until it releases in a tsunami of sensation.

As I'm riding the residual ripples of pleasure, he asks in a raspy voice, "Tell me your true name."

I almost do.

The sex is that good.

My lips part, but nothing comes out. I can't tell him.

He pulls out and rolls over, sitting up on the edge of the bed.

My head and body are still trying to recuperate from the third mind blowing orgasm since we woke up, so I take a second to sit up and press a hand on his shoulder. "Gabriel, I love you."

I hope it's enough.

I know it's not.

"I know." He sighs. "I love you too, and that's the problem. You love me, but you don't trust me the way you trust Phyr, and that hurts."

Gabriel had a year to gain my trust. Phyr had many human lifetimes in faerie. It will never be the same, but I thought he'd gotten past his jealousy of my relationship with Phyr.

"Do you really want complete power over me?"

He turns. The face of the were-nephil is heartbreakingly handsome. Sometimes I get lost in how that beautiful face regards me. Gabriel looks at me as if I'm the best thing that's ever happened to him, and he can't quite believe I'm real. Right now, all I can see is the pain etched into those features, and I've caused it.

Although we've known each other for years, we've held a lot of secrets from each other. Naturally, when we started out, we didn't trust each other implicitly after discovering those secrets. We have a territory to protect and as protectors of our community, we are constantly faced with problems most people don't have. Sometimes we don't see eye to eye. Phyr has played a large part in keeping us together in more ways than one.

I hate that. I wish he were here to act as an intermediary. How are Gabriel and I going to work if we need my closest friend for every big argument?

Gabriel blows out his breath. If I look inside his head, I bet I'll see he's having the same thoughts. I could. I don't. I value his privacy too much.

His face is grim as he says, "Powerless? You could control me. Take over my mind and make me never disobey you."

Ah, there it is. Even the children of angels don't like someone having more power than them. They're almost like the cheesy '80s Highlander movies. *"There can be only one!"*

I get behind him, wrapping my arms and legs around his thick, muscular frame, and then rest my head on his shoulder. "Do you think I'd use that power over you?"

"No." He swallows hard, and I can feel he's not being completely truthful. "I already feel like I'd do anything for you. I've let high fae in this territory. I support you mate bonding with another because we're not compatible, and trust that won't break us. I am letting go of so much I wouldn't have let go before. I feel like if I had the name Danu gave you, it would be our way of bonding."

"Would getting married be a suitable alternative?" I don't even know if I want to do as I suggest. I was married once, and still might be technically married since Raf ascended to godhood, but I wonder if it would help Gabriel.

Gabriel stops breathing and grows absolutely still. Finally, he lets out a breath. "I would marry you in a heartbeat *if* you could commit to just me. As long as we're not married, the media doesn't question the nature of your relationship with Phyr. You two are never apart."

"Why is this bothering you now?" I gesture broadly, indicating everything metaphorically.

His shoulders heave. "The way we appear to the world matters."

I monkey my way around his torso to his lap. No small feat. I'm not a lithe halfling. "How would knowing my true name make a difference?"

His shoulders slump. "My enemies grow in number, but I can face anything, even death, if I know that you have that sort of faith in me."

Gabriel's sincerity moves me.

"It's not that I don't have faith in you. I don't trust my siblings." Maeve and Nix could pluck my name from his head as easily as plucking a stray hair. They are old. From a time when fae walked this world. Gabriel knows this. However, I don't want to point out that he's weaker than them. Not when he's in this vulnerable mood.

"Couldn't they do the same thing to Phyr?"

Fair point. However--"Phyr has a geas on his soul. Danu has bound him to never tell." I add in a soft voice, "No matter the torture."

His features darken. "They tortured both of you, didn't they?"

I nod, a sad smile forming. "Him more than me. Probably more so after I left."

"Bind me by geas."

I cock my head. "I don't think it can be done."

"It can." The resolution in his eyes tells me he's asked Phyr. He smooths a finger over my lip, pricking it on one of my fangs.

I taste the coppery drop of his blood.

"Tell me your name, and I'll swear on my soul to tell no one without your permission."

Magic settles in the room like fog rolling onto a meadow.

"My name is Mórrígan. Danu says I'm the goddess of old, reborn."

His eyes flash with surprise and his mouth gapes. He takes a few moments to recuperate from the news. His lips curl into a lascivious grin. "I love a battle goddess."

"That's a modern perspective. I prefer the role of protector and healer." I kiss his finger, pouring my faelight into it, healing the wound. Gabriel is a hemophiliac. He could draw from his pack to heal, but I want to emphasize my point.

His gaze drops to my lips. His hands slide down my back and grip my backside as his mouth finds mine. Gabriel kisses me with the fervor of a devotee at an altar, begging their goddess for succor. He breaks free of the kiss, leaving me panting. Cupping my face, he says as if swearing an oath, "I love you so much."

"And I, you."

It's true. I do love him, too, but I can't help the feeling that our love will be tested again. I can only hope that what we're building is rock solid enough to survive the coming storm.

1

I didn't have opening Pandora's Box on my list of errands, but here we are.

A murder of crows that roost in the University of Washington Bothell campus fly overhead, darkening the evening sky as I make my way to check the mail. I hope they don't crap on my head. When a bird poops on you, it's supposed to be a blessing or lucky, but I think that's just wishful thinking.

A few of the crows break from the group, landing in the trees and on the mailbox.

One caws at me, likely expecting food. Sometimes I feed the crows unsalted peanuts.

I know. I know. I shouldn't be feeding wild animals, but I also feed cream to the sprites in my garden. I'm a sucker for all creatures. Actually, not all.

I don't feed Canadian geese. Those jerks can fend for themselves.

The crows remain at their posts, unafraid of my presence.

My mailbox is part of a huge communal locker of about forty individual boxes and two larger boxes for small packages. Busy with my bakery, I haven't checked the mail in about a week. I should punt the duty to my two acquired housemates, Rhiannon or Phyr, but I punt a lot to them so I can handle everything extraneous to the household. Besides, I like this being my task.

I have neglected mail for a bit, evidenced by the fliers, bills, and random junk stuffed tight.

A crow squawks so loud, I jump.

"I got nothing, buddy."

He takes off.

Fighting to work all the overstuffed mail out, I don't notice the prickle of unfriendly magic until it's too late. When I finally register something is amiss, I let everything drop. The contents of my arms fall to the wet pavement, cascading like autumn leaves. One envelope, however, sticks to my hand like a magnet to a fridge.

Like witchcraft.

While muttering a litany of swears that could make a sailor blush, I examine the envelope. Nothing out of the ordinary in the material, it's even weighted like a regular white envelope you might put a birthday card inside, except it's devoid of name or address. A tug of a compulsion spell urges me to open the envelope.

"Yeah right. I wasn't born yesterday," I say to the card because that's totally sane.

I was born to a witch and the High King of all fae, a long time ago. How long ago is anyone's guess. Nothing makes sense in faerie because it's all based on the beliefs of the fae who created it. If you aren't careful, that nonsense would kill you. Oberon, my father, always warned me to be aware of potential threats in even the most innocuous of settings. His advice kept me alive then, and I should heed it now.

"Miriam?"

I recognize the deep timbre of the voice and the worry. My neighbor Shawn made a promise to my late husband Raf to look out for me. Angels, like fae, take promises seriously.

I call over my shoulder, "Yeah. It's me."

Shawn comes into view under the streetlight. Judging by the keys in his hand, he's come to check his mail too. I didn't hear his Tesla pull up, sneaky electric cars, but I see the sleek gleam of the grey sedan across the street now. He stands two heads taller than my average height of five-foot-six. Looks, build, and killer wardrobe included.

In contrast, I look like Molly Ringwald—2020's Molly, not the Pretty in Pink version. Well, if Ringwald had a thicker build. Much thicker. I've been a size fourteen to eighteen for a few years now. Also, I have antlers, fangs, and my hair decided to turn pink instead of gray, but I don't want to get into that. Going through fae puberty in my forties hasn't been fun.

Shawn's eyes are so dark that there's little difference between pupils and irises in the low light of the setting sun. He takes in the mess at my feet, and the envelope I hold as far away from my body as possible. He squints. "You alright?"

No. No, I am not alright. Not. At. All.

I'd thought coming out of the supernatural closet would solve my problems. Instead, I had to face down a religious cult and a witch coven entering this territory. Not to mention the members of the former Paradise Center cult have given me and the other council members grief for getting their elders sent to jail—none of the True Believers seem to mind that their leaders kidnapped my daughter and imprisoned me for the heinous crime of having the magic we were born with. Also, I still have the Angelic Anocracy to contend with but haven't heard from them. I'm not surprised. The long-lived take their sweet time to react to major shifts, swooping in when the dust settles. Hence the witches taking a full year to do this.

The envelope may be the first of many evils loosed against me in retaliation for blowing up everyone's spot.

"Fine. Fine. I've been supernaturally served. Nothing big."

Shawn rubs his hand over his short-cropped curls. "What does that mean?"

I cast a pointed glance in his direction. "I would think a former archangel and a current lawyer would know what 'served' means."

"I do. This—" He gestures to the envelope clinging to my skin. "—isn't the way the Angelic Anocracy goes about summoning for a trial. *Who* is serving you a summons?"

No. The Angelic Anocracy wouldn't do this. Gabriel said they will eventually send assassins with flaming swords to strike me, and the rest of the council, down. Especially after Gabriel and I brought down a cult devoted to them.

I sigh. Shawn is only trying to help. "When witches commit a crime against witches, the elders of all the covens meet. Once that committee decides the person needs to be tried, they send a summoning letter."

He listens, worrying his bottom lip. "Are you certain that this is what we're facing here?"

"*We're* not facing this, Shawn. I'm going to figure this out."

He eyes me, grimacing. "We've been friends a long time, Miriam. Angels don't take friendship lightly. If you have a problem, I have a problem."

I take a deep breath. He's right. If the roles were reversed, I'd absolutely help Shawn any way I could. I've hidden what I am and so many secrets for so long, I'm still not used to having people have my back.

"Thanks."

He waves a dismissive hand while pocketing his keys. No mail pickup for Shawn.

A knot of guilt tightens in my stomach. He should be checking his mail and then driving around the block to his house, welcomed home by his kids and his husband Micah, not dealing with my family drama.

He eyes the envelope. "What will happen if you open it?"

"I assume opening it will activate a spell that will open a portal that will suck me to wherever a council of witch elders await to judge me."

More forehead rubbing. "Shit."

Shit is right.

I lick my lips, grinning. "There's always a chance Option B will happen."

His handsome face lights up with hope I hadn't meant to give him. "Which is?"

"The elders have already decided I'm guilty, and the envelope is a magical bomb."

I chuckle without humor. I'm panicking, and panicking will not get me out of this situation. Whatever I do, I cannot consider opening it. Not even hypothetically. Any intention in that direction will lead to the compulsion to do it.

A light blue BMW pulls up, a local punk band blaring from within. Kirsten, Roxy's mom, gave her a brand-new BMW for graduation, because of course she did. Just what I need. My kid is home from college.

My daughter Jada spills out of Roxy's car dressed all in black from her studded choker, My Chemical Romance t-shirt, ripped jeans all the way down to her Demonia platform boots. Her eye makeup and lipstick are dark, paling her brown skin. Her curly hair is currently teal, a halo around her shocked face.

"Mami, everything okay?" Concern colors her tone and her brown eyes are wide. Her expression shifts to excitement within a blink of an eye.

Jada reaches for the envelope. "Oh, that's for me!"

I whirl away, shouting, "Stay back!"

Her brown eyes light with the anger of a pissed off demigoddess. "Give it to me, mami. It's mine!"

Shawn puts himself bodily between my daughter and me.

"A compulsion spell coded for our bloodline is making you believe it's yours. Fight the urge," I say from behind the big, Graceless angel.

She furrows her brow and angles her head to the side, asking over Shawn's shoulder, "Do you want me to look up in the grimoire library to see if there's an unhexing I could do?"

"No. It's best if you and Roxy get as far away as you can. I don't know what this will do when triggered."

"I can feel the pull of a compulsion spell," she admits and then nods her head as if deciding something. "I'll get back in the car."

Roxy pokes her head out the window. "What's happening?"

"Call your father." Shawn says in a calm voice, "There's a magical terrorist threat, and we need his—"

"No!"

When they all gape at my shout, I add in a calmer tone, "I know what to do."

Shawn's brow furrows with concern, but he doesn't argue. He may have been a powerful seraph once, but all he can do now is sprout wings on demand. That's what "fallen from Grace" means, an angel stripped of magic.

Lucifer once told me what the Angelic Anocracy does to strip angels of magic. How they stripped him of magic. He eventually found a workaround-become the villain of the story. His power came from being the devil; not the fount the other angels' magical gifts sprang from.

Lucifer is also the reason I realized how to dismantle the magical bomb safely. Or rather, an encounter with him taught me something about faeries and their creators.

"What's the plan?" Shawn asks.

"Only what the fae believe can hold power in a faerie."

He cocks his head to the side.

"I'll explain after it's done," I say. "Right now, I need to get this thing out of here."

Light is what I call magical energy. Because my mother is a witch and my father is the king of the freakin' High Fae, I have a bit of witchlight, and a supernova's worth of faelight. Since fae are made of the stuff and I have a mortal body, I keep most of my faelight in what I call a cache. Caches are nulls, or the interstitial space between the fabric of the multiverse. I happen to have one inside me, or I can access it from there, but I don't like to think about it too much.

Quantum physics and magic make strange bedfellows but are bedfellows, nonetheless.

I take some of the faelight I have hanging around inside my cache and wield the magic like a blade to slice through the fabric of the multiverse, seeking my faerie.

"I'll be right back," I say and slip into my faerie.

Faeries rarely obey what we know as reality, because they are pocket universes based on the belief of the fae who created them. That is why the fae who could create faeries, called the High Fae, were worshipped by humans as gods.

Once inside my seedling faerie, I stand in a meadow, and the belief the envelope has no power against me makes the envelope becomes just that, a white unmarked envelope, dropping to the ground.

Spell broken, I create a flame with my faelight, burning the envelope to ash.

I sigh and turn around.

I am not alone.

ALSO BY T.J. DESCHAMPS

Midlife Supernaturals Trilogy

Eastside Hedge Witch (Midlife Supernaturals #1)

Eastside Mórrígan (Midlife Supernaturals #3)

Midlife Supernaturals Trilogy Box Set

Eastside Rock Witch (A Midlife Supernaturals Novella)

Midlife Olympians Series

Westside Oracle Midlife Olympians #1

Westside Harpy Midlife Olympians #2

Westside Titan Midlife Olympians #3

Faerie Tales Series

Tam Lin: A Modern, Queer Retelling (Faerie Tales #1)

Warrior Tittle (Faerie Tales #1)

Vow Unbroken (Faerie Tales #2)

The Ballad of Brave Janet (A Faerie Tales Novella)